An excerpt from *Master's Flame*

He leaned back in his chair and fixed her with a look. "Do you know what it means to inspire a man like me?"

Valentina wasn't one hundred percent sure she knew what it meant, but she acted on her best instincts, rising to her feet and crossing to kneel before him. She could barely keep her excitement in check as she reached to unbuckle his belt.

"No." His hands came over hers, stilling them. "No, my dear. Not that."

"Oh."

"Oh, indeed. You begin to alarm me. Is there some...condition? If so, we'll work with it as well as we can."

"A condition?" she asked, her cheeks flushing with embarrassment.

"A medical condition which requires you to have sex at least once an hour? Be honest, my dear. There will be no repercussions, and we will make allowances as we may."

"No, there's no medical condition." She straightened, wishing there was a way she could instantaneously be sitting back in her chair. "I'm sorry. I misunderstood what you were asking."

"That seems patently clear. When I want sex from my partners, I am very direct about it." He indicated that she should go sit down. "If I am not demanding sex from you, you may rest assured it is not desired."

"I'm sorry," she said again, miserably. His cool tone wasn't mocking, but Valentina nonetheless felt mocked. "I do have a bit of a condition. I am too...enthusiastic. Too impulsive and passionate, not just with sex, but everything."

"These are excellent problems to have, in my opinion. Before I knew you were called *La Vampa*, I sensed you had a bit more fire than everyone else. I need your fire, Miss Sancia..."

Master's Flame

Annabel Joseph

Cirque Masters
Book Three

For Lina
I would say more but I'd need too many words

And for Monsieur le Marquis, who started all this

Chapter One:
The Flame

Michel Lemaitre looked at the clock, then shuffled posters on his desk, rearranging the second and third. All of them were trite, lacking in creativity. Since the final choice would become the promotional face of Cirque du Monde's new show, *Cirque Élémental*, trite was not good enough. A waterfall? A white cat? Ridiculous.

He drew an engraved note card from his desk and composed a curt message to the art department:

If you ever send me another white cat on a poster, you will all be fired. Sincerely, M. L.

He piled up the posters and placed the note on top. "Jeanne," he said into his intercom. When his secretary entered, he held out the packet to her. "Art Department, *s'il vous plaît.*"

"*Oui, monsieur.*" She took the papers and bustled out.

Michel stretched back in his chair, then reached past his laptop and took a file from the left side of his desk. He flipped it open, leafing past clippings and documents to find the headshot. Heart-shaped face, large, luminous hazel eyes, and vivid red hair that had earned her nickname. *La*

Vampa—the flame. When a sharp knock sounded on the frosted glass door, he closed the file and barked, "*Viens.*"

Jason Beck, one of his Directors of Artistic Development, stepped into his office. You could take the coach out of California, but you couldn't take the California out of the coach. Even now, after years in urban Paris, Jason was tanned to a subtle bronze, his chestnut hair streaked with inexplicably natural highlights. At the moment, his healthy charm was sullied by a ponderous frown.

"Well?" Michel asked, pointing to a nearby chair. "How was the practice? What do you think of her?"

Jason threw himself into the armchair and scrubbed his hands over his face. "What do I think of her? She's a fucking maniac. She's fearless. She's terrifying. She's..." His voice trailed off as he searched for an adequate descriptor. "Insane. I think that's the simplest way to put it. Batshit insane."

Michel steepled his fingers and pursed his lips. "Insane is a strong word. Let's substitute eccentric, or visionary."

"No, sorry. Did you talk to her? Did you converse with her even a little before you hired her?"

Converse with her? What did conversation matter with a performer like *La Vampa*? At twenty-six, she had twenty years of performance under her belt with one of Italy's premiere circus families, starring in a banquine act that was considered the best in the world. When he'd passed her his card, he'd experienced a strange sense of recognition, or maybe precognition, that he was meant to meet this performer and bring her into his company. *I'm with Cirque du Monde,* he'd said. *Would you like to come?*

Yes, of course, she had said in luxurious English. With her accent it sounded like *off course,* and honestly, he had felt a bit off course as she held his gaze. Now, just in time for *Élémental,* Michel had procured his flame-haired flyer. Well, after he paid an ungodly sum to her family troupe as compensation for their loss.

He cleared his throat and frowned at Jason. "Whether she is insane or not, she is a highly skilled performer for whom we paid an exorbitant amount. Allowances must be made." Insanity didn't worry Michel Lemaitre, but Jason's exasperated expression did. He pitched his voice to a low, soothing lilt. "Tell me about your first practice with *La Vampa.* I'd love to hear what has you so worked up."

Jason's rough exhale shifted the hair that escaped his ponytail. "Okay, where do I start? She arrived on time in the company of a gentleman purported to be her father."

Michel raised a brow. "Purported?"

"I'll get to that in a minute. We talked for a while, got to know each other."

"Her English?"

"It's good, but when she gets excited she can be difficult to follow. And she gets excited a lot. By everything."

"How delightful."

Jason gave him a look that communicated a different opinion. "Anyway, she gave me a short demonstration of her skills."

"Her acrobatics are excellent, yes?"

The director's eyes shone with reluctant approval. "Her acrobatics are world class and her agility is astounding. Nearly as astounding as her lack of inhibition."

Michel waved a hand. "What need have we of inhibition? We are Cirque du Monde. What else did you discover? What are her strengths and weaknesses?"

"Strengths? She's athletic, with great natural ability. She's amazingly comfortable in her body. Flawless balance, flawless control. She's creative and energetic. Weaknesses..." He paused with a grimace. "Well, there's only one real weakness. She doesn't seem to possess an ounce of self-preservation. I spent ninety percent of the practice expecting her to break her neck. She's insane."

Michel shook his head. "She is an artist. The best art is fearlessly rendered."

"That's a real pretty saying. She still scared me to death. She also has the attention span of a flea. She stopped halfway through practice because she spotted a scrap of nylon fabric across the gym that she had to have."

"Had to have? Why? What did she do with it?"

"She stuck it in her gym bag, God knows why. She also spent a good bit of time flirting with Adei and some of the other gymnasts."

"Not you?" Michel asked, lips curling in amusement.

"Oh, me too. Halfway through practice I put a hoodie over my tee shirt because she was undressing me so hard with her eyes."

Now he laughed out loud. "How wonderful for you."

"Wonderful? First of all, I'm engaged to your daughter. Second, I'm supposed to be Valentina's director, not her love toy. Speaking of love toys, her father—"

"You said 'purported' father," Michel reminded him.

"During the break I found him with her in the locker room showers."

"Showering?"

"Fucking her against the wall. It didn't look very fatherly, but Valentina seemed to be enjoying it. She wasn't the least bit embarrassed either. She looked at me like she expected me to join in."

"Did you join in?"

"No!"

"Come now, confess. I'm not one to judge."

Jason ruffled with impatience. "Again, I'm engaged to your daughter. And I've never slept with any of my performers." At his boss's doubtful glance, he amended, "Well, except for your daughter."

Michel smiled at the correction. He'd sent Jason to scout his daughter last year at a circus in Mongolia, and by the time they returned, the two were embroiled in a relationship. Before then, Sara hadn't realized she had a father in Paris, or that he owned the world famous Cirque du Monde, and Michel hadn't realized he wanted to be a dad. At Jason's urging, Michel had grown close to the twenty-two-year-old woman, and given her the trapeze act in his new elemental-themed production. His daughter was air, wispy and ethereally lovely.

La Vampa, he hoped, would bring the fire.

Michel tapped at the file on his desk. "Aside from Miss Sancia's fearlessness and her voracious appetite for her fake-father, how did you find her artistry? Her tenacity? Did she take direction well?"

"Yes, but—"

"Did she seem capable of intricate technique and concentration?"

"Yes, but—"

"Energy, vitality. Conflagration," Michel said with a sigh of pleasure, enjoying the feel of the word on his lips. "She'll be perfect for *Élémental*." Michel flipped open her file to show Jason the sketches and notes he'd made while the talent department labored to bring her into the fold. "Do you know what they call Valentina in Italy?"

"What's the Italian word for 'nymphomaniac'?"

Michel ignored this. "She is called *La Vampa di Napoli*," he said. "The Flame of Naples, roughly translated. I imagine this 'Vampa' as a central character in our production, a motif. A woman of unbridled passion and strength, a blaze igniting inspiration wherever she goes."

Jason scratched his temple. "Okay. But she's crazy."

"*Excentrique*," Michel corrected.

"*Excentrique*," Jason repeated with a passable Parisian lilt. "However you want to say it. She's something else."

Something else. Michel felt the familiar rush of inspiration. "We have earth, air, water, spirit, and now fire," he said. "I see oranges and reds, a dynamic, vigorous act, a performer who embodies a blaze with flames reaching to the sky."

"A character called *La Vampa*?"

Michel nodded. "What do you think?" He felt heartened by his director's thoughtful expression. "These are just preliminary plans. Visions. I'll need your help, Jason. I'll need Valentina's most magnificent efforts and your expertise in refining them."

"And a magnificent insurance policy for *La Vampa*, who seems determined to break every bone in her body."

Michel stood with a smile. "Where is our flame now? Did you leave her in her father's arms?"

"Last I saw, they were headed to the cafeteria for lunch."

"Let's join them. I would like to welcome her personally to our community of artists."

Jason threw up his hands. "Sure. Why not?"

Michel strolled through the corridors of the main Paris complex with his usual sense of pride. He had begun his circus career as a traveler, a vagabond juggling on street corners. Even then, homeless and poor as a beggar, he'd found creative beauty in the ebb and flow of life. He'd built the Cirque empire from the ground up, scratched and begged and bullied until he achieved his perfect vision, until he got the results he wanted. It was a mode of operation he still practiced today, although he did considerably less begging and considerably more bullying.

The man beside him, Jason, was a trusted colleague as well as his future son-in-law. He could be depended on to whip the acrobatic acts into shape; his light manner belied a steely core. Perhaps he was an effective director because he shared Michel's dominant proclivities. As a player in the Cirque's BDSM subculture, the younger man's depravity rivaled his own.

No small feat, considering Michel's depravities.

They turned off the wide corridor into a community dining space dominated by panoramic windows and bright murals. A scan of the tables revealed no splash of red hair.

"I don't see her," said Jason. "But there's her fake-dad."

"I'd love an introduction."

Michel and Jason crossed to the man's table. Michel extended his hand. "Good afternoon, Mr..."

"Forenze," the Italian provided with a thick accent, leaning forward.

"Mr. Forenze, I am Michel Lemaitre, the owner of Cirque du Monde. Welcome to our happy little enclave."

"Happy?" Forenze leaned back again and made a disgruntled sound.

Michel looked around. "Where is your daughter?"

"She is not my daughter. She told me to pretend I'm her father so I can stay with her."

"You're not her father?" said Michel with feigned shock. Jason poked him in the back.

The Italian shook his head. "I meet Valentina last week at a café. She beg me to come, crying that she will not know anyone. She has already made several new *friends*," he sneered. "As for me, I have a ticket home tomorrow."

"Well." Michel turned to Jason, who'd flushed red around the ears. The American hated awkward scenes. "You'll be missed. Safe travels." He scanned the cafeteria once more. "Do you have any idea where she is?"

Mr. Forenze pointed to one of the doors. "She left that way holding hands with a large black man."

"Of course she did," Jason muttered under his breath.

"Adei?" Michel guessed.

"She did a lot of staring across the practice space at him. So probably. Yeah."

"This is serendipitous. He topped my list of prospective partners for Miss Sancia." The first meeting room in the hall was empty. Michel closed it and proceeded to the next. "I picture a hand-to-hand routine. Adei's strength and presence contrasted with her delicacy." He opened the next door. "Ah. You see what I mean?"

"Good lord," Jason said, turning away.

But Michel didn't turn away. Why would he deprive his senses of such a lovely tableau? Valentina sprawled atop a conference table, pants and panties around her ankles, her legs held open by Adei as he licked her bare pussy with abandon. "Lovely," Michel murmured. "See how he worships her?"

To say Michel Lemaitre was sex positive was like saying a fish was water positive. He didn't just love sex; he needed it to live, to breathe.

"You are not required to finish what you're doing," he said to alert them to his presence, "but I would enjoy watching the finale."

Across the room, the two performers froze, and two alarmed sets of eyes turned to him, Valentina's half-dazed with pleasure. Michel winked at Adei, who winked back and tightened his grip on the woman's thighs.

Jason made a noise behind him. "I'm out of here."

Michel was too absorbed in the scene to care when his director stalked away. He pulled the door closed as Adei hunched over *La Vampa*'s glistening mons. She held Michel's gaze another moment and then threw back her head in pleasure. Adei slid his hands under her legs and lifted her, bobbing her up and down on his tongue. There was nothing on earth like watching athletes fuck. They were so energetic and flexible. He envisioned an act in flame orange, Adei sending Valentina skyward with his thick, muscular arms so she flew like a comet, trailing that fire-red hair.

As he daydreamed, Valentina gripped Adei's head. "*Sì, sì, sì, sì, sì,*" she hissed. A moment later, Adei's efforts had her bucking through a prolonged climax. How beautiful she looked caught in the throes of orgasm. He watched the sleek muscles of her legs as she twitched through aftershocks. Her pussy glowed like a flower and he found himself wanting to take his own sample of her nectar. He found himself wishing to force open those shapely, strong legs and explore her many charms. He found himself wanting to tuck the delectable creature into a cage so he might fuck and torment her whenever he wished.

Such lurid fantasies. His cock ached, rock hard, but he smoothed a hand over it, willing it to subside. This little spitfire was not for him. Too young, too fresh, and certainly too undisciplined to satisfy his exacting tastes.

Michel gave her a moment to rest and compose her clothing before he held out his hand. "Come, Miss Sancia. We have things to discuss."

"You are angry?"

"Why would I be? I am not angry in the least."

She studied him, her light, gold-hazel eyes still glowing with pleasure as their fingers intertwined. Ah, he remembered that light in her eyes, that lively spirit from their single previous meeting. Her erotic hedonism, though, was a delightful surprise.

To Adei he inclined his head. "Bravo, young man. To give is sometimes to receive. Come to my office at four o'clock. We have things to discuss."

He turned back to Valentina. The reckless flirt blew Adei a kiss as Michel drew her out the door.

* * * * *

Valentina had to walk fast to keep up with Michel Lemaitre's purposeful strides—and she *had* to keep up, because he hadn't yet loosened his grip on her hand.

Not that she minded. She could barely believe she was walking through the halls of Cirque du Monde's headquarters on the arm of the powerful, sexy CEO. She'd liked Naples, and liked performing with her family as part of a traveling variety act, but they never left Italy. City festivals and community fairs were small time. She wanted to see the world and the surest way to do that was to join Mr. Lemaitre's company, with shows in numerous countries and touring productions that spanned the globe.

And the man beside her? He was nothing less than a genius, and that excited her. He exuded an intensity, an electric energy that made her heart pound. No, not her heart. Her sex. The moment she met him, the moment he took her hand so many months ago in Italy, she had recognized him as a sexual creature and responded in kind.

Mr. Lemaitre was tall and muscular, his swarthy physicality as attractive to her as his piercing, ice-blue eyes. He was in his mid-40's, seasoned, elegant and handsome, the type of man who commanded attention and knew what he was about. His features were prominent, finely carved, their aristocratic haughtiness softened by his head of unruly hair. Glossy black waves tumbled over his forehead and behind his ears, tapered and tamed to a neater arrangement in back.

It was an effort for him, she understood, this tame front. His exquisitely tailored suit, his styled hair, even his neatly manicured facial hair spoke of tamed impulses. Control. Nothing fascinated Valentina like an intriguing, complex man. Adei was charming and enthusiastic, but so much on the surface. So sweet.

Michel Lemaitre was not sweet. He was something else.

Mr. Lemaitre had stood and watched with no compunction as she enjoyed the pleasures of Adei's agile mouth. She knew it was bad behavior to steal away and have sex with Adei, but as always, in the moment, desire won out over reason. Anyway, Mr. Lemaitre had seemed far from scandalized. Another reason she wanted to be here. Performers talked, and Cirque du Monde was known around the world for its culture of sexual abandon. Adei had answered her come-hither stare without a second thought.

"Oh, I'm so happy," she burst out, skipping beside him. "This place is...*magnifico.*"

He dropped her hand so she could complete an exuberant pirouette. "I do not doubt you think so," he said drily, "considering how you spent the last half hour."

"Half hour? It was only twenty minutes."

He raised a brow. "And before, in the showers?"

"Oh. That." Perhaps he didn't completely approve. "I told Mr. Beck that man was my father, but he isn't really."

"I rejoice to hear it."

She couldn't pin down his tone. Angry? Teasing? Bemused? "My father is home in Italy," she said. "I met Lugo at a cafe and he wanted to come."

"He wanted to come, or you compelled him to come?"

"He had nothing better to do. He's very much a...what is the word? Slacker? Anyway, I think he's leaving."

She hoped he was leaving. Lugo's avid, clumsy lovemaking had thrilled her at first. She loved big, brutish men who grunted and groped. Then again, she loved cultured, urbane men too. She slid a look at *Signore* Lemaitre, who was large and had dark hair like Lugo, but was so much more attractive. She wondered what it would be like to share a bed with him. She'd heard that the Cirque founder was omnisexual and intensely dominant.

Fascinating. A fascinating and intriguing man.

15

He paused, bringing her to a stop. "In here, if you please."

He guided her through a set of double doors into an office complex. There was an outer waiting area with conference rooms and cubicles, and Cirque posters decorating the walls. She loved design and art, and the entire office sang with artistic energy. The area was flanked by a frosted glass wall and a door that read *Michel Lemaitre, Cirque du Monde.* She suppressed a frisson of excitement as he led her inside with a light touch on her back.

"Please have a seat." He nudged her toward a worn leather arm chair facing his desk as he removed his suit jacket and hung it near the door. She looked around at the memento-laden shelves, at polished wood furniture that spoke of refinement, wealth, and success. These walls too were decorated with photographs of Cirque performers in rehearsals and shows. She recognized some of them. They were the trailblazers, the outstanding ones. She hoped she would earn a place on his wall one day. He only had to give her a job to do. She would perform the hell out of it, whatever he wanted. Valentina was an adrenaline junkie who loved challenges. She lived for the high of performance, for that soaring feeling of expressing herself. *Please,* she thought, turning her eyes back to him. *Please let me express myself here.*

His gaze locked on hers across his desk and for a moment she felt frightened by the depth of his scrutiny, not that she had anything to hide. She lived in the open, true to herself as much as society allowed. She hoped he would respect that. "Well," she said, as silence spun out between them.

"Well," he repeated with a slight quirk to his lips. "First, I must commend you. Your English is excellent. Much better than my Italian."

She smiled at his compliment. "I have never had problems learning things."

"I'm glad to hear that."

"I can help your Italian if you like."

He tilted his head. Did he hide a smile? "I believe we'll limp along just fine in English," he said. "Miss Sancia—"

"You can call me Valentina," she interrupted. "Or Tina. My friends sometimes call me Tina."

"I am your employer, not your friend."

His curt reminder both devastated her and turned her on. "Of course," she said, sitting on her hands to keep them still.

He pushed a thick file forward across his desk. "Miss Sancia, do you know what this is?"

"My dossier?"

"Yes. Do you know what is inside?"

She bit her lip, thinking over his question. "Complimentary things, I hope. Any police reports...they are not to be believed. I did not vandalize that fountain, merely went wading in it because the water sparkled so beautifully that day."

"Miss Sancia—"

"And I was only naked because, well, I had on my favorite dress and I didn't want to ruin it. I was not even fully naked. Just mostly naked."

"Miss Sancia—"

"And that other time, no matter what the report says, I did not force the Sicilian councilman's sons into any inappropriate behavior."

His blue eyes widened. "Sons? Plural?"

"*Monsieur*, I never would have. I merely—"

"There are no police reports," he said, cutting her off. "Although we may continue this discussion at another time. This dossier contains my talent scout's notes, photographs, and my own notes from our brief meeting last year. Do you remember?"

She nodded, wondering about the purpose of this conference. Was she not officially hired? Had he gone over her dossier and decided she was not, after all, a Cirque du Monde-caliber artist? She was beginning to regret stealing private time with the handsome gymnast. "About before, about the man who was..."

"Going down on you on my conference table?"

"Yes. It was a matter of impulsive urges."

"Obviously."

"The man—"

"His name is Adei. Please do not disappoint me by stammering out excuses. I admire your carnal enthusiasm. However, we are not in the habit of constant, promiscuous, and public sex here at our headquarters. The focus must be on training for roles and performances."

"Of course," she said.

"That is not to say we don't satisfy our sexual urges at other times, in other, more appropriate locales," he added. "But while you are here in the training facility, please refrain."

"Yes, sir." She tried to appear duly censured but couldn't help looking at him sideways with a flirtatious smile. For a moment he gazed at her, a probing, prolonged study that wasn't flirtatious in return. Then he shook himself and looked down at the folder on his desk.

"Anyway, about your file. You have probably realized by now that you've not been brought here to blend into the background of some existing cast. Like many who see you perform, I find myself compelled. Inspired." He leaned back in his chair and fixed her with a look. "Do you know what it means to inspire a man like me?"

Valentina wasn't one hundred percent sure she knew what it meant, but she acted on her best instincts, rising to her feet and crossing to kneel before him. She could barely keep her excitement in check as she reached to unbuckle his belt.

"No." His hands came over hers, stilling them. "No, my dear. Not that."

"Oh."

"Oh, indeed. You begin to alarm me. Is there some...condition? If so, we'll work with it as well as we can."

"A condition?" she asked, her cheeks flushing with embarrassment.

"A medical condition which requires you to have sex at least once an hour? Be honest, my dear. There will be no repercussions, and we will make allowances as we may."

"No, there's no medical condition." She straightened, wishing there was a way she could instantaneously be sitting back in her chair. "I'm sorry. I misunderstood what you were asking."

"That seems patently clear. When I want sex from my partners, I am very direct about it." He indicated that she should go sit down. "If I am not demanding sex from you, you may rest assured it is not desired."

"I'm sorry," she said again, miserably. His cool tone wasn't mocking, but Valentina nonetheless felt mocked. "I do have a bit of a condition. I am too...enthusiastic. Too impulsive and passionate, not just with sex, but everything."

"These are excellent problems to have, in my opinion. Before I knew you were called *La Vampa*, I sensed you had a bit more fire than everyone else. I need your fire, Miss Sancia."

She stared at his broad, classically handsome face, his generous mouth. "You can have my fire, *signore*. As much as you want."

"What if I want all of it?"

Did he mean—? She rose to go to him again.

"No." He held up a hand. "I do not mean that. I mean that we are to mount a new production here in Paris. New cast, new performances, new blood. I have conceived a show about the elements, but it needs a central symbol. A flame, a fire, an explosion of life to anchor the rest of the acts. You understand? The show needs a spirit to drive it. You have this spirit and I want to use it to delight Paris audiences. The production will be named *Cirque Élémental.*"

"But..." She wasn't sure what he asked. "I'm an acrobat, a banquine flyer. I don't have an act to last an entire show."

"Not an entire show. There will be other acts, but you'll be the show's figurehead, the vision on the poster. We'll create an entire production with ten or fifteen other acts. Dance, lights, costumes, humor and pathos, feats of strength and agility. You know...circus."

The steady tone of his voice never altered, but some deeper challenge in his gaze excited her almost beyond bearing. At the same time, he'd made it clear he wanted her artistry, not her sexual advances. He hadn't wanted her on her knees before him. Very sad.

"I will do whatever you like, Mr. Lemaitre. Simply tell me." She gave him a look, one she hoped communicated that she was his vessel to use, artistically or otherwise. "Whatever you want from me, sir, I am yours."

Chapter Two:
Vesuvius

Valentina squirmed on the massage table as Priya dug relentless knuckles into her *latissimus dorsi* muscles. It was the end of November, six weeks since she'd arrived at the Cirque, six weeks since Mr. Lemaitre took her to his office and told her he needed her spark. No, not her spark. Her *fire*. Since that day, she'd been burning to please him, training hard and working with Adei and Jason Beck to develop an artful and intense hand-balancing act. Unfortunately, since that day, she hadn't seen him once.

The Cirque was building a venue in Brussels, so Mr. Lemaitre was needed elsewhere. During his absence, new acts for *Élémental* arrived from all corners of the globe. Valentina liked practicing her hand-to-hand act with Adei. He was alternately her pedestal, her trampoline, her stairs. He lifted her, supported her, threw her in the air and caught her. He held her motionless while she balanced on his upstretched arms. He was strong and steady for the most part, and when he wasn't, she let him have it. They were no longer lovers.

She had a regrettable habit of getting bored fast.

Because of that, Valentina spent most of her nights at *Le Citadel*, the Cirque's secret sex club. Jason had taken her the first time, along with his fiancée, Sara, who was Mr. Lemaitre's daughter. Valentina liked Sara because she was beautiful and exotic, with light blue eyes just like Mr. Lemaitre's, but she wasn't sure Sara liked her. Valentina never would have flirted with Jason if she knew he and Sara were engaged to be married. Even after Valentina apologized, Sara had given her baleful looks.

Valentina had a way of alienating people even though she tried to be warm and exuberant. Jason called it "recklessness" and he didn't like it. He warned Valentina that he would monitor her activities at the Citadel, and bar her from the club if she couldn't control herself. People laughed and embraced at the Citadel, kissed and flirted and fucked right in the open if they felt like it. In the back rooms, men and women played more serious games. Dominance and submission. Power exchange. Mr. Lemaitre had his own private dungeon built of stone and steel, where people bowed before him and called him *Le Maître*, a variation of his surname that meant "The Master." Valentina heard all this secondhand since Jason wouldn't let her go to Mr. Lemaitre's back room, or any of the back rooms.

"Not yet," he said. "Not until he approves it. Those are the rules."

But Mr. Lemaitre wasn't around and Valentina was dying to know what went on behind those walls. She wondered what it would be like to be one of his slaves, to yield to his barely-leashed sexual power. She'd never considered such things, but she thought, with someone like *Le Maître*, she might enjoy it. She loved trying new things and he'd said that she inspired him...

Speaking of which, she hoped she would inspire Mr. Lemaitre today. He was finally back in Paris to judge the progress of *Élémental*'s acts. She hoped he loved her work. In her fantasies, he loved it so much that he rushed over and took her in his arms and whispered, "I want you," or something gruff and demanding like that. But what if he didn't love her act? What if she fell or messed up? She moaned just thinking about it.

Priya paused and frowned down at her. "What? I hurt you, girl?"

"No, it's okay. Don't be gentle," Valentina said. "We're performing for Mr. Lemaitre today. I need to be really loose."

The masseuse's dark brows snapped together. "From what I hear, you are already loose enough."

Valentina ignored her, concentrating instead on relaxing her muscles and joints. She began a mental exercise where she visualized herself in performance, imagining her body's alignment, the placement of her limbs, even the graceful form of her fingers. Priya moved from her shoulders to her spine, digging her palms into the vertebrae and carefully realigning them. It felt so good that Valentina moaned again. "Priya, you're a goddess. Don't stop."

"Hush," said the Indian woman.

"Oh, *yes*. More. That feels so good."

Priya's magic fingers massaged away all the tension and worry, until Valentina sailed on a sea of relaxation. A good masseuse could make you feel like a brand new person. Valentina's moans rose with the increasing pressure of Priya's fingers. Suddenly, the door flung open.

Jason scowled at her, arms crossed over his chest. "Just checking."

Priya flashed him an irritated look. "Mr. Beck, I am almost done. She want to be loose. I'm making her loose."

Jason lounged against the door frame. "I think she's already loose enough."

"What?" Valentina's temper flared. "Priya made that same joke five minutes ago."

"You might ask yourself why."

"It's insulting."

"Insulting or accurate? I could hear you moaning all the way down the hall."

Director and artist scowled at one another as Priya gave her a final pat down. "Go, you," she said, helping Valentina up. "Do good for Mr. Lemaitre. You very loose and open now."

Valentina glared at Jason, daring him to make another comment, but he stayed silent as he led her out of the physical therapy office and down the corridor toward the practice facility. The relaxation of the massage ebbed away, replaced by the usual tension she felt at Jason Beck's side.

He looked over at her. "Nervous?"

"No. Yes." She frowned. "Priya doesn't like me. I've put in several requests for a male masseuse. They have stronger fingers."

He looked away to greet a passing coach, then back at her. "Males are called *masseurs*, and we don't have any who are appropriate for you."

"What does that mean?"

"We don't have any that wouldn't cave to your inevitable seduction."

Valentina set her teeth. "You know, I am tired of being made fun of. I am a single, healthy woman who enjoys physical pleasure and connection. I'm safe with sex."

"That's good to know."

"It's not hurting anyone."

"Isn't it? Adei just stopped moping over you last week, you almost ended Peter and Silas's twelve-year gay relationship, and now you've got the Russian juggling troupe at each other's throats."

"I didn't realize they were all brothers. I didn't know!" She thought a moment. "They are all very good in bed."

"Valentina," he said in a tone of warning. He pulled her into the smaller practice studio and shook a finger under her nose. "I appreciate that you're comfortable in your sexuality, but you're here to work, not seduce the entire company. If you keep causing havoc Lemaitre will step in and you won't like it when he does."

She jerked away and sprawled on the closest blue mat to stretch and warm up. Other performers did the same in various corners with other, nicer coaches. Because she was one of the production's stars, she had to work with stern, exacting Jason, who scolded her all the time. Her sex life was none of his business, and as for her various partners' interpersonal nonsense, that was no fault of hers.

Jason watched her, stepping closer from time to time to offer support or resistance as she worked her flexible limbs. She braced a leg on his shoulder and did a back bend, stretching and lengthening her spine. As much as he annoyed her, he was good at his job. And handsome. She liked the deep blue of Jason's eyes and the nature-tones in his hair. Gold, auburn, mahogany, dark-bark brown. She collected leaves the color of his hair from the autumn streets, which was weird, but she was always weird. That's probably why he was so snappy with her. When she righted herself and stretched her arms over her head, he narrowed his eyes.

"What?" she said in exasperation.

"Instead of taking the world tour of Cirque cocks, you should be in the gym lifting weights. You haven't gained any muscle mass. You need to be strong to do eight shows a week. Everyone's expected to be fit."

She did a couple back flips and faced him when she regained her feet. "I am not a strength performer. I'm an agility performer. If I develop big muscles I'll be too heavy to lift."

"Give Adei some credit. He can lift twice your weight without breaking a sweat. If you don't bulk up, Lemaitre—"

"Lemaitre, Lemaitre. Blah blah blah Lemaitre. I'll do my act, I'll do it beautifully, and he'll have nothing bad to say. He hired me as I am." She gave Jason an arch look. "He understands me better than you do."

Jason chuckled as she stretched her hamstrings and did another series of flips to warm up her back.

"What's so funny?" she asked when she finished.

"Your bravado," he said. "But whatever. This will be fun. Come on, you and Adei should run through it a couple times before he arrives."

* * * *

Michel headed for the practice studio. His train from Brussels had been gratifyingly prompt, and the construction there on schedule. Everything in order, just as he liked it, and now he got to view the seeds of what would grow into the new Paris show.

As always, he felt impatience mixed with a rousing sense of possibility. So many personalities, so much creative spirit to mold into a unified program. Creating art was, to him, an exercise in discipline. One took risk and inspiration and harnessed them for the enjoyment of audiences, controlling elements that resisted control.

Speaking of elements that resisted control...

Michel pondered the issue of *La Vampa*. He hadn't heard much directly from Jason, but word got around. She was every bit as disruptive as he had expected. She was either loved or hated by her colleagues, and sometimes loved and hated at the same time. Michel didn't have the luxury of forming any emotionally-based opinion of her. As with all his performers, he would support Valentina Sancia as long as her art and performance merited his care.

A few moments later he arrived at the practice space and took a seat on the perimeter with his artistic team. He scanned the large room, noting the various types of rigging and the groups of artists stretching on mats near the walls. He beckoned each act in the order he wanted to see them, saving *La Vampa's* act for last. He saw a fantastic high bar act, a Russian Swing routine with a lot of potential, a group of rhythmic dancers who were not as fey as he feared they would be, and a fire-eater that downright unsettled him. He watched his daughter's emotional solo trapeze act, developed over the summer in Marseille. As many times as he'd seen it, it still amazed him.

Overall, he was thrilled.

To his left, Adei stretched bulging muscles while Valentina bent backward and arched her minute frame into a near-perfect circle. He thought of the *ouroboros*, the snake swallowing its tail in a symbol of eternity and reinvention. She rolled out of the unnatural position and came to her feet with a grace he found arousing. Michel was a carnal man; when she did those things, he thought about sex. If she could do *that* with her body, what else could she do?

But this wasn't the time to fantasize about exotic sexual positions. He focused on Valentina and Adei's showmanship as the pair began their act. They already had music, West Indian in origin, with modern beats and dance influences mixed in. His musical director would refine and expand it based on the final version of the act. For now, it provided a blueprint as far as tempo and length. Michel was struck by Valentina's musicality as she twisted and strutted about the floor. Adei was the sun to her skittering planet. In a sensual bit of choreography, she shimmied up Adei's body and stood, perfectly balanced, on his upraised hands.

The lifeblood of his circus—any circus really—were artists who could do what other people couldn't. This hand-to-hand act fell firmly in that category, perhaps too firmly. Valentina's daring alarmed him. She went into a handstand on one arm—hers and Adei's—and bent her body back in a defined arch. She did splits and turns, her eyes locked with her partner's. She flipped in the air and Adei caught her on his upturned palms. It wasn't all his skill. She used her body to position herself perfectly and to land with a soft touch. With a grin, Adei flipped her up again, making it look like nothing more than schoolyard shenanigans. The things they did could only be achieved through the melding of two singular sets of talents. Even then, each new leap, arch, and stunt shocked him a little more.

"*Dieu*," he whispered at one point to Jason beside him. "How is it possible?"

"Because she's crazy," he whispered back. "Like I told you."

Then came the wobble. Adei's fault, not hers. Michel's practiced eye saw it nearly before it began. A falter in balance and concentration, a shoulder dipped too low. Valentina came tumbling down, landing on her feet like a cat—even that happened gracefully. The look she turned on her partner, though, was the least graceful thing he'd ever seen.

"You beast," she spat. "What's wrong with you? How lazy and stupid can one person be?"

Adei offered his hands to propel her back up but she slapped them away. He scowled and walked off the performance floor with a shrug and few choice words of his own. Michel watched with a measure of patience. This was how the best acts grew and changed—and Valentina's act would have to change. There was no way she could sustain that level of concentration and performance through eight shows a week. Even if she could, her partner couldn't. That seemed obvious from the way he willfully tuned out her ranting.

"We should go save him." Jason sighed.

"By all means. Partners must push one another to strive for excellence, but she may be pushing a little too hard." Literally, pushing him. The muscular black man was twice her size, and to Michel's mind, exercising laudable control in the face of her onslaught.

He crossed with Jason to the area where Valentina and Adei worked to settle their differences. Both men flinched as the petite woman let loose with a string of Italian curses.

Michel made a note of the ones he hadn't heard before, even as he frowned in disapproval. "Our own Mount Vesuvius. Charming." He made a sharp sound to get Valentina's attention. "Miss Sancia, do not injure Adei. You'll need him for future performances."

She ignored his order, waving a finger in her partner's face. From the looks of things, they weren't lovers anymore. He wondered if they were still friends. It became clear that Adei would need backup if he was to continue working with Valentina.

Michel turned to Jason. "Why do you not use spotters for the act?"

At those words, she left off Adei and turned on him. "Spotters?" she snapped. "I do not need spotters."

"Don't you? I could have sworn I just saw you fall."

"That was not my fault."

He couldn't remember the last time a performer had used such a tone with him. And here, in front of dozens of people. "It was your fault and that of your partner," he said with brisk authority. "You should not incorporate skills into your act that you can't replicate perfectly every time."

She straightened her shoulders, turning her wagging fingers on him. "I will perfect that skill, I just need time to do it. I don't want spotters milling around and getting in the way. There are lines that must be seen, movement that would be ruined by spotters lurking here and there. I know how to fall and not get hurt."

"You say 'I' a lot, Miss Sancia. You are not the only member of this act, nor the only person whose wishes must be taken into consideration."

"Perhaps," she said, "but I am part of the act, unlike you." At that retort, Michel heard gasps from the gathered audience of artists and directors.

He stared at her. Strong personality or not, she had crossed a line. "Miss Sancia—"

"Don't 'Miss Sancia' me—"

He held up a hand to silence her, then scanned the room. "Someone bring Andrew from the other studio to act as spotter. He's warmed up."

"No!"

Michel turned back to her with his iciest stare. "Are you speaking to me? I sincerely hope not."

The warning in his voice worked. She deflated a little, the blaze of her fury downgrading to billowing embers. "You're not listening to me," she said.

"I am listening to you. We can all hear you, but in this, you're not going to get your way. I won't stage this kind of act without spotters. At least, not the kind of act I envision."

"But—"

"I'm the director of this circus."

"Genevieve is the director of this show, not you."

Astonishing, the backtalk, the inability to show respect. Genevieve, slight and dark-haired, sent him an apologetic look. She looked terrified on Valentina's behalf, but Michel was rather enjoying the drama. He hadn't experienced this kind of mutiny in years. Ever, really. Was Valentina crazy, as Jason claimed, or only exceptionally brave?

He walked closer to her, inches away. She held her ground, vibrating with indignation. When he spoke, it was in a biting and resolute tone. "Miss Sancia, Genevieve might be the director of this show, but I am the director of all things Cirque du Monde. Perhaps you were unaware of this. Perhaps you are unaware of too many things. Let us proceed to my office, where I can explain these important matters to you."

Genevieve blanched and Jason got in his way as if to impede him. What did they think, that he would take her there and wring her neck? As tempting as the prospect might be, he'd worked too hard to get her here to choke the life out of her. It was only time to lay down some ground rules and teach her who was in charge. Without physical force, hopefully.

The only person in the room who did not look at all alarmed was Valentina. She stormed off ahead of him. Marshaling her defenses, he was certain. Planning her mode of attack. "You will wish to come too?" he asked Jason, who shadowed his side.

"I would like to, yes."

"Your protectiveness is one of your best qualities. Although you realize I would not behave inappropriately toward her."

Jason gave him a hooded look. "I don't think you'd be inappropriate, no. But you can be brutal all the same. She's new here, Michel. She's impetuous, and in some way, I don't think she lives in the same world as the rest of us."

"I know she doesn't. I intend to redirect her more troublesome behaviors, that's all."

Jason gave a skeptical grunt Michel chose not to analyze, and the two men headed down the hall after the fuming young artist.

Chapter Three:
Singed

Once in his office, Jason sat in one of the leather chairs in front of the desk and Michel sat in the other. Both of them watched her stalk back and forth across the room.

"Will she stop?" asked Michel. "Or should I make her stop?"

Jason raised a brow. "You can't make her do anything."

Michel believed he could, but his methods might upset Jason. Or Valentina, for that matter. He held out a hand to get her attention. "My dear, I need to talk to you. If you won't sit, then at least stop pacing."

She spun on him. "Why do you call me 'my dear'? I am not dear to you, that is obvious."

"If you were not dear to me, you'd be packing your bags right now."

"I'm upset, you know. Very upset."

"I sense that."

"I have a vision for the act. I've been working hard. Working, working, working, and you storm in, and you complain because I fell? It was Adei's fault. I need more time, more practice. How can you come in after only a few weeks and say, 'Show me something perfect'? How can you make me have spotters who will distract and get in the way? You are unreasonable, unfair. You do not listen, only give orders. Do this, do that, blah blah

blah," she barked, giving an exaggerated imitation of his stony critique face.

Michel ignored Jason's chuckle, steepling his fingers and studying her. His whip hand twitched. "Are you finished?"

"Will you answer my questions?"

"When you address me with the respect of an employee for her superior, I will answer your questions."

She turned to storm away. His hand shot out to catch her wrist. "*Mademoiselle*, I don't remember granting you permission to go."

The look she gave him could have melted rock. Blood rushed to his cock, a reaction to being challenged. *If you were mine, ma chère, the punishments I would deal you for this display...* But she was not his submissive, not his slave or plaything or anything.

Not yet, anyway.

The words whispered in his brain, and for the first time he admitted to himself that he wanted her. And it was terrible to want her, this hot-headed girl, because she would burn up both of them in a fire impossible to control.

He frowned and let her go. "I'm going to make you add to your act, Valentina. Three more men, Andrew and a couple others."

She looked devastated. "But...why?"

"It cannot remain as it is. Don't misunderstand me. Your skill is amazing and the work you've done so far is exemplary, but it isn't fair to Adei to shoulder such responsibility. More men—not spotters, but partners, like Adei—can expand the emotional interest of the act. More tricks, more possibilities, and the need for spotters disappears. Four strong men will make a beautiful visual, and you, their flyer, soaring across the sky."

"Four men?" He saw her consider this, saw her realize that more men could only increase the spectacle of her performance.

"But no more women," she said sharply. "Only me."

Michel spread his hands in a gesture of capitulation. "I don't know where you believe we could find another woman capable of doing what you do. Well?"

She bit her lip, thinking, dreaming, perhaps, of the possibilities. He waited a full two minutes with Jason silent at his side. "I guess it's okay," she finally said. "I guess it might work."

After a muted smile to reward her for her conciliatory tone, he hardened his expression and infused his voice with all the displeasure he felt. "Now, Miss Sancia, I would like to explain something to you. Here at the Cirque, we work as a team. We have no divas here, no rock stars, no supreme, inflated egos. No one lords over others here." He paused. "No one except me."

"I only spoke out for my craft," she protested. "My art."

"We are all making art here. That's no excuse for your unhinged and childish display. At Cirque, we consider multiple viewpoints and collaborate. I will always consider your point of view, but I will require you to also listen to mine because I'm your boss. I'll expect you to listen without raging and ranting. Do you understand?"

"What if I disagree with your viewpoint?"

"Do you understand?" he repeated, sharpening his already-taut voice.

"Yes, I understand." She made a face and rolled her eyes. "I speak English."

Oh, to be in a position to punish her as she deserved. He felt Jason shift restlessly at his side. His whip hand probably ached too. "Further, I will expect you to address me, your directors and coaches, your performance partners, in fact, everyone in this organization with professionalism and respect."

"But—"

Michel held up a hand before she could go off. "I'm not saying you have to bow down to anyone, or be falsely polite or solicitous, or any of those things. I expect you to speak to others as you would wish to be spoken to, and treat others as you'd wish to be treated. Would you like Adei to push you and hit you when you fall off balance in rehearsals and make a mistake?"

After a moment, she shook her head.

"What? I'm sorry, I didn't hear your answer."

"No," she said sullenly.

"I would prefer 'No, sir,' and in a respectful tone."

She squirmed, suffering. He was sorry for it, but she needed to understand that artistic license only stretched so far, especially with him.

"No, sir," she finally managed. "If Adei hit me I would probably kill him."

Again, Jason's inappropriate chuckling. Michel pressed his point, wrapping up his lecture with a rigid rat-a-tat of words. "If Adei cannot mistreat you, you cannot mistreat Adei. You will offer him an apology as soon as you leave my office. If you can't find him, you'll keep looking until you do. You will never, ever put your hand on another artist in violence from this time forward. Do you understand?"

"Yes," she said, adding the "sir" when his frown deepened. "It's only that I was upset."

"Undoubtedly."

"I don't like to do things wrong. I don't like to mess up." Her clear hazel eyes went liquid and her jaw tensed.

"Not many here do." If he kept her much longer, she'd begin to cry, and he couldn't handle that. "Go find Adei. Mend your fences. Tomorrow's another day."

She nodded and flew out of his office. He waited for the door to close before he turned to Jason and released a sigh. How unsatisfying, to only flay her with words.

Jason grimaced at him in sympathy. "Well done, Michel. I thought you showed admirable restraint."

"She exhausts me. I don't know how you cope with her day in and day out." He stood to get a bottle of vodka from a small refrigerator.

"Would this be the time to ask for a raise?"

Michel poured two shots of the ice-cold liquid and handed one to Jason. "If you hadn't just received one last month, then yes. As it is, be kind to me. I've apparently thrown in my lot with the devil's daughter."

Jason studied his face. "You know, I never realized how much her eyes look like yours. Not the color this time, but the shape. Are you sure Valentina isn't your daughter too?"

Michel spit out half a mouthful of vodka. "You're not funny."

"I thought it was funny."

"God forbid I would ever create such a contrary creature." He stared down into his glass. "Audacious little bitch."

Jason blinked at him once. Twice. "You want her, don't you?"

Michel took another drink, letting the liquor sit on his tongue while he weighed his friend's question. "Perhaps." He shook his head with a resigned air. "But I won't have her. My life is complicated enough. Do you think she'd want the kind of control I like to exert?"

"No. Although I think she needs it."

Michel bit his tongue, not trusting himself to speak.

"She's been asking about the private rooms at the Citadel," Jason persisted. "Are you going to let her back there?"

"God forbid," he said, crossing to put his glass on the desk.

"You won't be able to keep her out forever. Are you prepared for what happens then?"

Michel sank down in his chair, staring at the polished desktop. "You ask too many questions. You always have. She goes to the Citadel now, eh?"

"Almost every day. And Jesus, she's something. She would be something to play with. Just saying."

"Fire," Michel replied shortly. "She would be like playing with fire."

Unfortunately, he already felt singed.

"Speaking of the Citadel," said Jason, "Sara and I are planning to go next Saturday. If you want to...you know...not go that night. And the week after that, we're meeting friends there Wednesday and Friday, and we'll probably go Saturday since Theo and Kelsey will be in town."

Despite his desire to know nothing about his daughter's sex life, Michel had come to realize that Theo, Kelsey, Jason, and Sara were very likely a swinging quad. His lips tightened. "You and Sara stay very busy these days."

"She enjoys it," said Jason. "Do you want me to keep her away?"

"It's either that, or I'm barred from my own club." He said it with humor, but he felt prickly. What had become of his control? Since Sara, and now Valentina, he found his life taking twists and turns he hadn't foreseen.

"This is what happens when you bring your secret daughter to Paris after twenty-two years," said Jason. "She probably got her kinky genes from you."

"I'd prefer not to think about that." He rubbed his eyes, then drained the last of his drink. "But I suppose I owe the two of you some space. I'm happy that she's happy. That you're happy."

"And you're happy," Jason pointed out.

Yes, Michel was happy to have gained a daughter, but with her as part of the community, he didn't feel as much at ease in his carnal pursuits. He was famous for his dreaded back room, his carefully selected slaves, his depravity. All of it was legend. All of it was widely discussed, and until now, it hadn't mattered. He looked sideways at Jason. "Does it bother Sara that I'm so...public in my play?"

"I don't know," Jason said, but he knew the man was hedging. Of course it bothered her. Now they were scheduling their nights at the Citadel to avoid running into him.

"Maybe it's time I retired from the back rooms," Michel said, trying to sound as if it were no great thing. "Retired from the Citadel altogether."

"You don't have to do that. We can work things out."

"I'm a father now, you remember. My daughter's happiness is more important than mine."

Jason scrutinized him. How annoying, this grim-faced concern. Michel could play the martyr if he wished. He truly valued Sara's happiness over his own. His paternal devotion had surprised no one more than himself, but it would mean changes. Sacrifices.

"Just warn me whenever you and Sara will be at the Citadel," Michel said, turning away in dismissal. He needed some time alone.

"What about Valentina?" Jason asked.

"What about her? Find the men she needs for her act. Men of strong constitution, without girlfriends or wives. Work up something new, something more practical, and let me see the preliminaries in a few weeks. I trust you, you're an excellent director." As an afterthought, he added, "If possible, keep her out of my hair."

"And the back rooms?"

Michel tried hard not to imagine Valentina in cuffs and chains, begging for his mercy. "If she likes she can visit the other back rooms, but I'm not inviting her into mine."

Jason hesitated at the door. "Is she worth all this, Michel?"

All this. The risk to the performers she worked with? To poor Adei, who still pined for her? Or did Jason speak of the danger to him, the danger to his sanity? The risk that he'd pursue her against all caution and reason, enveloping both of them in flames?

"I don't know," Michel said. "I'm not sure if she's worth it. It's too early to say."

Chapter Four:
Suffering

Michel should have returned to Brussels that evening rather than stay in Paris. He should have, but he did not. He most certainly should not have decided to make an appearance at the Citadel just after one in the morning, not in his present mood.

The erotic playspace was his creation, his escape, his legacy, and his joy. He'd wanted to take fantasy and decadence and make it real. With the circus he came close. With the Citadel, he hit the mark square in the center. For years now, he had scened and fucked alongside his more adventurous employees, taken the most tantalizing ones under his wing when it amused him and played with them until he grew tired of them. He favored boys for sadism and girls for sex. It was strenuous work, being one of his pets. He was sorely tempted to make a pet of Valentina. She fit his prototype: beautiful, reckless, and utterly uninhibited.

No, Michel. Think. It would not be wise.

Even in the darkness of the club, through the smoke and noise, he could pick out *La Vampa* from his vantage point near the bar. She wore a black push-up bra and a matching garter skirt and stockings, her red hair pulled back in a careless twist as she danced, grinding her hips against a female friend. She was normally pale but the club's lights made her look even paler. She looked like an otherworldly creature brought to life.

He turned away, scolding himself for his fanciful musings. He needed sex, that was all. Sex to soothe and distract him, and fortify him for the near future when his daughter's presence would force him to leave these games behind.

His St. Petersburg boys were there, fine, blond, strong Russian submissives waiting to be beckoned. They could satisfy him expertly, take his full length down their throats and then prostrate themselves for his whip or flogger. They lived for pain, for subjugation. Unfortunately, he was in too unusual a mood to risk playing with them. His eyes roved, weighing his options. There were three or four women he could take to the back room, even a lesbian couple who enjoyed submitting to him together.

He could take Valentina, if he wished.

That was the worst part...he could do it. She wanted him, and Jason wasn't here to stop him. There was no one to guilt him or hold him accountable. He could take her back and play with her, and discover just how she felt about his stringent brand of mastery. As he stared at her, thinking dark thoughts, he realized his two blond slaves had worked themselves across the room to her vicinity. He frowned as Maxim and Leonid started to flirt with her. The two of them had less-than-zero interest in women, but they would have noticed their Master's interest in her.

He disliked acts of initiative in his slaves.

He ordered another drink and watched the three of them dance together. He'd been distancing himself from his Russian slaves lately. Were they trying to attract him again by seducing his newest obsession? Were they being petty and flagrant in order to get his attention? Were they acting out in hopes of being punished? Valentina allowed them to fawn all over her, a blissful smile on her face. He couldn't blame her for enjoying their attentions. Both men were extremely skilled with their hands. He could tell she didn't know who they were or the significance of their horny little tryst in the center of the dance floor, but others did. Furtive glances fixed on him, then flitted away.

Very well. She ought to know who she was dealing with. He finished his drink and beckoned his slaves to head for the back room, knowing Valentina would follow. If Jason were here, he would have run over and dragged her out of the Citadel by her ear. But Michel had no intention of playing with the young woman, only letting her watch. Surely that would cause no harm, and hopefully it would strike some healthy fear into her soul. Fear of him.

Soon the four of them were gathered in the small anteroom outside his private dungeon. He gave her a look both fond and reproachful.

"You shouldn't be here, Miss Sancia. Do you have any idea what goes on inside?" He nodded toward the door as his slaves stripped out of their form-fitting fetish wear.

Her eyes skimmed their way. It was difficult for a normal person to ignore the sight of their nude bodies, much less this sex-crazed woman. "I know what goes on, *monsieur,*" she said. "I've heard."

"What have you heard?"

"That there is dominance and submission. That you have slaves. I know about the lifestyle, of course."

Off course. "What do you know?" he challenged. "Have you ever dominated anyone?"

Her eyes strayed again to his slaves, the two men waiting for orders with a servility so natural it seemed inborn. "I'm not dominant. I'm a submissive, like them."

He respected people's self-identification in all things, but in this case, he couldn't keep a straight face. "Does it come easily to you? Submission?"

"I don't know. I've never tried it," she admitted after a moment. "But I don't like easy things, and I think I'd enjoy being overpowered if someone could actually do it."

This, he could believe. People submitted for many reasons, all of them fascinating, all of them deeply personal. If she liked the challenge of submission, she would enjoy watching him play with his slaves. He took in her skimpy, sexy outfit, his eyes catching on the lines of the black garter belt set off by her pale skin. Such clothing was power, protection. Distraction in her case, with every curve emphasized and on display. "You must undress if you want to come in. No clothing is permitted within my inner sanctum."

He didn't expect Valentina to balk at the regulation, and she didn't. She undressed until she stood before him as proudly naked as his slaves, her acrobat's body a wonder to behold. Next to his broad, muscular playthings, she appeared an ultra-feminine pillar of eroticism. Her small, firm breasts jutted forward, tipped by taut nipples. At a signal, his pets collected her clothing, folding and stacking it neatly next to theirs. Another gesture and the men knelt, heads bowed, one at either side of him.

Valentina looked impressed. She regarded their naked splendor hungrily, the little nympho. He cleared his throat to get her attention. "What draws you to power exchange?" he asked. "Only enjoyment? Only sex?"

"I know there's more to it than that. I know there must be trust, and negotiating, and safewords."

"Safewords?" He gave a tight smile. "There is nothing safe about words. Something to remember if you ever give your body over to a dominant's will."

"I don't care about being safe." Her fingers twisted together in the intensity of her confession. "I want pain and surrender. I want to be subdued, pushed to my limits. Forced to obey."

"Do you?" How he wished to reach out and touch her. *You will harm this one*, his conscience whispered. *If she does not destroy you first.*

The warnings blared in his brain each time he thought about taking what she so blatantly offered. He must turn her off. He looked away, feigning disinterest in her body, in her submission. He undressed in silence, giving each article of clothing to his fastidious pets to put away. Valentina made no attempt to disguise her curiosity. He would have been disappointed if she did. Her eyes caressed every part of his body, lingering on his thickening cock. He enjoyed her admiration but seduction wasn't the point of this interlude.

What is the point, Michel? Besides lying to yourself?

With great effort, he silenced his misgivings and led *La Vampa* into his most sacred space.

The "Back Room" as it was called, was of stone and concrete. It was smaller, quieter, but no less depraved than the rest of the club. Chains hung from wood beams in the ceiling, and racks, benches, a cage, and a sex swing decorated the stark space. In the corner, a large chair dominated a raised platform. It was his chair, the throne from which he surveyed his kingdom of kink. Sometimes, at his invitation, this space was filled with a hundred people. Today, it held only him, his slaves, and her.

Valentina drew a deep breath beside him. "It's so beautiful."

Odd. He had never considered it beautiful. Dark, forbidding, even claustrophobic, but beautiful?

"Look around if you like," he said, because he could tell she wanted to. With a soft sigh she left him, circling the perimeter of the room. She studied everything, touching and tracing, making exclamations of delight. His slaves remained motionless, one at either side of him, awaiting instructions. They were much better trained than Valentina. For all her claims of submissive tendencies, she had no training at all. *And it must stay that way. Do not imagine her kneeling down, conquered. Do not imagine her whimpering at your feet.*

He let her explore the room as she liked, but when she would have reached to grab a flogger off his wall, he made a sound that arrested her and she moved away. Her eyes were huge, bright with curiosity. She made her way to his large chair, the deep, embossed leather chair that no one ever dared sit in, and made herself at home in the seat. What must his slaves think? But they were not allowed to judge or react, or do anything but obey his orders.

He crossed to her and held out a hand, pointing with his other to a place on the floor. "I sit in the chair, my dear. You may sit here. Do not move a millimeter without my permission, do you understand?"

Valentina settled beside him without argument, hugging her knees to her chest. She showed no reserve or alarm. Somehow he wanted to change that. How could she be so glib here in his dreaded dungeon room with two of the most masochistic slaves he'd ever owned?

"*Soixante-neuf,*" he commanded, gesturing between them. "Make it beautiful for our guest."

The young men fell into one another's arms, so eager to please. Even so, he was about to let them go, release them from their servitude to *Le Maître*. He would have to stop thinking about them as the pets, the boys, the slaves, and let them return to being the strong and intelligent human beings they were. He tilted his head to the side as they wound themselves into a grasping sixty-nine position. He would miss them, but they would have each other, along with a great deal of erotic memories.

Beside him, Valentina gawked. She was no sexual innocent. He could only believe her intense regard was due to their handsomeness, their grunting avidity. After some time, she looked up at him. "Why don't they come?" she asked. "Their cocks seem about to burst."

"They only come if I allow it. Otherwise, they are punished. In this room, they obey me in all things. They'll fuck me if I ask them to, or fuck you if I demand it, however and wherever you like, even though they are both homosexual. They do as they are told."

"Oh." Her breathless *oh* sounded like a question.

"Is there something else you'd like to ask?"

He expected her to request a Maxim and Leo sandwich, but instead her brows drew together. "What do they get from all this? I mean, if you deny their pleasure?"

Michel shrugged. "They get pleasure from suffering, and from pleasing me."

"What happens if they refuse to do as you ask?"

"They're punished."

"Punished how? If you are already hurting them?"

Her barrage of questions both amused and annoyed him. "They are punished in various ways," he said, waving a hand toward the wall of implements. "Harsh punishments, because they're masochists. They get pleasure from being hurt and humiliated. The trick is to be cruel in a way that excites them."

She eyed their red, thrusting cocks. "So they feel pleasure and pain at the same time?"

"Precisely. How quickly you learn. In addition to not letting them come, perhaps I will force them to make us come while they remain unsatisfied. What do you think?"

She looked impressed. "I think you're very good at being cruel."

She was starting to get the idea. He turned to the two men, still hard, burning with lust. Grasping for control. Objectification had always been their favorite kink. "Stand up. Let her look at you." He reached down and stroked Valentina's soft red hair. "Choose the one you like most, dear."

She looked taken aback. "But if they're gay—"

"Choose."

"Well…which one is least gay?"

He laughed, and noted that even Leo's lips twitched in the hint of a smile. "They are both exceedingly gay. Which one's cock do you find most pleasing?"

She looked at his own lap, at his increasingly stiff rod, then back up to meet his gaze. "Yours."

"I see the concept of obedience escapes you. I asked you to choose one of my slaves for your sexual pleasure. If you won't do it, I will."

Now his authority—and displeasure—was focused on her. She shivered. "If it pleases you, yes. You choose for me."

What a submissive thing to say. Perhaps, despite her bold personality, a submissive spark curled inside her, waiting to be fanned into flame. He didn't need any more reasons to want her, not as he tried to keep her at arm's length. This little display on the rigors of slavery didn't seem to be putting her off at all.

With a sigh, he beckoned to Maxim. "Lie back," he said to Valentina. "Let him have your pussy. He may only use his mouth."

"Not his cock?" She stared at it, disappointed.

What a greedy little wanton she was. "Not his cock," he said acerbically. "He isn't deserving." Michel didn't admit that he was too jealous to let Maxim fuck her, even though the young man was gay, and his slave. Michel didn't believe he could stand by and watch someone else fuck Valentina without suffering for it, and he didn't like to suffer.

"That's a good girl," he murmured as Valentina lay back and spread her legs. He trusted Maxim would make things good for her. It wasn't the first time Michel had made his slaves go down on a woman, although he imagined it would be the last. He watched Maxim for a while to be sure he performed with adequate enthusiasm before he ordered Leonid between his legs. Still he watched the other pair as Leo sucked his cock, drawing it deep into his practiced throat. Michel reached to touch Valentina's hair, stroking the wavy strands in time to Leo's bobbing strokes. His cock filled with heat and anticipation, his whole body given to sensation. Valentina's cries and moans of pleasure heightened his own enjoyment of this sweet interlude, as did the knowledge that both his slaves' cocks ached for release.

In the end, Valentina's glorious lust undid him. He wanted to draw out this sensual moment, feel the waves of his climax as she too climaxed, but it was not to be. The way she grasped Maxim's hair, pulling his face into her, the way her whole body quivered as the slave licked and teased her clit... Michel's orgasm roared to life and exploded with greater intensity than he'd felt in a while.

As soon as he'd emptied himself in Leo's mouth, Michel nudged him back and then pushed Maxim away from Valentina's pussy. She made a small "oh" sound as he grabbed her thighs and opened her wider for his pleasure.

"Ah, *mignonne*," he sighed as he took her with his mouth. She tasted sweet and piquant, unique. She was provocative beyond his ability to bear, provocative enough to drown out the clanging alarm bells in his brain.

No, no, no. When had he last behaved with such poor discipline? She quaked beneath him, but he didn't want her fear. He wanted her surrender, her capitulation. He licked every inch of her and teased her pearly clit until she shuddered. The sounds she made were as delicious as the taste of her, as exciting as the feeling of her fingers twisting in his hair. When he growled, she opened her hands and dropped them to his shoulders. He drove into her with his tongue, consuming her, memorizing her flavor and all the secret spots that made her twitch.

He was generally capricious about his slaves' pleasure, denying orgasms as often as he allowed them, but in that moment he needed her climax like he needed air and water. When she dug her nails into his neck and cried out in ecstasy, he wished to begin all over again, but he didn't dare. Instead, he pulled her up into his arms and gazed at her. She melted against him, locking her arms around his neck. How sweet she was. How dangerous to his continuing mental health.

"You must go," he said.

She stiffened, her pretty mouth turning down in disappointment, or perhaps horror that after such heights of pleasure, he would summarily send her away. "Why? What have I done?"

"Nothing. It is merely time for you to leave. I have no more need of you here."

"No, I want to stay," she begged, clinging to him. "Please!"

He ignored her, carrying her to the door. "You can't stay." He let her down and nudged her out into the anteroom. "No arguments. Get dressed and go back out into the club. Dance a little before you go home. Everyone loves to watch you dance."

He closed the door on her wide-eyed shock. He heard her kick the door, once, twice. Silly girl, to think she had any choice in this matter. He turned to his two boys, his valued slaves who had given him so much of themselves through the years. Maxim looked at the floor but Leo met his gaze. To Michel's horror, the man's eyes said, *I understand.* How dare he? How dare he presume to understand what Michel could not? He felt endangered, enraged. He felt a need to expend energy that had no other place.

"On the floor," he barked at the men. "Now."

He went to the wall for the snake whip. He marked their backs first, reveling in their pleading groans as they writhed on the floor. Then he had them stand, taking measured shots at their exposed, straining cocks. He didn't injure or draw blood, didn't leave them with anything more than a few welts. The whip was one of his favorite toys and he knew how to wield it with a delicate touch. Then he took up the flogger and beat them until they pleaded for mercy. Respite. Orgasm.

Before he'd allow that, he fucked both of them in the ass, first Leo and then Maxim, a long, brutal session that emptied him out with a mind-blowing climax. Then, finally, because this was the end of so much more than this one night, he let them come, tormenting them again with the whip until they shot onto one another's rigid, muscled bellies. By the time they stumbled from the room, they'd been used in all the ways they best liked to be used. He didn't say goodbye, and they didn't say goodbye, although the finality of this parting was mutually understood. None of his slaves had ever resisted when they left his private room for the final time. It was for that quality Michel chose them in the first place.

He crossed to sit in his chair and rubbed a hand over his face. Why wasn't he in Brussels? Why had he released Maxim and Leo on the very night he'd brought Valentina here? Why was he suffering? His life was not in balance for the first time in many years. It was her fault, Valentina's, and his fault too. He was acting weak, pathetic, and obsessed. She was a hazard to him, a threat from the crown of her blaze-red hair to the tips of her toes. If he allowed her to conquer his restraint and his reason, it was no one's fault but his own. With a muttered curse he stood and went to the door. He tore it open and nearly tripped over the small figure huddled on the other side.

She was not dressed, and she had not gone back out to dance and have fun as he'd commanded her. She gazed up at him with her large hazel eyes. Her expression was as bleak as his slaves' when he'd released them.

"Oh, please," she sighed. "Why won't you do that to me?"

He sucked in a breath. "You were supposed to leave. You were supposed to dance and go home." He pulled her up and reached for her clothes. "For God's sake, at least get dressed."

She shook her head and set her chin. "I don't want to get dressed. I want to be yours, like them."

"No." He threaded her arms through the straps of her bra and clasped the front closure, avoiding her gaze. That finished, he leaned down and made her step into her garter skirt.

"I don't care if you hurt me and make me do awful things," she said as he pulled the skimpy garment up her legs. "I want to be your slave, like them. Can't you have a girl too? I heard that you like both men and women."

He grimaced. "I like people. People who excite and inspire me."

"Then why not me? You said I inspired you."

To his chagrin, *La Vampa* started to cry. Not the volcano of tears he expected, but silent, sparkling trails running down her cheeks. She buried her face in her hands as he smoothed her stockings up her legs and attached them to the garters. Her body shook with a misery he could not understand.

"Why?" he asked in frustration. "Why must this be?"

"Because I belong with you." She pushed his hand away, fastening the last garter herself. "Why did you bring me here and show me this if you weren't going to give it to me? Why are you doing this?"

"Stop this, Valentina. Stop fighting with me and making demands. If you must know..." His voice trailed off. He was about to hurt her. "If you must know, you are not the type of submissive I'm attracted to. Your uncontrolled dramatics are not to my taste."

She gazed up at him, her eyes dilating in pain. He bit back apologies, excuses. Amorous protestations. *Everything about you suits my tastes, little Vampa. The truth is, you set me on fire, which is why this cannot be.*

He turned away from her to dress, and by the time he turned back she was gone, leaving nothing behind but an irritating sense of loss.

Chapter Five:
Drama

Valentina lay awake in her dormitory apartment feeling suffocated and confused by everything. Mr. Lemaitre didn't want her. Why? Why had he taken her back to his private room only to tease her and show her what she couldn't have?

She pulled the covers over her head as images of the evening's events replayed in her mind. Mr. Lemaitre's fine, strong body revealed to her in all its magnificence, the bodies of his slaves on display for her. *Choose the one you like the most.*

Couldn't he understand that he was the one who called to her with his creativity, his sexuality, his force?

When he went down on her, she'd been caught between pleasure and shock—shock at the way he'd pushed his slave aside to crouch over her, pleasure at the intensity with which he took her. The fine, strong muscles in his shoulders had flexed and strained as he'd pulled her to his mouth. She'd wanted him to fuck her so badly. She liked oral sex but she loved being fucked so much more, and his cock was glorious. Thick, heavy, and perfect in length.

But after he had made her come...he sent her away. Even now the feeling of devastation curled inside her. She'd sat outside the door and listened to him torment his slaves, listened to his sharp voice and all the terrifying noises. He'd hurt them, whipped them, fucked them, cursed at them and made them cry out for mercy. She'd heard everything, and wanted more than anything to be them, struggling with sheer willpower to meet his demands.

More than anything on earth, she wanted Mr. Lemaitre for her Master, but he didn't want her. She wanted to be his toy, his plaything, the canvas for all the colors of his power. His parting words had crushed her. *If you must know, you are not the type of submissive I'm attracted to.* The same cold authority that thrilled her had turned against her in rejection.

Very well. Valentina couldn't stay where she wasn't wanted. After a restless night, she woke and packed everything she'd brought into suitcases and boxes, and stacked it beside her half-finished art projects. She felt bad for Adei and Jason and all the work they'd put in, and bad for the other performers in *Cirque Élémental*, because her absence would wreak havoc with the production schedule, but she couldn't bear to face Mr. Lemaitre again after his rejection, couldn't bear to endure his judgment of her work. She would go home to Naples and...

And what? Continue her family's banquine act? Sign on with some lesser competitor of Cirque du Monde? She stared at her disordered stack of luggage and boxes, imagined it sitting in her room back in Italy. If she left now, she could not come back. She would be breaking her contract and behaving with an utter lack of professionalism. She kicked the nearest box and hurt her foot so badly she burst into tears. She collapsed on her bed and pounded the pillows, helpless to control the violence of her emotions.

In the midst of her breakdown she heard a knock, soft at first, then louder. Had Mr. Lemaitre come for her after all?

"Valentina. It's Jason. Open up."

Damn it. She batted a lock of hair from her tear-dampened face. "I don't want to talk to you."

"Open the door or I'll kick it down. Open it right now."

His sharp words sounded frantic. As miserable as she was, none of it was his fault and she didn't want him to worry. She wiped away her tears and went to crack the door. "What do you need?"

He studied her through the narrow opening and then pushed inside, so she stumbled back against her suitcases. He caught her arm and looked at the pile. "What do I need?" he asked. "I need you to show up on time for practice, for one. I need you to answer your cell phone when I call."

"I turned it off." She lifted her chin, hoping she didn't look as ghastly as she felt. She swept a hand at her things. "I'm leaving today. I'm going home."

"Like hell you're going home." He stood facing her, his hands braced on his hips. "What happened? What did he do to you?"

Valentina knew who he meant but she couldn't bear to recount the story. She turned away and sat on her bed. "I'm leaving. That's all you need to know."

"Oh, no." He sat down beside her and tilted her face to his. "I need to know everything. I heard Lemaitre took you to his back room last night. Now, today, you're packed up to leave. Something happened and I need to know what it was."

"Nothing happened!" The rage in her voice surprised even her. She shrugged off Jason's hand. "Nothing happened, except that he rejected and insulted me. He humiliated me. He said I didn't..." Her voice roughened with the tightening of her throat. "He said I didn't suit his tastes."

Jason made a small sound beside her, a light exhalation that sounded suspiciously like *Thank God*.

"I have to leave," she said, hugging a pillow to her waist. Her chest hurt from all the tears. "I have to go. I can't bear to stay here."

"Why? Because Michel Lemaitre rejected you? Welcome to Cirque du Monde. He rejects ninety-nine-point-nine percent of the people who offer themselves to him, and there's a reason for that. Listen." He took her shoulders and forced her to face him. "If he rejected you, it was to protect you. He has reasons for everything he does."

"What reasons?" she cried, pulling away. She paced in a circle around her sad pile of belongings, old luggage and boxes of clothes and scraps and half-finished projects. That's what she was—half-finished. She turned to Jason, throwing up her arms. "He says I am fire, that I inspire him. He does a whole show based on me, on my act. He...he..." She couldn't say the rest, that he'd knelt before her and taken her pussy with his mouth, and made her come harder than she'd come in her life. "He had me, all of me, but he didn't want me. I would have given him *anything*."

Jason leaned back on her bed with a frown. "Do you think you're the only person who feels that way? I know you think you're special somehow, that you're better than everyone else—"

"I don't think that."

"You do, and I understand why. You're a completely unique person. But listen to me—when it comes to Lemaitre, that isn't enough. He either chooses you or he doesn't. If you're not strong enough for him, he won't play with you, point blank. If you're not steady and well-adjusted, he won't take the risk."

Valentina ground her teeth together. She wanted to deny his words, refute the insinuation that she wasn't steady and well-adjusted, but her actions in the last twelve hours spoke louder than words. She sank down on the bed beside him and threaded fingers through her hair. "He thinks I'm crazy. He thinks I'm insane."

"Everyone thinks you're insane," he said gently, rubbing her shoulders. "That's who you are, a crazy, impulsive person who's not afraid of anything. It's also the reason you can't be with him." His voice softened the slightest bit. "If he rejected you, you should be thankful. I am."

"Why are you thankful?" she asked, trying to untangle the puzzle of his words. "Because you want to be with me?"

Jason gave her an exasperated smile that made her feel rejected all over again. "Have you ever heard of a thing called fidelity, Valentina? I don't know the Italian word, but you should look it up. Also, the word 'restraint.'"

"I know you're engaged to Sara, and I know what restraint is, I just..." A hopeless sound escaped her. "I just don't have that. I never have. I don't know why."

His arm tightened around her shoulder. "Because you're crazy. That's my theory. At the very least you're hot-headed. Maybe it's the color of your hair. Whatever it is, you have to understand that you won't mesh with Lemaitre. He's the most controlled—and controlling—person on the planet. The two of you will never work out. You're too different."

"But we're different in the right ways." She thought a moment, trying to put her feelings into words that Jason might understand. "It's like...when you feel drawn to someone, and you know they have something you need, something you want. You understand in your heart how perfect you would be for them. That's how I feel about him. I feel like we belong together. I want to be close to him. I ache for him, Jason."

"Why? Because he's Michel Lemaitre? Because he's a badass, and your boss? This is a classic case of lusting after what you can't have, merely because you can't have it. And once you received it—if you ever did receive it—you'd realize it wasn't as great and fulfilling as you built it up to be. I think you experienced a little of that last night. There's always a letdown after you sample forbidden fruit."

"Oh, really?" She pursed her lips. "Those are your words of wisdom?"

"Do you or do you not feel like shit this morning? If Lemaitre was so great, you wouldn't be feeling this agony. Believe me, he's not the godlike figure you envision. He has no magical powers, no Midas touch that's going to turn everything in your life to gold. He's only a man, and he has the same weaknesses and drawbacks we all have. He's just better at creating this image of power and fantasy. It's also the formula for creating spectacles, for magic acts and circus. That's why he's so good at what he does."

Valentina took a deep breath in and out. Magic. Was Lemaitre's overwhelming appeal only some engineered sleight-of-hand? A circus trick? A falsehood?

Somehow that upset her even more than his rejection. "Do you think he ever cries?" she asked. "Does he ever doubt himself?"

"Yes to both questions. He's human, like you and me. If you find things about him to admire, then admire him, but don't feel like he's some god you have to touch for your life to be complete." He shrugged and leaned away from her. "Anyway, you've already touched him. He brought you here and made you the subject of an entire show. How greedy can a mere mortal be?"

His teasing tone brought a much-needed, if weak, smile to her lips. She looked up into her director's incisive sea-blue eyes. "You're right. This isn't the end of the world. I think I'm calmer now."

"Good." He glanced at his watch. "Because I'm late for my next practice. Damn it. Are you really okay? You're not going to hop a plane to Naples?"

She shook her head. "I guess I'm staying here."

"Then I suggest you take a day to get your head back on straight. Unpack, go out for some lunch, soak in the tub. Maybe go to Priya and get a mind-numbing back rub. Whatever you do, don't think about him. He's gone anyway, back to Brussels."

That thought comforted her. He wasn't even here, and probably wouldn't be for any length of time until the construction project wound down. That gave her some leeway to get over him, at least the deepest pangs of misery and rejection, but she thought she'd always feel a little pain when she saw him. Feelings that strong never went away.

"Wait," she said as Jason moved toward the door.

He looked uneasy when he turned. "What now?"

"If he won't have me because I'm too hot-headed and crazy...well...what if I became less crazy? What if I worked on being calm and sedate?"

"Calm and sedate?" He made a face. "Even if such a thing was possible, you couldn't keep it up long-term. You wouldn't be you."

"People can change."

"You'll never be calm and sedate, Valentina. I'm sorry, but that's the truth. My advice? Forget about Lemaitre and find someone who wants you as you are. I mean, there are a ton of men and women who would love to top you. You could take your pick of a dozen D-types at the Citadel if that's what you're into."

"That's not true."

"It is true. I've seen the way they look at you."

Valentina tuned out his words because they meant nothing to her. No one else was like Michel Lemaitre, and they never would be. She barely noticed when Jason said goodbye and closed the door, because she realized she'd hit upon the answer. She only had to remake herself in the image of Maxim and Leonid. She had to be calm and clear-eyed, silent and utterly self-effacing. If he didn't like her as she was, she would transform herself into his image of a perfect slave. She would pour herself out to make room for whatever Lemaitre wanted, and once he filled her up, she'd finally feel complete.

She would practice being calm and sane while Mr. Lemaitre was away, and practice submission at the Citadel until she was great at taking pain, as great as Leonid and Maxim, then she'd win his regard when he returned to gauge *Élémental*'s progress. He wouldn't be able to resist her when he saw how much she'd changed.

It was so simple a solution. Thank God Jason had come by to open her eyes.

* * * * *

Michel stayed away almost a month, until there was nothing else to do in Brussels and the Christmas holidays brought him home. The new year found him holed up in his office, concentrating on business. Margins were good. It was a perfect time to launch a new production and there were plenty of tasks to be done.

Even sequestered in his office, he heard company news, but nothing of *La Vampa* aside from the usual status reports on the development of her act. He found this shocking—he had expected her to run rampant while he was away. He wondered if she still went to the Citadel, if she was still cutting a swath through all the sexually available men of the Cirque. He hoped so. He hoped she was having fun. He hoped it had not been too difficult for her to come to terms with his rejection. The way she had looked at him that night...like he was eviscerating her soul.

If Valentina was not so central to the upcoming production, he might have sent her to some other show, only to free himself of temptation. As it was, he could not. By now all the acts were in place and proper rehearsals were underway, with new sets and equipment constructed by the art department. Huge stage pieces filled the Cirque's workshops, and red, orange, and gold paint covered everything.

He scheduled time in mid-January to see an overview of the show before they moved into the practice theater. The directors and coaches huddled around him as the performers demonstrated their progress and awaited his critique. Of course, nothing was ever perfect, not at this stage. Michel was as blunt as he could be without disrespecting his staff and performers. He shared many positives to balance the negatives, but Jason seemed strangely subdued as the order of acts led up to Valentina's routine.

"So, how is the hand-to-hand coming, now that you've added extra men?" asked Michel. Had he tried too hard to sound casual? He didn't want to admit how anxious he was to see her perform, how many times his gaze had strayed to the side of the room where she stretched to stay warm.

Jason's expression gave nothing away. "The act is coming along. They've been very focused. Working hard." He paused, looking up from the page of notes before him. "I understand the 'twins' have been put out to pasture."

"Is that what people are saying?"

"It's true, isn't it? You sent them away."

"They were needed for the Los Angeles show." Indeed, Maxim and Leonid had volunteered with just a little urging from his direction. "They have earned it, don't you think?" he asked Jason. "If you stay too long in any one show, or any one situation, life grows stale."

"Hmm." Jason made a non-committal sound as Valentina entered the performance area. The costumes were one of the last components to be created but she was dressed in the spirit of the show, in a bright orange-yellow bodysuit that was still not as eye-catching as her hair. Jason explained the progress on the act, new stunts and nuances that had been added. Michel listened with half his attention. Valentina and her partners would show him the heart and soul of the performance, which was all he really cared about.

A moment later, the quintet took the floor. The first thing he noticed was an inexplicable slouch to Valentina's shoulders, a deflation, as if she were half asleep. Performing for the boss should have had her at full charge. He narrowed his eyes as the music began and Adei and Danil drew Valentina into the first lift.

The performance had no errors, no hesitations or confusion. There were no wobbles or bobbles and the stunts themselves were graceful and creative. He could not say what was wrong with the act except that it had no life. Valentina had no spark, no joy, not even a smile.

"What is she doing?" Michel hissed under his breath to Jason. "What's wrong with her?"

Jason grimaced and rubbed his neck. "She's trying to please you, I think."

Her face was a blank, pretty mask, and her body, while capable at the tricks, expressed no deeper artistry. She wasn't on fire. His *La Vampa*, his inspiring flame, had fizzled out.

"*Arrête*," he shouted, jumping to his feet. "Stop."

Fifty faces turned to him. The recorded music came to a halt mid-note and Valentina slid down Roman's chest. She turned to regard her boss with a flash of irritation that immediately disappeared back into that unsettling mask.

That was when he realized she was doing this on purpose, punishing him, perhaps, for rejecting her before. She was not ill, she was not tired, she was simply hiding her charisma behind this polished, expressionless shell. It infuriated him.

"Where is the energy? Where is the soul?" he yelled. "I almost fell asleep in the middle of your performance."

Her four partners looked accusingly at Valentina.

"I was trying to be controlled," she said in a stilted manner that sounded nothing like her usual tumbling speech. "Precision and grace are the foundations of a good hand-to-hand act."

"Precision and grace?" His voice edged up to a roar, his temper goaded by her level explanations. "Do you presume to educate me on the vagaries of performance?"

"I don't presume anything," she said, her voice faltering. "Why are you angry with me? Did I fall? Did I make any mistakes?"

"You can do every movement perfectly and still put the audience to sleep." His gaze swept over her partners but it was on Valentina that he focused his ire. "We must have emotion and spirit from you most of all. You are the anchor of this show, the focal point of the act, and you're like a mannequin being passed around and arranged in static poses. How boring and depressing. Where is the life, the risk? The drama?"

"Oh." She gave him an arch look. "My apologies, *monsieur*. I thought uncontrolled dramatics were not to your taste."

Michel heard a small sound from Jason, a light sigh over the furious racing of his blood. "Michel—" Jason began in a warning tone, but *La Vampa* had pushed him beyond temper into indelicacy. He yanked her away from the others, marching her toward the corner of the rehearsal space. He tried without success to collect himself before he leaned down to glare into her sullen gaze.

"Are you playing games with me, Miss Sancia?" he said between his teeth. "You may find such strategies blow up in your face."

She crossed her arms over her chest, not backing down in the slightest. "Playing games? I am not the one between us who plays games, Mr. Lemaitre. I have not forgotten that night, not one second of what happened, even if you choose to act now as if nothing took place. *Miss*

53

Sancia," she mocked, affecting a low, French-inflected voice. "You will call me Miss Sancia, as if we're mere acquaintances, when once you called me *mignonne*, just like a caress, and knelt between my legs?"

"Enough." That bark, that command was generally enough to bring any disorderly person to heel. But Valentina was not any disorderly person. She batted his hand away.

"No, it's not enough," she yelled. "I thought you were different. I thought you were brave and that your heart was open to everything in the world. You disappoint me, Mr. Lemaitre. No, disappointment is not a good enough word. You devastate me with your manipulations and lies. I've tried to please you but you won't be pleased."

He looked over at Jason as if he could save him, but no one could save him, not now. The entire room—fifty people or more—stood still as statues, watching and listening to every word that passed between them.

He tuned them out and fixed his eyes on his dream and his nightmare. Knelt between her legs, had he? How novel of her to throw it in his face. "You have no concept of professionalism, do you, *Miss Sancia?*" he asked in a cutting tone. "Or discretion, for that matter." He took her arm, pulling her right against him, and lowered his voice so no one else could hear. "If you have private things to say to me, you'll make an appointment and meet me in my office like any sane person would."

"Why not your back room?" she sneered.

He squeezed her arm, unforgivably hard, but this insubordination couldn't continue. "My office, *mademoiselle*," he said, giving her a little shake. "There, and only there, will we discuss the personal issues between us. You will never air them publicly again or you will find yourself on the first flight back to *Napoli*. Do you understand?" His tone had gone from cutting to vicious. She nodded without comment, going white about her lips.

He released her and pointed to the center of the practice space, where her partners stood waiting. "Now, you will go and repeat your act, and this time you will perform it with the spirit and artistry of which you are capable. Go."

He stalked to stand just on the perimeter of the performance space, his arms crossed over his chest. Her partners regrouped and took their positions and Valentina straightened her slouched shoulders. If she hadn't, he would have gone and done it himself, and added a great whack to her backside for good measure. How could she imagine he'd be pleased with her lackluster, robotic performance? *My apologies, monsieur. I thought uncontrolled dramatics were not to your taste.*

Little hellion. He could not allow a battle of wills between them. He couldn't allow her to win. He watched her repeat her performance with the same accuracy and control, but this time she let her flame burn. My God, she was incomparable in her artistry.

He ought to have congratulated the five of them on an improved performance, but his temper burned too brightly. Instead he returned to his place at the table and called for the next act, not sparing Valentina a look.

Chapter Six:
Mastery

Michel leaned back in his chair. His private dungeon was busy, filled with friends and a selection of his past and present slaves. None of them appealed, but he had to be here to reassert his authority after Valentina had publicly dressed him down. *Was Lemaitre going soft?* everyone wondered. *Losing control of the company?*

No. Just control of one crazy girl.

He stared across the dungeon at the delightful brunette waiting in chains against a St. Andrews cross. Why didn't Kaiya's beautiful body stir him? Why did her hair, which he'd long admired, suddenly seem a drab, dark shade?

He pushed out of his chair and approached her, willing himself to find excitement in her bondage, her submission. She pulled at the chains, putting on a lovely show. Male slaves were good for enduring his darker impulses, but for connection, for beauty, women possessed a softness men couldn't match. Their bodies were, by default, vulnerable, composed of tender orifices. Women were designed to be invaded.

His organ stirred at the thought, not yet erect, but heading there. Was it the chains? The fear in her eyes? The voyeurs around them, studying their every move? Then someone stepped in his way, one of the more experienced Masters.

"*Monsieur*, forgive me for interrupting."

Michel stared at the man. He would never have entered a scene in progress, except in an emergency. "What is it?"

"There's something going on in one of the other rooms. It's...causing a stir." Another man stood behind him, also a respected Citadel player.

Michel blew out a breath. "I don't want to be bothered. Have someone else handle it." Of course, Valentina would be involved. Who else would create such chaos that they would come here and interrupt him?

Something flickered in the glance between the two men before they turned to go. Something telling. With a curse, Michel turned from his pretty, trembling victim and strode across the hall after them, toward the last of the back rooms.

He heard Valentina's screams first, shrill, wild shrieks that made his hair stand on end. He threw open the door with a bang. People scuttled out before he could even take stock of what he was seeing. A pair of men wielding whips, marking their victim. Too many welts, some of them bleeding. Manacles. Red curls pulled up in a messy twist. A knife in another man's hands, and a noose around the slim column of the woman's neck.

Valentina's neck.

Michel cursed in French, because it was the first language that came to his lips, and then in English because the men were Americans, part of a high wire act. They dropped their whips and scattered back as he crossed to Valentina and lifted her with an arm around her waist. The blood on her back and thighs smeared warm against his skin. He ripped the noose off her neck with a shudder. Damn them. If she'd passed out during their onslaught...even lost her balance for a moment...

She collapsed against him, moaning, weak, and sub-spacey. A quick inspection assured him the worst of her injuries were the angry cuts on her back. He was furious with her, but this was Valentina, who was crazy. Her tormentors should have known better. He turned to the two men who'd been throwing the whips.

"What in holy fuck possessed you to play this game with her? A noose?"

"She a-asked us," one of them stammered. "She said she wanted to play hard. She wanted it."

"And you said yes?" Michel tightened his grip around her waist. "We have rules here, even in the back rooms. Safe, sane, consensual."

The men looked at each other, then gestured to the third man holding a knife. "If she fell, we would have cut the rope."

Michel eyed the weapon, then snarled at the asshole holding it. "What good it would have done, once she snapped or injured her neck?"

"She asked us to do this," repeated the first guy. "It was consensual."

"But not safe or sane," he barked. "Get out, all of you. You're banned for one year from the Citadel. Go."

The last man hesitated before he left, gesturing toward Valentina. "Is she going to be okay?"

"I'll deal with her," Michel said. "Get out of the Citadel before I have you dragged out with a fucking noose around your neck."

"It was my idea," Valentina protested weakly. "Don't be angry at them."

"I'll be angry at them as much as I like, and angry at you." He looked down at her in despair. What was he to do with this woman? How was he to control her erratic behavior? "How much did you drink?" he asked, shaking her from her subspace stupor. "Answer me."

"Nothing. Half a drink."

"Then why? Why would you participate in such a scene?"

"Because I wanted to," she yelled, trying to struggle away. "I wanted to feel something. Something horrible. Something bad."

"Why?" he shook her again so her teeth rattled together.

"You should know," she said, her voice rising to a shriek. "You insulted me today. Rejected me."

"Oh, this is my fault?" He bit back sharper words, words that would have maimed her, words he would have regretted. The idea of her risking her life because of something he'd done to her? God, it flayed him raw, and he didn't deal well with that feeling. He focused instead on the bleeding cuts on her back. He would have to take her home and treat them, not because he blamed himself for them, but because he didn't trust her to do it herself. "Do you think before you do anything?" he said, giving her a sharp shake. "What did you imagine you'd accomplish with that scene?"

He wanted to shy away from the pain in her eyes. He didn't want it. He didn't want any of this. "Don't look at me that way," she screamed.

"Don't touch me. I hate you. I hate you, and you don't care about me anyway! What I do outside of work is none of your business."

"When you try to kill yourself in my goddamn dungeon, it becomes my business," he said, wrapping a blanket around her. "Now shut your fucking mouth before I'm tempted to whip you some more."

* * * * *

Valentina lay nude, face-down, on a poster bed in a half-lit, white-painted room. An identical bed stood in stark relief against the opposite wall. Besides the four tall posts making up the frames, both beds were enclosed on three sides—and on top—with iron bars.

Cages. These weren't beds. They were cages.

No, they were beds. She was going mad, even madder than she'd been when she'd incited Jake and Damon into scening with her in the back room. She'd been hurting and she'd wanted to hurt worse, and now she hurt so bad she almost couldn't draw breath. She felt empty, like some vast hole had opened inside her that could never be healed. She hated when she got this way, when she did dangerous, impulsive things because she didn't have a name for the emotions inside her, or any way to control them as they swarmed in her brain.

Look, Mr. Lemaitre had thundered as he held her in his bathroom. *Look what you've done to yourself.* Horrible, garish cuts and welts covered her from her shoulders to her ass and hips, and even to the backs of her thighs. It hadn't seemed like so much in the moment but now it looked awful. There would be bruises, he said, and then he'd said a lot of other very cruel things. He'd stood with her in his white-granite guest room shower and washed off the blood, and lectured her until tears mixed with the water coursing down her cheeks. *You don't even know them*, he'd said. *They are nothing to you. How can you give this much of yourself to them?*

He didn't understand. He didn't understand that she'd been giving herself to *him*, not them.

But that only went to show how crazy she was. She'd wanted his attention, perhaps his regret. Even his anger. Well, she had that. She wanted Mr. Lemaitre but he didn't want her, and she didn't know how to process that, how to get over it.

She winced as his fingertips salved a cut on her shoulder blade, and knew she needed to say true things to him. It was the only way to reverse this horrible slide and make up for her mistakes, so when the first truth came to her she spoke it aloud in the oppressive silence. "If I could go back in time, I wouldn't do it again."

He moved from her shoulder blade to a cut on the tender skin near her spine. "I'm glad to hear that." His voice was tight, dripping with something like sarcasm, but not the roar of disapproval it had been before.

"It's just... My brain... When I start to feel—"

"If you are going to make more excuses, save them."

She fell silent, biting her lip. "*Monsieur—*"

"I don't want to hear excuses. I need to understand what's driving this behavior of yours. I need to know how to stop it, because it can't continue."

"My grandmother said I had *il Diavolo* inside me. How do you say it? Diablo?"

"The devil," he murmured. "What a lazy excuse."

She sighed and turned her face into the pillow. It smelled faintly of lavender but it wasn't girly. It smelled fresh and crisp, like the towels he'd dried her with, like the pristine white robe he'd shrugged into. Like him. His house, what she'd caught of it as he dragged her to this room, was also very crisp, with no color, no clutter. It was so unlike her own place, trashed with the various detritus she compulsively collected. What would it be like to let go of all that and stay in this plain white room, in this cage bed, forever? She started to cry. She knew why she wanted him. She wanted control, and he could control her. Not forever. He wasn't a man to stay with a slave forever, but he could teach her to balance her behavior, to think first. To *wait* before she acted impulsively.

"I need you," she mouthed against the pillow, too softly for him to hear.

"What?"

She curled her hands into fists as he moved to her buttocks, rubbing the warmed medicine into her cuts. His fingers were as strong and masterful as the rest of him. Her pussy reacted with a tingling warmth, even in her misery and pain. She pressed one of her fists into her eyes to smear away the tears.

"I'm sorry," she said. "I didn't know how else to get your attention."

His fingers stopped still. "You did this to get my attention? You risked your life and endured this abuse *to get my attention?*"

"Mr. Lemaitre—"

"If you needed my attention, you could have come to my office as I said. You could have sent me an email." He massaged salve into a smarting cut on the back of her thighs. "I am available to my performers. You need only ask for an appointment."

"You know that's not the type of attention I'm talking about. It's not the attention I need."

"You *need*. It's all about your needs, isn't it?" Again, she caught the scent of heat and clean lavender. His robe was stark white against his tan, furred chest. She tried to turn to him but he stopped her with a hand on her back. "No. Give the cream a moment to absorb before you roll over and smear it everywhere."

That hand holding her still...it was everything she wanted. Control. Protection.

Possession.

"I want to be yours, Mr. Lemaitre," she cried. "I want to be yours so badly."

"Do you? I never would have guessed."

She twisted to meet his eyes. "Don't mock me. Don't laugh at me, please. It's the truth, and it's killing me that you don't want me."

"You mustn't mock *me*," he replied, the thunder back in his voice. "You don't want to be mine. You haven't the first idea about submission. You want a thrill, an experience. You want me to fuck you until you get your rocks off. You want the adrenaline rush."

"No. Yes." She sighed, following him with her gaze as he went to the bathroom to wash his hands. "I want you to use me and control me, like you did with your slaves. I want your power, your possession."

"You want my cock, because you're a nymphomaniac with poor impulse control."

"That's not true." She lay back down. "Well, it is true, but there's so much more than that in my heart." Her voice roughened in her frustration. "You won't even try to understand what I'm feeling."

"I don't think *you* understand what you're feeling." He returned and sat in the chair beside her, looking over her whip-marked body. "This is an ill-fated attraction, Valentina. How can I make it stop?"

Oh, those words hurt her. She had to make him see... "Make love to me. Just once," she begged. "Touch me just once so I can know the feeling of your...your magic."

"My magic?" He shook his head. "Jason's right. You don't live in the real world." He stood and paced away from her.

"Mr. Lemaitre, I would give anything to belong to you."

He turned back, holding up a finger. "Don't. Don't say you would give anything, especially to someone like me, because I'll take you up on that offer and you won't like it."

"I would like it. I'd do anything for you. Anything, anything, anything." She yelled the word at him, her heart pounding. "You know how I feel, I know you do. I only have this one life and I want to experience everything I desire."

"Everything *you* desire?"

"Yes, and you are keeping me from doing it."

"And you need this to be fulfilled in life? You need to be mine? To be taken by me, used by me? Possessed by me, as you so dramatically put it?"

"Yes," she cried. "That's what I need."

He crossed his arms over his chest. "What will you offer that I need? What will I get out of this possession, besides a recurrent headache?"

Valentina's face flushed red, because she hadn't once, not once, considered his side of things.

"Ah, but you see, my dear, that's the rub," he said quietly. "I'm not a service top. I take slaves for my pleasure, not theirs. I have less than no interest in your *needs*, Valentina, except as they intersect with what I desire."

She swallowed hard. "Well...what do you desire?"

His piercing gaze transformed from something reproachful to something more speculative. It scared her a little, the assessment in his expression.

"I think you're a selfish hedonist who wants what she wants," he said. "That's not slavery, you know. It isn't even power exchange. It's topping from the bottom and I don't tolerate it in those I 'possess.'"

Valentina tried not to be distracted by the growing tent in his robe. "You...you would have to teach me to be better. I need control."

"*You would have to. I need.* You're still not listening, Valentina," he said, coming back to the bed. "The only one having their needs met in a relationship between us would be me."

There had to be some flaw in his thinking, because she was sure he would meet her needs. His mastery would fulfill her as nothing ever had. "What can I give you?" she asked. "How can I prove that I'll do anything for you?"

"There you go with the 'I'll do anything' again."

"Mr. Lemaitre, please! What can I offer that would satisfy your desires? What would make it worthwhile for you?"

Again, that slow, almost threatening gaze of consideration. His eyes traveled over her, his lips drawn into a contemplative line. "You'll do anything?"

"Anything, I swear. There's nothing you could ask for that I wouldn't gladly do."

The air seemed to grow heavy between them. She knew she was being impulsive again, but she didn't care. Everything she'd said was true. After a moment, he made a small motion of annoyance. His expression hardened to something like stone.

"If that's how you feel," he said, "then I want a no-limits arrangement. Complete and utter ownership, no holds barred. No negotiation, no contracts, no release clauses. Your body is mine for one month, for whatever I desire."

Whatever I desire. The idea excited her so much she could barely breathe, but she forced herself to stop, to clarify his terms. "So I would have no rights in this relationship?"

"None."

"You could do whatever you wanted to me, and I couldn't stop you? What if you decided you wanted to kill me?"

"Then I get to kill you. Honestly, the way you perturb me, I would put the odds of a murder at 2 to 1."

She decided he was kidding, although he didn't have the slightest hint of humor in his demeanor. "Do you really want that?" she asked. "You really want...me...for a month? Does that mean..." She could barely say the words. "Does that mean I would become your slave?"

Some wary expression flitted across his face. His voice was light, almost a whisper, when he answered. "You have been my slave for some time now, haven't you? You might think on whether it's what you really want."

She didn't have to think. "I want it. I'm sure of it. Completely sure."

"You have no misgivings? No questions to ask?"

"No. If this is what you want—"

"Ah, finally, she is thinking about what I want," he said to the ceiling. "Perhaps there is hope." He looked back at her, shifting so the bulge beneath his robe grew even more apparent. "I believe in information, in negotiation, so let me tell you this. You will not be my play slave. You will not be my lover, girlfriend, or funslut. You'll be my real slave. You'll do what I say, whatever I say. You'll put aside any wants, needs, desires, and uncomfortable feelings that get in the way of me getting what I want. You'll eat what I say, you'll sleep where I say, you'll wear what I say, and you'll submit to every single act I choose to visit upon your body, whether it horrifies you or not. I'll fuck you when I want, I'll beat you when I want, and I'll ignore you when I want. I'll make you wait for my company until you're in agony, and then I'll ignore you some more just because it makes me hard to play with your emotions. I'll do everything in my power to fuck you up because that's what brings me pleasure. If you want to belong to me, Valentina, that's what it entails."

Every word out of his mouth made her wetter, not that she understood why. She only knew she wanted to be his, and if that meant giving up everything else, well...it was only for a month. It was twenty-nine days more than she'd ever expected him to give her.

"I want that." Three words. She couldn't come up with any more. There was very little blood left in her brain.

"I'm going to make you sign something. You're going to give me your word and your consent, and you're not going to back out of it. You're not going to be able to cry, beg, or plead your way out of this if we proceed. This isn't a game. Do you understand?"

"Yes, *monsieur.*"

"Yes, Master," he corrected.

"Yes, Master," she said, a thrill shivering through her. He was going to do this. He was going to master her, make her his slave. She could barely contain her excitement.

He blinked at her a moment, then stood. "Don't move."

She lay where she was on her stomach, aroused by the curt command in his voice. He left the room and returned a moment later with a black marker in his hand. It wasn't the fine-tipped kind. It had a great big cap on a wide, slanted tip. He gestured her over.

"Stand up. Stand here beside me." He pointed to the floor at his right.

She scrambled off the bed to stand where he indicated, and then her mouth dropped open as he put the pen to the pristine white wall between the two beds. In a large, scrawling hand he wrote *I belong to Le Maître*, along with a beginning date—today's date, January 15—and an ending date, February 14. With a slash of his arm he made a line.

"Your full name, *ma mignonne*," he said, handing her the marker.

She paused a moment, turning the pen in her fingers. Did she trust him?

Yes.

She put the pen to the smooth, white paint and signed *Valentina Maria-Rosa Sancia*, and in a fit of whimsy, dotted all three i's with hearts.

He met her eyes with a warm smile, and she returned a giddy grin.

"May I have my pen?" he asked.

"Yes, Master."

He took it from her and capped it, and tossed it on the bed, then turned back to her, shrugging off his robe. He was so perfect, so strong and finely formed. She took in his proud shoulders, his flat abs tapering down to defined pelvic furrows, and his cock... He was so big and thick, that even hard, his cock pulled downward. It bobbed back and forth as he turned to the nightstand beside the bed and yanked it open.

"Bend over the bed," he said, drawing out a condom. "Brace yourself on your arms."

Yes, oh God. Yes. *Finally*. She couldn't wait to have him inside her. All this time she'd dreamed of it, hoped for it. She moved obediently to the bed and bent over it, wincing a little at the sore areas of her back.

Behind her, he made a tsk of a sound. "Why did they do this to you? Idiots. I won't be able to mark you for a few more days, until your skin has healed." He traced a few of the cuts, light whispers of sensation. "I think the medicine's well enough into your wounds for a good fucking though, eh?"

"Whatever pleases you, Master," she said. Yes, that sounded very slavelike and good.

"I don't need your agreement," he snapped. "It was a rhetorical question. Eyes forward. Look down at the bed."

Valentina bit her lip, afraid to say anything else, even "Yes, Master." She heard the rattle of the condom as he unwrapped it, and some other wet sound. Lubricant?

She felt one hand at her waist. The other nudged between her ass cheeks. Oh. *God.*

"Master," she whispered. "I—"

"Silence. Not a word. If you can't be quiet, rest assured I'll find ways to punish you that don't involve your back." His hand left her hip and wrapped in her hair, jerking her head back. She cried out, feeling a rush of fear.

Don't hurt me, please. But he was going to hurt her. She'd expected pleasure, like when he'd gone down on her in his dungeon. She'd begged him to fuck her. Well, she was getting fucked all right, but not in the way she'd fantasized. She keened through her teeth as he pressed his cock to the tight bud of her ass. *You'll submit to every single act I choose to visit upon your body, whether it horrifies you or not.*

Her ass ached at the pressure, the ring refusing to admit him. When he made no forward progress, his hand tightened in her hair. "You asked for this," he taunted. "Submit to me. If you can endure being bled by a whip with a noose around your neck, you can endure being sodomized by a slightly outsized cock."

Slightly? she thought. With the help of copious lube, he slowly pried her open. She braced against the bed and groaned, her hands in fists against the rising agony. At last the head popped in, but it offered no relief. He stopped, letting go of her hair to grasp both her hips. She prepared to scream. If he drove into her she knew it would tear her, perhaps even kill her…

But he didn't. Instead he rocked in her, a centimeter forward, a centimeter back as he worked himself inside her. She'd had anal sex before but never with such a large man. She waited for the muscles to relax, to accustom to his girth, but the adjustment never came and he drove deeper and deeper. Her toes curled against the cold floor.

Finally, she couldn't bear it. She reached back, twisting to look up at him. "Please, Master."

"Please what? You must have realized my attentions came at a price."

She sucked in a breath, making little pants. "It hurts. It really...please... I'm trying to submit to you but...it really...hurts."

She was lifted and pushed toward the wall, driven by his hands and his cock still buried inside her tender place. He pressed against her back and put a hand on either side of her head, and turned her face so her nose landed on one of the hearts of her name. "You signed that not five minutes ago. Now look at it while I fuck you, and remember you promised to do *anything*. Relax your goddamned asshole so I can get in." On the words "relax" and "goddamned" he slapped her flank, sharp, hard cracks that made her cry out.

Because he was so much taller than her, he had to spread his legs to angle his cock into her ass. It gave him that much more leverage to fuck her. As he eased inside her, he took her hands and trapped them against the black words. *I belong to Le Maître.* My God, what had she agreed to? He moved against her back, pressing his thick cock forward until she groaned in entreaty. This wasn't the fucking she wanted, or the mastery she wanted. This wasn't pleasure.

This was submission.

"Stop it," he said, cracking her flank another time. "Stop shying away from my thrusts. Stop flinching."

"I'm afraid you'll hurt me."

"Oh, I'm going to hurt you, but you'll survive."

"Please, Master," she whispered, trying to move her hips. He held them fast. "I'm scared."

"Hush and be still, or I'll tie you down so you can't move an inch, and then I'll fuck you like this five times in a row."

The frightening thing was that she knew he would do it, that he meant every word he said. He had no pity or concern for what she wanted, just as he'd warned her. Helpless whines and pleas fell from her lips as he drove deeper. There was a bit less pain, but still the frightening pressure as he filled her. He put a hand on her neck and tilted her head back, rasping in her ear. "You're mine, little firebrand, for thirty whole days. You asked for possession. Do you know what I'm doing right now?"

"You're possessing me," she said with the little air he allowed her.

"Yes, I'm possessing you. Every part of you belongs to me, even your reluctant little asshole, and I'll take you there whether you want it or not." As he spoke, his fingers traced over the trails of her tears, then down to her hips and waist, where he held her for his thrusts. The lube made it easy for him to slide in and out. It was her flesh that resisted, aching from the stretch and invasion.

He might do this to her every day over the next month. Three times a day. Five. She shuddered, coming to a full realization of how dire her situation was. He'd tried to warn her that this wouldn't be fun, but she'd been so turned on at the idea of being his slave she hadn't remembered just how brutal he could be. He'd tried to warn her so many times. She'd seen him interacting with his male slaves, heard him being horribly brutal to them through the door of his back room.

She stared at the black words on the wall, and even as the pain made her cry and grit her teeth, she felt an empty, throbbing need in her womb. Her clit felt heavy and sensitive. As much as this hurt, something about it excited her too. Perhaps it was how powerless and vulnerable she felt, and the way he controlled her. She clung to the wall, wondering how long this would go on. There was no question of coming, of trying to take any pleasure from this encounter. He would give her pleasure if he wanted to give her pleasure, and otherwise, she was fucked. Literally. She wanted to reach down and finger her clit. She could have come just from the heightened sense of being a sexual creature—his sexual creature—but she didn't dare take her hands from the wall where he'd placed them. She was too afraid of what he'd do.

At last his breaths lengthened. She felt his heat against her sore back as he drove into her faster, frightening her with the depth of his thrusts. When she whimpered, he sighed against her ear and circled her neck again, pressing his thumb and middle finger up against her jaw. "I've wanted to fuck you like this for so long," he said. "Against the wall with my cock in your ass, with tears running down your cheeks. You cry out for this, Valentina. To be treated this way."

"Yes." It came out a whisper. She said it again, louder. "Yes, Master."

He rocked against her, going still. His garbled groan of pleasure almost made the pain and hurt seem worthwhile. If she was a true slave, she wouldn't even think about the pain. Would she? Or was that part of being a slave...reacting to the pain with all the fear and agony she felt, because that's what Master wanted, to hurt her?

She hoped he would explain these things to her. But tonight, this night, he didn't. As soon as he pulled out of her ass, he took her to the bathroom and cleaned her up again, and applied more antibiotic, and gave her a toothbrush and toothpaste and privacy. She leaned against the sink muttering *dio mio, dio mio* over and over until she managed to calm herself.

Then she went out into the bedroom and started freaking out again. The beds were *cages.* The fourth side of the bed, the open side, had sliding bars which he'd closed most of the way, leaving just enough space for her to crawl in. He stood waiting for her in his robe, every inch the exacting Master.

When she met his gaze, he looked back at her with a half-smile. "Where else would a slave sleep but in a cage?"

For a moment, just a moment, she almost lost it. She almost turned and ran, and tried to escape, but she knew he would have chased her and brought her back again. He was *Le Maître* and she'd signed her name on his wall. So she didn't refuse or run away. She crawled, naked and hurting, into his bed-cage and lay under the stark white counterpane and covers like a good slave.

Her Master drew the bars the rest of the way over. She saw now that they worked on a slider at the top. Ingenious. There was plenty of room inside. She could stand up and not hit her head on the bars at the top. Perhaps she could even jump up and down for exercise if he stored her there for long hours. She was really losing her mind now. He wouldn't do that, would he?

She was too afraid to ask. She only stared through the bars as he hooked a padlock around the post and secured it, effectively trapping her for the night. He went to the door and put his fingers on the light switch, then turned back to her. "Are you afraid of the dark?" he asked.

She shook her head. "N-no, *monsieur.*"

"Master," he reminded her. "Always, from now on."

"No, Master. I'm not afraid of the dark." *But this cage...*

"Sleep well," he said, flicking off the light. The room went black. The door closed behind him and he was gone.

Chapter Seven:
Well and Good

Michel left the white room, his senses alert for any sound of panic. He'd had slaves freak out in there. Not many, but some, one of whom had wrenched a leg between the bars and sprained her knee.

He didn't believe Valentina would lose her composure. For all her rash, impulsive behavior, she was easy to control with sexuality. One look at his cock and she'd gone all soft and submissive, surrendering to a rigorous round of sodomy. While he'd taken care not to injure her, he knew he'd hurt her. He'd felt the tension in her muscles, particularly the tight ring of muscle he'd forced open, and heard the pain in her panting, frantic sounds.

His cock twitched and began to thicken at the memory of it, lazy aftershocks of lust tingling in his balls. He brushed a hand over his swelling organ, willing it, like everything in his life, to submission. Valentina had been through enough for one night. The scene at the Citadel... *Dieu*, it could have been a disaster. It would have gutted him to lose Valentina, both as a person and a performer. As cruel as he'd been to her tonight, he hadn't done what he really wanted to do, which was beat her into a cowering ball and rail at her for her foolishness. But he had been that cowering ball once upon a time, and he would never do it to anyone else.

He shook such thoughts from his head. He had controlled himself, honed the restraint he'd practiced as long as he could remember, and tucked Valentina away in her cage for the night, clean, whole, and thoroughly assfucked. He went into his bedroom and checked the video monitor. Yes, still calm. She probably didn't realize the white room—his slave room—was wired and sound monitored. Every sound she made would come to him through the speaker beside his bed, every movement picked up by a night vision camera mounted in the corner. She would understand tomorrow when she lay in bed waiting for him. The equipment stood out against the white walls, as apparent as the words he'd written, securing her in service to him.

Oh, it wasn't a legal contract. It wasn't binding. He had to do the binding part himself, and he thought he'd made a good start. He stared at her prone form, her small movements as she tried to find a comfortable position with the cuts on her back. *Your fault, ma mignonne.* With the whipping she'd taken, she wouldn't be able to work for a few days. A bother, but he would keep her busy in other ways.

His cock swelled again, thinking of those ways. This time he let it fill to hardness, grasping it in calloused palms. A few pulls and he was already halfway to orgasm. As he pleasured himself, he thought about Valentina's softness, the femininity of her curves. He fucked men when he wanted to master leashed power, when he felt rough and aggressive, because men were difficult to hurt. Women...women were different. They were thrilling precisely because they were so easy to hurt, especially for a large man like him. It took skill to threaten and frighten a woman but not really hurt her. Valentina had been a quivering mess as he sodomized her, and yet she fit him perfectly. He had made her fit him and now she slept, secure in her submission to his will.

Soon, he'd take her pussy and perhaps even let her come. That wouldn't be as painful for her, the little nympho. She'd go mad with happiness. There would be times he'd bring her so much pleasure she'd nearly explode with it, only because it would amuse him to see her that way. *Just wait, little slave girl. With great sacrifice comes great reward.* He came in his hand with a sigh, imagining Valentina in the throes of ecstasy, her vibrant red hair thrown back on a pillow, her legs spread wide, offering herself to him, offering everything to him...

He cleaned himself up with a rueful chuckle. It wasn't the first time he'd masturbated over her, and certainly not the last. For his part, he would make sure she felt rewarded by the end because that's how he operated. He'd reward her with skills learned, with greater confidence and inner strength. With affection, and lifelong friendship if she wanted it. He never abandoned his slaves, only set them free to find more fulfilling masters or mistresses, because there was one thing he couldn't give his slaves, no matter how much they pleased him—romantic love.

Romance? Ugh. Love? He distrusted the very word. He distrusted the idea, the concept. His daughter Sara had forced him, kicking and screaming, to become a father, and he had to admit the experience had greatly enriched his life, but romantic love? It was slippery and risky, the very antithesis of control. His parents had loved one another. Michel understood that, saw it in the way they related to one another, the way they returned to each other, fight after fight, arrest after arrest, like magnets drawn together. He remembered them fucking on the floor, on the couch, wherever the urge struck them, not caring that he watched. By four or five he'd learned to leave the room.

He understood now, as an adult, that normal parents didn't act that way. Normal parents didn't fight and fuck and try to kill each other. His parents had been a particular brand of people, and addicted to a plethora of substances. He learned that at a young age too, not to eat the powders and pills they took, after a traumatic trip to the hospital to have his stomach pumped. He learned so many things young children shouldn't have to learn.

He was barely seven when his mother killed his father in a jealous rage over another woman, or perhaps because he'd stolen her drugs. She'd stabbed him in the heart with a dull kitchen knife. He'd screamed at her until the life blood ran from him, and she'd screamed back, and little Michel Leveille had watched all this and told himself, *never*. He would never love anyone as his parents loved each other. He would never scream and hit and throw things. He would never use drugs.

He would never lose control.

His mother went to prison and he became a ward of the state, assigned to various temporary homes. He sought solace in control, and practiced managing people both older and younger than himself in order to create some calm in the chaos of his life. When he was old enough, he left the last of his temporary homes and traveled, entertaining strangers and saving money until he could pay to change his name from Leveille to Lemaitre.

From the youngest age he had lived a calculated and careful life, free of strong emotion, because the alternative—blood and screaming and terror—did not suit him. *Never*, he had told himself as a seven-year-old boy. For many years, it was the only word that kept him sane. Now, nothing thrilled him like taking an uncontrolled situation and making it neat and controllable.

He gave another rueful laugh and studied the green-tinged monitor. Valentina Sancia, a raw, shrieking, crying, emotional mess of a headstrong woman, his newest slave. Had he felt this need to corral her, to control her, from the very moment he met her in Naples? He had denied himself her charms because he feared chaos, but Valentina needed him, pure and simple. She lacked control and he had it in spades.

And she'd be worth the struggle, he knew. She was strong and yet soft and sensual, an erotic combination he found intoxicating. She gave herself over to hedonistic urges with no qualms or inhibitions, another necessity in a good slave. She was beautiful too, with her flaming red hair and porcelain smooth skin. He would enjoy training her and transforming her, teaching her to control her impetuous passions. Perhaps best of all, this arrangement solved a problem for him. Keeping a slave at his home would offset his urges to go to the Citadel, and allow Jason and his daughter to come and go as they pleased. They were newly engaged and needed time to explore one another and be with their friends, without the worry of running into dad in the back rooms.

It was all well and good. He fell asleep with a sense of satisfaction, a sense of everything being exactly as it was meant to be.

* * * * *

Valentina awakened in the bare, white room, sun peeking through slatted white blinds. It took a moment for her to remember she was at Mr. Lemaitre's house. Her Master's house. She lifted her head, her eyes focusing on the black words on the wall, then on the small, blinking camera mounted in the corner across the room.

Was he watching her? Observing her like some animal in a zoo? She resisted the urge to pull the covers over her head. Her back stung worse today than it had last night, and her ass... She felt the faintest twinge of soreness. It was more of an ache, a physical memory of pain and intrusion that made her whole body tense.

A wave of horny response swept through her. He had fucked her ass last night, pressed her against the wall and thrust into her over and over with no thought to her wants and needs. He'd used her and hurt her and then put her in a cage and walked away as if she meant nothing to him. So fucking hot. She slid her hand down between her legs, only meaning to soothe the tingling there, but her light touch added fuel to the flames. She sought out her clit, rubbing it to life with gentle stroking. With her other hand, she squeezed her nipples under the covers, first one, then the other...

The door crashed open. Well, it didn't crash. It opened wide, and Mr. Lemaitre stood there naked as a Roman statue, providing the mental crash in her brain. Instinctively, she curled her hands away from her pussy and her nipples.

"No, continue," he said. "Our conversation can wait." He crossed to the bed and unlocked the cage, and threw the covers back so she felt stripped. Attacked. His light blue eyes seemed dark as he put his hands on her legs and spread them open. "Continue. Masturbate for me until you come."

She stared at him, still half lost in horny fantasies and daydreams, until he leaned down and slapped her across the cheek. It wasn't a hard slap. It didn't send her flying—she'd slapped men much harder, many times. No, this was a delicious, kinky slap, meant to tell her who was in charge. She put her hand on her pussy, feeling hot and cold as he stared down at her with an intent look on his face. She was awake now, under his power, and he wanted her to masturbate. Okay.

His eyes roved over her as she fondled herself, pausing at her nipples as she pinched them, then moving lower to her pussy. His regard alone was almost enough to make her come. She rubbed herself harder, toying with her nipples in a light, soft touch that usually got her off. She closed her eyes, then opened them as she sensed him move again. He brushed her fingers away from her nipples and grabbed them himself.

His touch was not light or soft.

She cried out as he twisted the sensitive peaks, and shied away from the torment.

"Don't stop," he scolded as her hand left her pussy. "Spread your legs wider. Masturbate as you were told. You were all too eager to do it a few moments ago."

Yes, but then she'd been under her own control. Now, she was one hundred percent under his. *Give yourself up to him. Give him your pleasure.*

He let go of her nipples and took her face in his hands. "Come, damn you. That's what I asked you to do."

She wanted to, but there was some fear or embarrassment that stopped her, some performance pressure she'd never had to deal with before. The longer she took, the more displeased he looked, which made it even more difficult. Finally he went to the nightstand and got a condom, and rolled it onto his rigid cock with an impatient sigh.

"Come here." He took her legs and dragged her toward him, not being careful of her cuts or bruises. "If you are going to be a sexual creature, then be one. No self-consciousness. No shame." He nudged the head of his cock against her sensitive pussy, gathering her close. As she stared into his eyes, he pinned her hands above her head and pressed inside.

Valentina drew in a sharp breath, arching her pelvis to accommodate his thick length. He was so solid, so impossibly firm sliding against her spasming walls. It seemed an eternity before he pushed all the way in, but she loved that it took a long time, because this was a joining she wanted to remember. He moved so slowly it was like the world turning, like nature breathing in and out. She counted every inch of his invasion, every measured breath. Sometime in the midst of this, he leaned down and caught her lips in a kiss. Not a tender, sweet kiss, but a biting and demanding one. This was challenge, not sweetness. He was driving her to be the "sexual creature" he claimed she was.

She did her best to give him everything. People said she had no sense of self-preservation, and perhaps they were right. She welcomed every rough, pummeling thrust, sinking down into his possession. When the waves built, when her body started to tense and reach for that peak, she closed her eyes and drifted away on sensation, only to be drawn back by a sharp sound. He stared down at her, insisting on her attention.

She lost herself in his gaze. She could have cried for the trembling pleasure he brought her, the completion of her fantasies, the fiery response he created every time he stroked her clit. She made noises she couldn't control, pleading, moaning noises, but to look at him...to reveal herself to him this way was novel and frightening.

And he knew it. Every time she looked away, he nudged her face back again. He persisted, forcing her compliance until the pure skill of his touches and strokes overcame her fears. She stared at him, wanting to cry, wanting to struggle, wanting to laugh and scream and explode as he braced himself over her, pounding into her. She loved being pinned down and forced to obey. She wanted to attack him as much as she wanted him to subdue her.

When her orgasm came she did attack him, sinking her nails into the muscles of his arms and shoulders, trying to pull him down. He fought back, pushing her hard into the bed as her walls collapsed around him. He gave a shout that sounded very much like a roar. If her climax was powerful, his must have been doubly so. She could feel his cock pulsing inside her and she clamped down on it, wanting to hold this moment forever. *Don't leave. Never leave me.* But he pulled away from her with a grimace of...disgust.

Valentina didn't understand. Tears formed in her eyes, weak, silly tears. Slaves didn't cry, did they? He stood and walked away. Valentina lay where she was, staring at the bars on top of the bed as they went in and out of focus. She stared at them until the tears dissipated and the bars seemed stark and black again. By that time Mr. Lemaitre had come back. He stood over her, the tube of antibiotic cream in his hand.

"Turn over. Lie face down on the bed."

"What did I do, Mr. Lemaitre?"

"Master," he corrected her.

"Master, how did I anger you?"

"Don't make me ask you again. Not in my current mood."

He glared at her until she rolled onto her stomach. He'd just fucked her, just given her the strongest orgasm of her life, and he wasn't in a good mood? He checked her cuts again, muttering things in French she didn't understand. She wished she'd put more effort into languages growing up, but she'd been preoccupied with the only thing she was good at...balancing on top of her father and brothers' hands and flying through the air.

"Since you can't work, we'll use this time to get you a physical," he said, drawing her from her thoughts.

"A physical? When I came to work for the Cirque, they gave me a million physicals. They checked my conditioning, my muscles, my joints—"

"Not that kind of physical." He put the cream away and sat on the bed beside her. She turned onto her side and couldn't help staring at his cock. Even in a flaccid, relaxed state, it was large. His balls hung down, heavy and ponderous. No wonder he communicated so much virility. He was designed like a bull.

"Valentina, are you listening to me?"

She flushed, meeting his eyes. "I... Well, I was a little distracted."

"I wish I could beat you."

She flushed hotter, staring at the floor.

"Soon," he said, as if to reassure himself. "I'll be able to punish you soon for all these lapses of propriety. You desperately need it. For now, as I said earlier, I want you to have a physical and STD tests. I'll be tested too so we can safely have unprotected sex."

"Unprotected sex is never safe," she pointed out. She'd learned that long ago and she'd always been careful.

"You're correct," he conceded. "A lot of things between us will be...how shall we say? Quasi-safe. You're on the pill?"

"The shots," said Valentina. "Yes, Master." She swallowed hard. "What do you mean by quasi-safe?"

He gave her a long look, then a derisive laugh that wasn't comforting. "Perhaps it's not too late..." He shook his head. "I suppose it is far too late for both of us." He leaned over her, staring at her very directly. She couldn't help shrinking back on the bed. His tousled black hair made a dark halo around his head. "Someday you'll wish I'd left you alone. Many times in future days, you will wish it."

"No. I'll never wish that."

He groaned and leaned his head back. "Don't be so fucking naive and innocent. I can't bear it."

She felt hurt for a moment, until his hint of a smile reassured her. "I've always wanted you, and I will always want you," she said, believing it.

He cupped her face, rubbing a thumb over and across her chin. "You must learn that 'always' is a word to tempt demons. 'Never' is the same." Again, he gave that sharp, derisive laugh. "But all of this is lost on you. Listen, I have appointments this afternoon, so we're going to your place this morning."

"My...my place?"

"Yes, your place where you live, to get whatever you'll need to stay here for the next month."

"I can pack my own things," she said, sitting up in the bed.

"I'm coming to help you. Or rather, I'm coming to keep you from bringing too much."

This was a disaster. One look at her apartment and he'd think she was a lunatic, even more of a lunatic than he already thought, especially considering the stark, uncluttered organization in which he lived. "I—but—but I have nothing to wear. I came here wrapped in a blanket."

"No matter. I've accumulated a lot of female clothing over the years." He took her arm and hauled her out of the bed. "We're sure to find something in your size."

Chapter Eight:
Very Bad

Valentina sat beside Mr. Lemaitre in his gleaming, expensive car. She didn't know much about cars but she supposed his car was expensive by the way it hummed and eased around downtown corners, and by all the lights and buttons on the dash. He was dressed now, a sophisticated, urbane businessman going about his day, fetching his slave's things from her apartment. She was dressed too, in some other woman's clothes.

It upset her a little, that an entire section of his closet overflowed with the abandoned or forgotten clothing of other women he'd enslaved, fucked, or otherwise been involved with. She assumed the garments were clean but she didn't like wearing the clothes of a woman she was jealous of. *Valentina, you idiot. You're no more to him than any of them were.*

But she wished she was. She wished she could be special to him, not just another slave to train. Oh well. She'd take what she could get. She was young. There would be time for other things later. For now, for these thirty days. Twenty-nine days...

She stole looks at his hands, at his thighs, too shy to turn and stare at his face the way she wanted to. She wished she could huddle right beside him but he was driving. She would have loved to sink into his arms but no arms were opened to her. He glanced over at her instead, his expression cool, unreadable. "You're trembling. Are you cold?"

"Yes. No." She shook her head. "I don't know. I'm only...shivery."

She didn't know the right word for how she felt. She was too agitated to think of words in English, or even Italian. She could barely think at all. Winter's morning light filled the car, striking his knee, her shoe, the herringbone upholstery of the seat. A spot of sun hit something on the floor and it sparkled red. When she leaned to get it, he reached for her as if he thought she was falling.

"What are you doing?"

Collecting things. It is something I do. "Nothing," she said aloud, palming her treasure. When he looked forward again, she glanced down and found she had a piece of speckled cellophane, something like a scrap from a Mylar balloon, or a holiday gift basket. It lifted her spirits—the red color, the sparkle. It was just what she needed. She slipped it into her pocket, watching Mr. Lemaitre's profile from her peripheral vision to see if he noticed.

No, not Mr. Lemaitre.

Master.

Valentina ached this morning. She ached from being fucked, she ached from spending the night in a cage. Her heart felt weary and excited and confused. She wanted to be Mr. Lemaitre's slave, wanted to be one of his best slaves *ever*, but good intentions didn't guarantee success. You could intend to conquer the most daring circus stunts in the world, but unless you were physically capable of doing them...

She shifted on her sore ass and turned to look out the passenger window. He had said he would train her, that she desperately needed it. He had seemed warm at times last night, but then so withdrawn that he frightened her. Some of the things he said...well, she didn't understand him in the slightest. Being with him was like being in a cage with a wild animal you admired but didn't really trust.

Thinking of cages reminded her of his white room and his cage-beds. It was so depraved, so very sexy, the way he took whatever he wanted. So many people hid or denied their desires, but Mr. Lemaitre reveled in them and brought them to real life. She pressed her legs together against the rising heat in her pussy. She wished she could thrust her hand down her borrowed jeans and stroke herself until she came. Better, she wished he would do it, reach over as he drove and force his thick fingers inside her.

He put a hand on her knee and she jumped, and wondered if he had somehow known the direction of her thoughts. He said nothing, only stroked over her jeans, up and down her thigh.

As they neared the residences, Mr. Lemaitre withdrew his hand and drove to her building without asking the number. Did he know where everyone lived, or just her? He parked the car and Valentina realized it wasn't that big of a car, for all its luxury. "Where will we fit everything?" she asked, turning to look at the back seat.

"As I said, you're not bringing much. You'll spend the majority of your time serving me."

"Oh. By serving you...you mean..."

"Giving me pleasure, satisfying my whims. Taking my cock in your holes. A job you were born to do, don't you think?" He looked at his watch, cool and distant again. She scrambled out of the car and tried to match his long strides as they walked to her door.

"My place is kind of a mess," she warned him at the threshold.

"I expected it to be."

She turned the knob. He frowned as she pushed it open.

"No key? You don't lock your door, Valentina?"

"I needed the key for something else. I have nothing valuable to steal, anyway."

He made an annoyed sound and insisted on entering ahead of her to check things out. It was a kind, protective thing for him to do, but she never locked her door and thus far, no intruders had ever come in.

While he prowled her small living room, she turned on the light, embarrassed by the clutter. All her mess was here and there...her clothes and sketches and silly things she put together for fun. She had boxes of scraps and tools on the table, and worst of all, a half-completed likeness of Mr. Lemaitre. She furtively placed the red cellophane into a box with other bits of things.

"You see," she said when he turned to her. "Nothing is disturbed. I needed the key for that."

She pointed to a collage she was working on, a portrait of Jason Beck constructed of bottlecap eyes for his hardness and brown and gold leaves for his hair. She used papier-mâché to create the form of him, and the key to represent his heart. Mr. Lemaitre stared at it hard.

"I can get another key," she said, following his gaze. "Or maybe find another one and take that one off."

"What is it?" His voice sounded sharp. "Explain it to me."

She walked closer to her work. She'd been putting it together for weeks now. "It's Jason. You see, the eyes and the hair..."

His lips twitched. "The hair is a good likeness."

"I collected the leaves in the fall."

"Naturally." He reached out as if to touch it, but he didn't. "This fascinates me. I like it, but at the same time I find it disturbing." He turned to her with a reproachful glare. "You never told me you were an artist."

"Oh, I'm not an artist. I only do this for fun."

He backed up and bumped into a bird made of matchbooks. It fluttered over his shoulder until he reached to make the wings still. "How long have you been doing this...for fun?" he asked.

He tilted his head to read the matchbooks. She'd collected them from all over Italy, traveling with her family's circus. "I don't know," she answered. "I've always liked to take things that feel special to me and make them into something new. It's a way of keeping memories."

"But these leaves and paper scraps, my dear, they will not last forever." He crept around her small apartment, being careful not to jostle her things, even though he was much bigger than she was and she jostled them all the time. He stopped at a sculpture of a woman she'd made of slender branches, a dancer she'd seen at the Cirque. He scrutinized the wood, tracing a finger over the body's delicate joints. "Why make art this way? These sticks are weak and breakable."

"I know," she said sadly. "It doesn't stay."

"It's a shame. It's beautiful work."

"Well, beauty doesn't stay either."

He straightened and turned to her, thinking. Considering. She didn't understand what puzzled him. If anyone should know about the vagaries of art and creativity, it would be him. Like a circus act, the things she made were delicate and ephemeral. Laden with meaning and sometimes difficult to process. She could tell he didn't know the work on the table was him. It was large and bold, obviously made in his likeness, but so often people didn't see what they looked like through other people's eyes.

Ah, well. It didn't matter. It wasn't nearly finished.

His attention caught on her self-portrait, a canvas in mixed media. Eyes, nose, mouth, strong chin and heart shaped face. Hair of ribbon and paper and candy, because it had been the precise color and shape she needed. Pretty soon the ants would come.

"That's you," he said, gesturing to it. He recognized her when he couldn't recognize himself. Strange. She nodded, reaching without thought into the box with the paper scraps. She fished out the scrap of red cellophane and held it up to the outline of the hair.

"This belongs here," she said. "I will do it later."

He moved closer, scrutinizing the mish-mash of discovered materials, then looked over at her with an expression that spoke of resignation. "*Alors,*" he said. "What a remarkable creature you are."

She put the scrap back on the table, watching the sparkles catch the light. "Is that a good or a bad thing, to be a remarkable creature?"

"It's very bad for me."

She looked up at him, then stepped back from the intensity of his gaze. He caught her with his hand and drew her close again. He felt so solid, so warm and bracing, the scent of his cologne a subtle tease. He stared down at her mouth as she studied his face. How intent he looked, how tragic and stern. She couldn't tell if he was pleased or angry as he wound his fingers in her hair and pressed his lips to hers.

His kiss felt like a storm, like something dangerous. He muttered in the middle of it, then took her lips again, holding and twisting her hair hard. His other hand pressed into her back, hurting her, but she didn't care. She wished this could go on forever, this violent embrace, but then it ended as abruptly as it had begun and he pulled away from her.

"I have meetings," he said.

She gazed at him, limp and out of breath. He turned from her, turned in a full circle, then back again. He took her wrist and shook it. "I have meetings, did you hear me? We'll have time for this later. Go pack up your things."

* * * * *

83

Aside from practical, necessary items—work clothes, toiletries, etcetera—Michel allowed her only one set of drawing pencils and one sketchbook. Thirty days, he told himself. It was only thirty days.

But long after he left her in the care of his houseboy and returned to work, that single sketchbook stayed on his mind. Before today, he'd had no idea she was an artist. A performance artist, yes. A visual artist, no. He stared into space, second-guessing himself. Would he harm her, taking away her freedom to create? Keeping her in a cage for thirty days with only one method to vent her artistic impulses? Was he doing it only to see what happened? Whether she would crack, or break somehow? Was he *experimenting* with her?

He wasn't sure. He didn't know.

Twice, he zoned out in the middle of meetings with the artistic heads of *Cirque Élémental*. Bad behavior, and people noticed, although no one said anything. Jason gave him irritated looks. Michel stared back at the man, imagining a key where his heart was.

Ah, well. He'd pay better attention once he'd worked through the thoughts in his head. He had things to consider, choices to weigh. He enjoyed mulling over conundrums and puzzles, and things that couldn't be explained.

Like her.

A few hours ago, in her cluttered, messy apartment, he'd taken her in his arms and kissed her in a way he'd never kissed any other slave. He'd breathed her in like a drug, all his senses in overload. He had curled his hands in her hair and pressed her against him and even whispered *ma chérie* against her cheek. In truth, he'd barely stopped himself from taking her on the floor.

Pathetic.

Not even twenty-four hours in, and he'd already made his second serious mistake. The first mistake had been in the white room, when he'd fallen on her and fucked her without the least bit of control over his impulses. He was disgusted with himself. He'd shaken it off, determined that would be his last weak act as her Master, and then he'd followed it up with the kiss of the ages beside her ridiculous self-portrait.

Not ridiculous. Fascinating, and half made of candy.

He might have withstood the temptation if it was only her beauty and her physical talent that attracted him. He knew scores of people who were beautiful and physically talented. He was rich in that currency, perhaps too rich. He might have withstood her sensuality and bubbly personality, her daring. He loved risk-takers, but even that he might have dismissed as a dearth of common sense.

But no. In her apartment, he'd been confronted with something he was helpless to stand against—soaring creative genius. Her brain didn't work like everyone else's, and neither, he suspected, did her heart. Her art was unsettling and original, and best of all, without preciousness or reflection. She simply did these things, in the same way she fucked every man she fancied and danced without fear on no greater surface than her partners' upturned palms.

"Michel?"

He looked around the conference table into ten pairs of questioning eyes. He cleared his throat and scratched his forehead. "Let's reconvene in a week," he said. "My apologies. I'm scattered. I didn't sleep very well last night."

"Is everything all right?" asked Genevieve in concern. Jason scowled at him.

"Everything's fine," he assured them. "If you have any specific questions, make an appointment to see me in my office."

With that, he shut his laptop and escaped with most of his dignity intact. It was his company. They worked for him. If he wanted to blow off a meeting because greater problems were demanding his attention, he damn well could. He retreated to his office, determined to salvage at least part of the day for work. He put Valentina, her art, his kiss, all of it out of his mind and focused on an emailed spreadsheet.

Five minutes later, a knock interrupted him.

"See my goddamn secretary," he yelled. "I'm busy."

Another knock, and then Jason stuck his head in. Of course. At his dire glare, his future son-in-law shrugged. "You said if we had any specific questions, to come to your office."

"I said to make an appointment." He stood and crossed the room, intending to shut him out, but Jason put a hand on the door before he could close it.

"I heard you left the Citadel with Valentina last night."

"You heard it from whom?" he asked with a sigh.

"Everyone. Do you have a minute?"

Against his better judgment, Michel admitted Jason and gestured him toward a chair, then sat behind the desk, crossing his arms over his chest. "What, then? What is your question?"

Jason narrowed his eyes. "What ever happened to 'My life is complicated enough'?"

"What are you talking about?"

"Valentina. You spent the night with her, didn't you? You wouldn't be acting this way otherwise."

Michel stuck out his jaw, then heaved a frustrated sigh. "You're like a woman. You have to know everything."

"I wouldn't normally care who you're locking in chains, but this is Valentina Sancia. She's not really your type."

"I have a type?"

Jason snorted. "Yes, you do. Submissive, obedient, attractive. She's only one of those things."

"Perhaps I've grown bored with my usual type."

"So you gave them a farewell check and relocated them to California. Who else are you playing with right now?"

"That's none of your business." That was what he said aloud, but the question jolted him, because the answer was no one. The past few weeks he hadn't played with anyone, except...

"Is there a point to all this?" Michel asked in as bland a tone as he could muster. "If not, I have some gripping figures to look at from the set-design department. I'm sure you understand."

"I heard she had a noose around her neck when you found her, and that she was too injured today to work."

Jason wasn't asking if these things were fact. He knew they were. He was asking what Michel intended to do about them. Jason was fiercely protective of his performers, which was one of the reasons Michel put up with him. The other reason was that his daughter adored the man.

"Okay," Michel said, leaning forward. "Shall I tell you what I have planned for our little hellion? Will that put your mind at ease?"

"Probably not, but tell me anyway. I'm curious."

"I'm going to take over her for thirty days. One month."

"Take over her?" Jason sat up straighter.

"She agreed to it. She wants it. I'm going to keep her in the spare room at my house and attempt to train some of the craziness out of her."

"You mean, train away that fire that attracted you to her in the first place?"

"It attracted me to her as a performer," Michel clarified. "As a person, we both know she's aggravating as hell. She needs...mellowing."

Jason leaned back, considering. After a moment, he shook his head. "No. This is bad."

"What? There's nothing bad about it." Michel turned back to his laptop. He'd never been so anxious to return to the tedious crunching of numbers. "It's consensual, and I have no intention of hurting her."

"Said the man who unhooked her from a noose in one of the back rooms last night."

"I didn't do that to her."

"Didn't you? You don't think you had anything to do with it?"

"No, I did not." Michel's pulse had risen with Jason's aggressive line of questioning. He willed himself to calm, falling back on the basic truth of the matter. "I think this is a great solution for both of us."

Jason arched a brow. "How so?"

"I help transform Valentina into a content, obedient slave, and you and Sara don't have to worry about running into me at the Citadel."

"Because you'll be with Valentina at your house."

"Exactly."

"So you're doing it for us, then."

Michel scowled at his sarcastic tone. "And for me, damn you. You know I enjoy developing slaves. I like the power of it. I like that I've changed them by the time I'm finished with them. I suppose it's my megalomania that makes me want to do it, but even so...I mean her no harm. I intend to make her better. As you know, it's the whole point of the game."

"Yeah. Just remember it's a game, and that you're toying with another human being's life."

"I never forget that. How can I, with you poking in my business?"

"I'm going to keep poking you as long as she's with you. How long did you say? Thirty days?"

"Twenty-nine," Michel answered smoothly. "One day down, and thus far, she's survived. Give Sara my love, will you?"

It was a dismissal. Michel had work to do, and Valentina had occupied too many of his thoughts already. He didn't want any more questioning, any more dire warnings from Jason or anyone else. He had to get his mind—and his thoughts—into proper order and get home to Valentina.

Not to kiss her or fuck her. No. The time for that romantic nonsense was over. It was time to start training up his slave.

Chapter Nine:
On Track

Valentina sat on her bed in the white room, scuffing at a small drawing in the corner of her sketch pad. She worked in conservation mode, rationing the pages in case he didn't allow her more when she ran out. She had the sketch pad and her phone, and that was all. No books, no computer, and no TV. His snippety houseboy-slash-minion wouldn't let her go out, wouldn't even let her take a walk around her Master's picturesque neighborhood. He took her clothes away, for God's sake.

"Your Master's orders," he'd said. The man's name was Galvin. He had beautiful clear skin and large eyes, and a permanently placid expression. He was about her age, and his physique suggested a fellow athlete, but any attempts to get to know him petered out right away. Valentina prayed that Mr. Lemaitre would let her return to work the next day, or she might die of boredom.

She closed the sketch pad and flopped on her back. Michel Lemaitre was too hard to draw. It was impossible to capture his air of capability, and virility, his beautiful perfection, and any lesser likeness wasn't good enough. How long had she been in this damn white room? Three, four hours? This slavery thing bored her. She did a few exercises to keep her muscles in order, a few handstands just to amuse herself, and then she considered masturbating...but...

Her eyes flicked to the cameras. Did Mr. Lemaitre review the footage at the end of each day? Was Galvin watching right now? As if she had summoned the man with her thoughts, he stuck his head in the half-opened door.

"Mr. Lemaitre is coming. He's five minutes away."

Valentina gawked. "What does that mean? What must I do?"

"He wants you waiting in the living room." He held up his phone, pointing to a text in French. Mr. Lemaitre couldn't have texted *her*? He was her Master, after all. But no, he had to text this stranger so the man could give her orders. It annoyed her, mostly because her mind was about to snap from boredom. She stomped to the bathroom and brushed her teeth, fingercombed her hair and put on a little lip gloss. She turned to check out her cuts. Healing quickly...the cream he'd applied must have helped. Out in the living room she flung herself sideways on the couch and frowned at Galvin. "Can I sit down while I'm waiting here?"

"You can," he said with a small incline of his head. "But you'd better be on your feet when he comes through that door."

Something about the way he said it cut through her bored irritation and started a little thump of arousal in her clit. *You'd better be on your feet.* She was Mr. Lemaitre's slave, here to serve him from the moment he got home.

Well, at least it would give her something to do.

The door opened a moment later. Valentina leaped up, struck, as always, by the sight of Mr. Lemaitre. Tall, elegant, in a fine wool coat that hugged his shoulders. He didn't look at her right away, although she was sure he knew she was there. Instead he greeted Galvin, shrugging out of his coat. He took off his jacket next, and handed them both to the younger man, who carried them out of the room. Only then did he turn his gaze to her. "How are you, Valentina?" he asked.

"I'm bored."

His lips curved in a hint of a smile. "I don't doubt it. You might have worked today if you'd made better choices last night. You were missed by your colleagues. Jason in particular asked about you."

"What did you tell him?"

His smile faded. "The truth. That you've bargained away your freedom for the next month in a regrettable act of foolishness." His gaze flicked toward the kitchen. "You've become acquainted with Galvin?"

"He's been staring at me all day," she sniffed. "Lurking around. I think he wants me."

"He's gay, my dear." Mr. Lemaitre tugged at the knot of his tie. "I wouldn't have left him alone with you otherwise. He would have spent all day fucking you rather than watching you." As he pulled off his tie, Galvin drifted back in and lifted it from his fingers. She watched him leave again, feeling piqued.

"I don't need a babysitter, you know."

Mr. Lemaitre stopped in the act of unbuttoning his top button. "Do you think I would leave you here to your own devices?"

"Why not? What would I have done?" The man's house was so empty and boring, she couldn't have found many ways to get into trouble.

He grimaced and flipped through some mail on the table by the door. "While you belong to me, I'll want to know everything you do. It arouses me to monitor and control you. I pay Galvin to keep my home, and as a bonus, he serves as my eyes and ears. Get used to it."

"Why don't you use slaves for your housekeeping chores?"

He threw down the stack of mail and turned to her with an annoyed expression. "Because most of them are useless at housework. They do shoddy jobs only to be punished. It's tiresome, just like your unending questions. Come here."

She crossed to him, unsure if he was going to embrace her or slap her. What he did was turn her around to look at her back. He said a few words in French, words she recognized as expletives. "Still not healed enough to beat you as I would like. But you could bear a spanking."

Before she could process his words, he dragged her toward the couch. With an efficient grace, he pulled her down over his lap. Okay, a spanking wouldn't be that bad, surely. If she could survive a whip...

Whap! The first smack sounded obscenely loud echoing off the bare walls. And oh, it was way worse than she thought. *Whap, whap, whap.* His hand rained down in an unending barrage of crisp, sharp slaps to her ass cheeks. Her determination to remain still, to bear it with dignity, soon flew out the window. She wiggled and arched against his strong thighs and the smooth, fine fabric of his pants. "Ow, Master... Please."

He stopped, rubbing his palm over her heated ass cheeks. "'Please?' We're only getting started. You need this, my dear—I find it a tried-and-true method for silencing questions. There's only one thing you need to know here. I will rule and you will submit. When I am anywhere near you, your entire concentration will be focused on what I want, what I need. When you annoy or question me, you will be punished and instructed how better to behave to my liking. This will be lesson number one, to be followed by others."

Her heart fluttered and beat harder at his firm warning...while other parts of her fluttered in a different way. "How many others?" she managed to ask, pressing her legs together.

"As many as it takes, until I've molded you into my perfect slave."

"Or until my time is up," she said shakily.

"I promise you, I'll accomplish my aims long before then."

With those words, he resumed spanking her. His hands were so large, and his arms so powerful. She didn't think a spanking could hurt worse than being marked with a snake whip, but she was reconsidering that assumption. She cried and fidgeted, wondering if Galvin would come help her if she screamed his name.

No, he wouldn't.

Her Master tightened his grip on her arm. "Stop pulling away. You must accept whatever I choose to do to you. I own you." The spanks rose to even greater intensity. "If you can't remember that, I'll sodomize you against the wall again, while you stare long and hard at the terms you agreed to. I did warn you before you signed, girl. I did offer you escape."

Valentina swallowed a sob. Escape? Why would she want escape? His discipline and demands were the necessary antidote to her tormented wildness. Her whole life she had lived for this moment, for the person with the will and stubbornness to subdue her and show her she had no other choice but to shape up. She was wet and hot for him, and anxious to be molded into his vision of the perfect slave. She *wanted* that. She belonged here with him, even if her ass cheeks stung so bad she could hardly bear it. She stayed as still as she could, surrendering as far as her body would allow. But oh...it hurt like fire, like irons being laid against her skin. Tears squeezed from her eyes and dripped onto the hardwood floor below.

Finally he stopped, and used those big, punishing hands to guide her to her feet in front of him. She felt herself curling in, assuming a defensive posture. "Don't slouch," he said. "Stand up tall. Your posture should always be one of presentation. Do you understand what that means?"

She shook her head, wiping away tears.

"Presentation. Display. Display yourself to your Master for his pleasure. Don't slouch and cower." As he spoke, he poked and prodded her, straightening her hips and pinching her breasts. Then he held up his hands. "Put your nipples against my palms."

She had to thrust her breasts out to do so. Apparently it was the effect he sought, because he dropped his hands and said, "Stay. Yes. Just like that."

Her nipples stung from his pinches, but her face stung worse, from embarrassment. No, not embarrassment. Exposure. She wasn't in charge of her body anymore...all her limbs and curves were for him. It gave her a frightened, bereft feeling, at the same time it made her desperate to be close to him. He watched her as if waiting to see if she would comment, or question him again. She didn't.

He pulled her right between his legs, reminding her to maintain her presentation posture. She did her best, holding her spine taut even as her ass throbbed with lingering heat.

"Let's begin with some words, little slave. Four words, easy to remember." He grasped her face between his fingers. *"I serve you, Master."*

She got lost a moment in his eyes. He had to give her a brisk slap on the cheek to refocus her. "Repeat it. *I serve you, Master.*"

"I serve you, Master," she said in a loud, clear voice. It was sinking in, the totality of it. She wasn't the old Valentina anymore, but someone else, someone he was creating to his specifications.

"Say it again," he said. "I don't want you to forget it. *I serve you, Master.*"

"I serve you, Master." She flinched as he took one of her nipples between his fingers and pinched it even harder than before. The pain grew in intensity until she quailed away from it. He tsked and cupped her neck.

"Who do you serve?"

She tried to think through the pain he gave her. She'd just learned this! "I serve you, Master," she finally cried.

"Show me. Don't flinch when I hurt you. Accept it."

He pinched her other nipple, so, so much harder than before, and she ground her teeth to stay her pleas of mercy. Her body tensed with the effort to stay still.

"Does it hurt?" he asked, staring into her eyes.

"Yes."

"Yes, Master," he corrected, tightening his fingers until she felt hot, aching pain.

"Yes, Master," she gasped, holding his ice-blue gaze.

"Do you deserve to be hurt?"

"Yes, Master."

"Why?"

This was the most painful part—understanding why she needed this, and facing the fact that she was so often out of control. Could he train her to be better? To control her temper, her passions, to think before she spoke? She wanted to become worthy of his affection, so his disdainful prompts were a nightmare beyond the pain in her breasts.

"I deserve to be punished because I...I'm bad," she said.

Something in his eyes flickered. "No. Try again."

"Because...because..." She started to cry because he was hurting her so terribly and she didn't know the answer he wanted. "Because I ask too many questions."

"Getting closer."

She broke into open sobs. "I don't know. Please, help me."

"'*Because I serve you, Master*,'" he provided in a tight voice.

"Because I serve you, Master." Hadn't he just taught her that? She was so awful at this. So stupid. Her lips trembled and she bit them to keep them still.

"It's not that hard, Valentina. The answer to the lion's share of my questions will be '*Because I serve you, Master*.' The answer to a great number of your questions too." He released his biting clinch of her nipple. "You deserve to be hurt for no other reason than it amuses and arouses me. Sometimes you'll be hurt for punishment and sometimes because I want to listen to you cry and beg for mercy." He smiled as he forced her to her knees. "I enjoy crying and begging."

She stared, her mouth going dry at the sight of his thick cock straining at the front of his pants. She wanted to open his fly, release him and kiss and caress him, but she still remembered the embarrassment of their first meeting, when she'd knelt before him and he'd stopped her. *No, my dear. Not that.*

Instead she waited, straightening her back and pushing out her average-sized breasts. She wished she had big, bountiful breasts for him but she could only be as she was. When she dropped her gaze to the floor, he tapped her chin up.

"No, you must look at me. Always look at me. I do not like retiring, introspective slaves who stare at the floor and obsess about their purpose and their feelings. This slave purity is nonsense. You have one purpose here—to please me. To do that, you must be attentive and stay in the moment. You must observe and be ready at any moment to fulfill a request. Above all, you must have energy when you're with me."

"Yes, Master."

Don't look at the floor. Have energy. Be ready to fulfill requests. While she drilled these directives into her memory he crossed to the far wall, muttering in French. She could only hear a few words, and none of them were comforting. She sensed she was about to be subjected to a trial, an ordeal, to learn if she was strong enough to be one of his slaves. One of many.

She wasn't going to delude herself. A man like Michel Lemaitre took what he wanted, to include multiple play partners. She herself enjoyed many partners, at least before. Now...

Now she didn't want to.

She wanted to be his and only his.

He returned with a pair of nipple clamps, a clear glass anal plug, and an unopened vial of lubricant. "Hold out your hands." When she did, he placed the plug in one hand and the lube in the other. "Hold those for me."

She knelt, arms outstretched, staring at the plug in her palm. She hadn't used a lot of anal toys before, and this one wasn't beginner sized. She swallowed hard as he flicked at her nipples, preparing them for the clamps. When he attached the first one she sucked in her breath at the pain but managed not to flinch or draw away. He put on the second one and let the chain between them drop against her belly, a cold tug at her aching peaks. He squeezed her breasts, avoiding the nipples. The squeezing hurt but the heat and pressure of his fingers somehow made it better. When he knelt to grope her, forcing a palm between her thighs, she stared down at the thick plug in her hand and began to shake.

"Be still," he said. "I've barely hurt you yet."

"Yes, Master. I'm s-sorry." Her voice stuttered as he thrust his fingers into her pussy. She dripped with arousal, embarrassingly slick against his hand.

"Someone is excited," he said. She flushed as he took the plug from her palm and slid it between her legs. He probed her pussy with it, roughly, so she swayed a little on her knees. Then he held it up in the light so she could see the sheen of her juices on the surface. As she stared at it, he brought it to her mouth. "Lick it off. Taste yourself."

She did as he asked. When he pressed his fingers against her lips, she sucked them also, happy to touch and caress some part of him. When he was satisfied, he drew his hand away and took her face in his palm. "Who do you serve?" he asked softly.

For a moment she forgot the words, but they came to her just in time. "I serve you, Master."

"Turn around and show me your ass."

He took the lube so her hands were free. She skittered around on her knees until she faced away from him and then she paused. Did he mean her to bend over? Or just stick her ass out? He solved her conundrum by shoving her forward so fast she nearly thunked her head on the floor. Two smacks of fire attacked her ass cheeks.

"Show me your ass," he repeated with annoyance. "Point it up in the air and reach back to open yourself. You can balance on your shoulders. I know you know how to balance." She heard him flick open the lube's cap. She arranged herself as well as she could, flinching as her position forced her clamped nipples against the floor. She gripped her ass cheeks and parted them, feeling humiliated and punished. He was so good at this. She thought she should tell him that, and tell him how excited she was to be doing this scene with him.

But she wasn't supposed to be daydreaming about how hot he was and how raw and abject she must look. She was supposed to be alert to him, ready to obey and submit to his urges. When she felt cold lube drip on her asshole she arched a little more, accepting the slow intrusion of his finger when it came. He worked it around inside her and then added another.

She clenched around his thick fingers, nervously remembering the pain yesterday, the struggle to accommodate her Master's size.

He withdrew and added more lube, and then she felt the plug against her hole. Her legs tensed and she drew her knees together, not that she could halt this invasion. The plug was going inside her no matter how long it took, of that she was sure. It was nowhere near as large as his cock, but the pressure of it burned as he tested it against her sphincter. The lube eased the way a little but her body didn't want it inside. *Relax. Relax! Let him do what he wants.*

"You see," he said, as he worked it in and out, a little farther each time, "I hurt you, but I also help you. This plug's size will make it easier for you next time I fuck your ass."

When will that be? she wanted to ask, but at the same time, she was afraid to know. She almost let go of her cheeks, not because she meant to disobey but because she was shaking again. She gritted her teeth as the widest part of the plug breached her. In and out, a little more each time. It never got any easier, only more painful. With a heartless grunt, he pressed it in all the way and she clenched around the narrower neck of the toy in relief. It felt heavy and thick inside her, but at least she wasn't so stretched anymore. When he'd fucked her, she'd been stretched around his huge cock the whole time, pained and terrified. She couldn't think of that now.

"You can release your ass," he said. "Stand up and look at me."

She did as he asked, flushing hot. Her ass felt stuffed. Under his unblinking regard, she tried to display and present herself, tipping her breasts forward and squaring her hips. *I serve you, Master. I serve you, Master.* Thinking the words made it easier to bear the ache in her nipples and the sore discomfort in her ass. And the fear. He reached out and pulled her back to the couch, back over his lap.

Oh no, she'd thought this part was over. She took some panting breaths and braced herself as he grasped her arm, holding her down. His other hand brushed lazily across her ass cheeks. "Pain is not a game to me," he said after a moment. "I use it to get what I want. I'll use it to change you, Valentina. I'll use it to make you better and stronger. You want that, don't you?"

"Yes, Master. More than anything."

"Reach down and place your palms flat against the floor. You are not to move them. You are not to pull away from me. You are to maintain your position over my lap until I'm finished." He paused, cupping the curve of her ass. "Why do you deserve this, Valentina?"

This time the words were right there. "Because I serve you, Master."

"Good. You're learning." The first spank landed in a slap of fire. It was harder this time. She wasn't imagining it. The next one came even harder, and the next one harder again. He paused a few seconds to rearrange her, making her arch her ass up after she'd tensed against him. As she waited, the heat of the spanks spread out, radiated. Her ass clenched around the hard glass plug, sending an intense flush of shamed pleasure to her pussy. She was so wet she could feel the moisture creeping down the insides of her thighs.

Fuck me, please. Don't spank me. Fuck me. She wished he would fuck her the way he had that morning, grabbing her legs and driving into her pussy with pure unbridled lust. She was ready for him, so ready. He was hard—she could feel it—but he wasn't letting that break his stern control. The spanks continued hard and loud, spread out across her ass and the underside of her cheeks, and whenever she clenched away from the punishment, a sharp *Up!* had her arching for more.

She was working so hard to deal with the pain that she didn't even think of the obscene plug in her ass until he spanked right over it so it bucked inside her. She wanted to cover her face and cry because she hated and loved this at the same time, but she wasn't supposed to move her hands. When she curled her fingers into fists, he gave her an especially sharp crack. "Palms against the floor."

It had been five minutes perhaps, that was all, but the pain was building faster than she could process it. It was growing beyond what she could bear. She twitched her bottom to the side and was rewarded with a sharp spank on the side of her thigh.

"Oh, please!" she cried out. "It hurts so badly."

"Does it? Remind me who you serve."

She choked down another cry. "I serve you, Master."

He spanked the backs of her thighs then, near the top where her tender flesh was so much more sensitive, and where there wasn't much lingering damage to check him. Each blow burned like a hot poker from a fire. With a half-whine, half-cry, she tried to hold her position but it hurt *so much*. She pounded her palms against the floor in frantic agony.

"Who do you serve?" he asked, walloping her across both cheeks, right over the flange of the plug.

"I serve you, Master." She practically screamed it. He gave her three more hard whacks and then stopped. He pushed her off his lap onto the floor, not in a violent way, but not gently either.

"Kneel in front of me. Sit up straight, back on your heels."

She obeyed. When she moved to wipe away her tears, he stopped her. "Leave them. I like them. Now put your hands behind you and spread your cheeks again, nice and wide. So many tight, luscious holes, all of them available to me whenever I want. We are coming to understand one another, aren't we?"

"Yes, Master." She gingerly gripped her painful cheeks and spread them. Her toes curled against the floor. Her ass and thighs felt nuclear from the spanking and the plug felt twice as big inside her now. Since she had to hold herself open, there was no chance of her forgetting it was there.

"Don't move," he said, leaving the room.

What? Really? She waited, dreading, wondering what would come next. Since she'd reached behind her, her breasts were thrust forward, the chain between them dangling almost to her navel. He returned with a slender, whippy black crop. Valentina's jaw constricted in panic as she stared at it.

He put his hand under her chin and lifted her eyes to his. *Oh, Master. Please...it's not enough yet?* It was all she could do to meet his gaze, as scared and vulnerable as she felt.

"Keep your chin up," he said, and then with a deceptively economical movement, he flicked the tip of the crop against the middle of her chest, between the vee of the dangling chain. She yelped, but before she could move or even draw breath to say more, he was dealing biting little flicks to her breasts also, underneath, above, all around. Each one made her jerk, but the barrage was so constant she couldn't define exactly where she hurt. Before, the clamps had faded to a dull ache; now the pain was revitalized tenfold. She wanted to protect herself but she knew she'd get in trouble if she made any kind of defensive movements. She let go of her ass and made fists against her side.

"Are you holding your ass open?" he scolded. "No matter the pain, you must remember your instructions. You must obey."

She reached back to part herself again, not certain if the shame or pain was worse. Oh, definitely the pain. The flicks continued, one after the other in an endless, horrible tattoo. Every once in a while he'd strike her hips or her belly but then he'd go right back to the shocking, stinging bites on her breasts.

"Oh, God," she cried. Tears squeezed from her eyes but she didn't dare do anything about them. They dropped down, hot and slick, onto her chest.

"Who do you serve?" he asked. His voice sounded terrifying. "Look at me and answer."

She focused on him through the haze of her tears. "I serve you, Master. But...oh..."

"No buts. I'm barely hurting you. If this is too much—"

"It's not too much!"

But it was almost, *almost* too much. He looked down at her over his aristocratic nose and started flicking her right on the nipples, one and then the other. She arched back, hating it but forcing herself to take the pain. One of the clamps was knocked loose, dangling down her front, and blood rushed to her tortured peak. In the midst of that agony, he managed to flick off the other one. While her nipples throbbed, the clamps slithered over her knee and onto the floor with a clink.

"Spread your legs," he ordered, never stopping his assault. She stared at his face, at the crop, at the full, hard cock outlined behind his tailored work pants, and did as he asked. The next blow landed right over her clit. She threw her head back and cried louder, tears flowing down her cheeks and past her ears.

"I find I am able to beat you after all," he said, his tone light. Amused. "As long as I avoid your back. How does it feel?"

She couldn't think of an answer. All her energy was focused on keeping her legs open when what she really wanted was to snap them shut. With a start, she remembered she was supposed to be spreading her ass cheeks. She wanted to please him. She wanted to be a good slave.

She spread her legs wider and closed her eyes, accepting two sharp flicks on each inner thigh. She clamped her mouth shut against frantic muffled noises as he continued. Left, right, left, right, then her pussy again. Her fingers dug into the flesh of her tender backside. That, at least, was a pain she could control. Oh, how she wanted to cover herself. Her arms shook from the need. Again and again he flicked her clit, sharp strokes meant to punish and not pleasure.

"Who do you serve?" he asked.

"I serve you, Master." She could barely form the words. He dropped the crop and opened the front of his pants, releasing his engorged cock. Valentina watched as he rolled on a rubber.

"Open your mouth."

She obeyed, woodenly, blindly, gagging when he pressed the swollen organ toward the back of her throat. In, out, in, out. He held her head and forced himself deeper. When she choked, he drew away and picked up the crop again. Flick, flick, flick. Left, right, center. She gazed up at him, begging for respite. He paused, still holding the crop, and thrust into her mouth.

This time she tried harder. The face fucking was so much better than getting cropped on the insides of her thighs. She opened her throat and used her lips and tongue as best she could, but eventually she choked again and he drew away to resume the cropping. By this point, between the oral and the pain, she was going a little out of her mind. *This is a test, Valentina. What are you made of? Don't fail him. Don't fail yourself.*

Again, he stopped and brought his cock to her lips. She sucked him in a panic, still holding her ass cheeks wide. If she made him come, would this ordeal end? She deep-throated him for long, industrious moments, controlling her gag reflex. His pleased moans sounded in her ears, a balm to her frazzled nerves. As the fever of pain calmed, she allowed herself to appreciate the hardness and scent of him, the clean, musky smell. She was subsisting on very little air, drawing deep gusts through her nose, but still she sucked and licked his cock with all the abandon she could muster.

"*Dieu*," he said, drawing away from her. She coughed as air rushed into her lungs. "Turn around." He positioned her again on her hands and knees, her face to the floor. His hands replaced hers, spreading her cheeks wide. He held her hips and impaled her pussy with a deep groan. It felt so tight, almost unbearably tight with the plug still inside her ass. But, oh God, it felt so good too, so wicked. Her walls clenched and her whole body trembled with the need for release.

"Don't come," he warned. "Not until I say."

No, she wouldn't come, not ever, if he didn't want her to. At this point, all she wanted to do was obey.

* * * * *

Michel held his breath, counting slowly to ten in his head. He wasn't ready for this to be over, but his cock was about to explode from the sensation of stuffing her tight, hot cunt.

"Jesus Christ, will you be still?" he bit out. He slapped the outside of her thigh, over the lone spank mark lingering there. Her ass and the backs of her thighs were uniformly red. He'd wanted to push her to her limits, past her limits. He'd wanted to assure himself that she didn't have many limits, which seemed to be the case. He'd seen stronger women crack long before now. He had a feeling Valentina could endure another hour. Another day. Whatever he required. He groaned in his throat at that delicious thought.

He wasn't going to ease up on her now, no matter how sweet her pussy felt. The first lesson was always the most important lesson—the breaking lesson, so to speak. He wanted her to leave off questioning and give herself to him completely. He wanted her to sleep tonight with one thought and one thought only in her mind. *I serve my Master.*

Michel steeled himself, drilling into her pussy without a care for her pleasure or her completion. Tonight, that was unimportant. Tonight was about showing her who was on top. He pulled out of her pussy and set about working the toy out of her ass. She was tight and small as hell and he had to go slowly. Once he had it halfway out, he started to piston it in and out of her sphincter. "Do you like that?"

She shuddered on her knees. "Not really."

"*No, Master* will do just fine."

"No, Master," she whimpered.

"I don't care whether you like it or not, as you know. But I am heartened to hear that you don't, since I enjoy testing your submission." He teased her with the plug a full minute longer, asking her at the end, "Who do you serve?"

And she answered in that avid, sweet voice, laced with tears: "I serve you, Master."

He set the toy aside and moved closer to her, fisting his cock, pressing it against her asshole. He knew she didn't like this either but it was important for her to understand she was going to endure it anyway. It was important for her to fear him and the things he might do to her.

When he couldn't ease the head inside, she made a sound of dismay. "Hush," he told her. "Open yourself up to me."

He put a hand across the backs of her shoulders, pressing her down. With his other hand, he continued to probe the head of his dick into her hole. Her whines were turning into frightened cries.

"Damn it," he said. "Why must this be so difficult?"

"Please, Master. I'm trying. Please try again."

She slaughtered him, the way she never, ever gave up. "I've already tried," he said, leaning back. "You're too small and too tight. You won't relax."

She stayed still, a hunched up, reddened, shivering, slavey mess on the floor. "I want to serve you. Please, Master. Please just put it in me. I'll bear it."

Mon Dieu, she would bear it too, the little idiot. He gave her a sharp slap to the ass and stood to get more lube. "I'm not going to rip you. I'm not going to force it in when it doesn't fit. You need to open to me." He knelt behind her and slathered more lube on her hole, and then onto the condom. "You're going to undergo anal training, do you understand? Until you can take my cock in your ass whenever I want it. We're not going to have these struggles."

"I'm sorry. I'll try harder." She was sobbing now, so anxious to submit to anything he asked. He believed she would push an icepick a little farther into her forehead every day if he asked her to, until she'd succeeded in giving herself a lobotomy. He wanted to be annoyed about it, but as he finally eased the head of his cock into her ass, he felt a certain tenderness, a pang of admiration wrested from the pit of his black, cold heart. She drew up beneath him, her sobs turning to moans as he pushed deeper.

"You're a pathetic little slave," he murmured as he fucked her. "There is so much you need to learn. But I'll teach you." He held the tail of his shirt out of the way, watching her tiny asshole stretch to accommodate him. His earlier conflicts were forgotten, washed away by her tearful submission, by the change he saw in her already. She was under his power, at least for the moment. Thirty days. Twenty-nine, now. She'd survive.

"Don't come," he said as he got close. "You are not allowed to come tonight because you're pathetic and untrained, and because you're too small to take Master's cock in your asshole. I could barely fit in your mouth."

He taunted her because she needed to hear it and because it was the only way to keep her from reaching climax. As for him, he binged on pleasure like it was Christmas Day. When his orgasm roared up from his thighs and his balls, he shuddered from the agony of the long-awaited release. He had intended to withdraw and mark her with his cum, puddles of it all over her slender back, but in the end he came inside her conquered body, thrusting deep. He collapsed against her back, spent, and felt her give a little sigh.

Poor unsatisfied slave girl. But now she knew. He was cruel and heartless. He rejoiced in her frustration and basked in her cries of pain. "Stay there." He pulled away, discarded the condom and took his time readjusting his clothing. When he finally went to stand back over her, he was dressed and deliciously satisfied. She was naked, wet-cheeked, and covered in red from his hands and the crop. "Do you see now?" he asked very, very gently. "It is not fun. Being my slave is not unbounded happiness and pleasure. It is *tres difficile, non?*"

She looked at him through tears and said, without the least hesitation, "I serve you, Master."

Very well, he thought to himself. *We are back on track.* "Get in the shower and clean up," he said aloud. "Dinner is at eight o'clock."

Chapter Ten:
The Reality

Michel didn't take wine at dinner, nor did he give her any. The sex and her submission had intoxicated him enough, and there was wine in Galvin's exemplary sauce. Lemon chicken with capers and roasted asparagus, and a naked, freshly-fucked slave at his right hand. Pure bliss.

The crop kisses on her front had already faded. The crop was a handy tool when marks might be an issue...the stinging attack of the tip felt much more damaging than it actually was. But now, he wished she were marked a little, with *his* marks, not the ones from the club. He would have enjoyed looking over to see her welted and punished like a proper slave. When those cuts on her back were healed, he'd bring out harsher implements, straps and paddles, tawses, canes, whips, floggers. He would be judicious in his use of them, as always. His slaves were all performers too, and he needed them whole. He only ever imparted surface damage to their bodies, although he was skilled at making it feel like he was punishing them a lot harder.

Lovely Valentina. What a miracle she'd be when he was done with her. All her headstrong angst, transformed into beautiful, obedient serenity. He was capable, she was capable. He could make this happen.

She was *his*.

Only for thirty days, he reminded himself. No, twenty-nine. Would he count down each day as it came, dreading her eventual release? Or would he say goodbye with a sigh of relief? He imagined the latter more possible. Either way, his time was limited, which was why he'd come on so strong, moving her into his house so he could control every aspect of her existence.

You've never had a slave move in before.

Well, there was a first time for everything. And it wasn't so different from having slaves spend the weekend, or a week here and there. He told himself that, but some vague, niggling warning still pinged in his brain, some realization that Valentina was different from the others. It was her hair, probably. It wasn't normal.

He reached over and traced a lock of it, absently, like an owner touching one of his things. She looked at him with so many questions in her gaze. She was still edgy from the tough scene he'd just led her through. He found her anxiety arousing.

"You have no idea how beautiful you are," he said, and he meant it, because she really didn't know. She didn't understand the way he saw her. She didn't realize how lovely she seemed to him, with her nervousness and the rigid way she held her body. He could tell he frightened her. She wanted to escape him but she couldn't. Or wouldn't. The truth was, he hadn't locked her in with anything other than her mind. She could walk out anytime she wanted...although the thought of that made him very, very upset.

"How's the food?" he asked. "Good?"

"Yes, Master. I'm glad you have a real cook and not a slave cook."

"Slave cooks are the worst."

"I'm glad you don't have slave food either," she added.

He halted with a piece of chicken halfway to his mouth. "What is slave food?"

"You know, slave food. Muesli and table scraps. The end part of celery that no one likes to eat."

"*Mon Dieu*, Valentina." He shook his head. "I'm a sadist. I enjoy being cruel, but the end part of celery?"

She gave a small strangled laugh, like she wasn't sure it was allowed in his presence. He smiled to let her know it was, and she studied him as if he'd grown a second head. Did he smile so infrequently?

Yes.

"You'll find I do my own thing," he said, sobering. "Perhaps you've read books or seen movies about how Masters and slaves are supposed to go on. They're fine as entertainment but I do things my own way."

"Are you going to give me a slave number?"

"No."

"A brand?"

He rolled his eyes.

"A collar? All slaves wear collars."

He reached over and wrapped a hand around her neck. "Here's your collar. It's called my will." He gave her a little squeeze and released her. "I don't put my slaves in collars. They can be lovely, but collars suggest permanency."

She gave him another of those studious looks. "You don't have permanent slaves?"

"No. I do not make promises of happily ever after." He shrugged, taking a sip of water. "It always ends in broken hearts."

"It's not such a great thing to survive a broken heart. My heart has been broken dozens of times, and you see I survived."

"Dozens of times? How indiscriminating you must be."

She toyed with a stalk of asparagus. "I don't know. Perhaps it's only that I see so many things to admire in so many people."

"Do you see things to admire in me?" As soon as he said it, he wished he could unsay it.

She looked up at him in surprise. "Of course I do, Master. There is your power. Your strength and directness. Your intelligence. Your creativity and..." Her eyes swept down his bespoke shirt and four-hundred-dollar pants. "The fine way you dress, and the careless shadow of your beard when it's late and you haven't shaved. Your elegant fingers and fingernails, the way they touch and move things."

He looked down at his hands, but she wasn't finished yet.

"And your eyes, they're light and beautiful. When they fix on me I feel frightened and warmed at once." She paused. "I loved the way you took your tie off by the door. Not because it made you seem more human, but because you seemed as godlike as ever, doing casual everyday things."

Ah, but he'd forgotten that she was an artist, with an artist's whimsy. "Godlike, Valentina?" he echoed, bemused.

"Yes. And there are many more things I admire in you, too many to name. I suppose that's why I'm here."

"Very flattering words. You're wonderful company to have around. I look forward with great pleasure to the remainder of our—" *Experiment.* He almost said experiment for some reason, then he caught himself and substituted "engagement." He smiled at her but she didn't smile back.

"Will I get any breaks?" she asked, twirling her last stalk of asparagus on her fork.

He glared at her hand until she stopped. "No, you're my slave. You don't get breaks. And you'll use proper table manners or you'll eat from a dog dish on the floor. Sit up straight and stop playing with your food."

She picked up her knife and started slicing what was left on her plate into numerous tiny pieces. So, so tempting to go for the dog dish.

"Can I earn a break with good behavior?" she asked when her chicken and asparagus were diced and sorted into separate piles.

He took her plate and removed it to the other side of the table. "No. But these silly questions have just earned you another assfucking against the contract wall. Eventually this will sink in. You are my slave. You belong to me from now until February 14th." Valentine's Day. He'd only just thought about that now. "Do you have any other questions?"

She stared across the table at her plate. He wouldn't have taken it if he didn't believe she'd eaten enough. Well, perhaps he would have.

"No, Master," she said in a defeated voice. "I don't have any more questions."

She looked down at the mahogany table top while he finished eating. Poor, sad slave. "Sit up straight," he murmured when she started to sag. "It's only twenty-nine more days."

She glanced sideways at him. He watched her throat work, heard the faint sniffles she tried to hide. He knew she was given to theatrics, but he didn't think these were theatrics.

"It's not as fun as you thought, is it?" He reached out and touched her hand where it rested in her lap. "Perhaps some nipple clamps would make it more fun?"

She looked up at him with such dread, such agony that he felt sorry for a moment.

Only a moment.

"Take a deep breath, Valentina, and stop crying. I can't eat while you're crying."

She blinked through tears. "I thought you enjoyed making your slaves cry."

"I do." He took her hand and placed it over his hardening cock. "That's exactly my point. If you don't stop crying, I'll have to carry you off and fuck you, and I haven't had my coffee yet."

She lifted the napkin out of her lap and mopped it over her face in a breach of etiquette that normally would have resulted in some scolding words. Well, it was day two. There was such a thing as pushing too far.

"I think you can go back to work on Wednesday," he said once she'd composed herself. "You'll enjoy that, won't you?"

"Yes, Master. I don't want to fall out of shape."

"Oh, you're getting exercise. Just not the usual muscles."

Galvin entered and poured coffee for both of them. "Go ahead," he said when she looked to him for permission. "If you think it won't keep you awake later."

Valentina took little sips of the rich brew, gazing at him over the rim of her cup. He wondered when she'd last sat so still and quiet for so long, and the caffeine on top of it.

As for him, he felt a great sense of relaxation. Still and quiet suited him perfectly, perhaps because of his loud and hectic childhood, or perhaps because of his natural tendencies. He'd been half hard all the way through dinner, an enduring, pleasant feeling of arousal he didn't need to fight. He was going to have her again, directly after the coffee, and then clean her up and store her neatly away in her cage.

Calm. Clean. Controlled. Did she realize how euphoric it made him feel?

"Come," he finally said. "Let's go back to your room."

He escorted her upstairs, checked over her cuts and found them without infection, and then steered her over to the wall, to the black writing of which he'd become very fond. He wondered if she felt the same fondness as he pressed her against the words. "Stay."

He went to the nightstand for the usual supplies. He'd already buzzed through nearly an entire tube of lubricant. Valentina's mouth fell open as he slathered it over the condom.

"Again? Tonight?"

"Yes, I told you. Tonight, and any other time going forward that you ask for a break. There are no breaks in this sort of slavery." He nodded toward the wall. "Eyes there, my dear. Right there on that line you signed with your little hearts."

"But—"

"There are no buts either. No buts, no breaks."

"I understand now," she said as he parted her and lubricated her asshole. Lovely, how she closed up so tight in the space of a couple of hours, so he could force his way in again. "I understand, okay? I won't ask for any more breaks."

"Wonderful," he replied, blithely and intentionally ignoring her point. "I asked you to face the wall."

She turned and let out a sigh as he pressed against her from behind. His hands caressed her hips, her waist. Ah, but her body was lovely, her breasts high and full, her ass so round and strong, and still tender from her spanking over his lap.

"I don't care if you punish me for saying this," she said. "But I think you are way too obsessed with anal sex."

He didn't answer, only put a hand over her mouth and smiled into the soft, fragrant mass of her hair. With his other hand he pressed his cock between her ass cheeks and availed himself, once again, of her tightest, most sensitive orifice as she groaned and whined, pinned against the wall. "*I belong to Le Maître*," he read, breathing against her ear. He let go of her mouth to tap the wall. "Signed, *Valentina Maria-Rosa Sancia*. Do you know what that means?" He eased deeper into her ass, as deep as he could go. "It means no breaks, *ma mignonne*. Ever."

He put his hand back over her mouth, not that she had anything to say besides soft pleas of entreaty. He just liked fucking her that way.

* * * * *

Valentina had always loved work. Even when it was tedious, or challenging, she'd loved showing up for practice, but never, ever had she loved it more than today.

Oh God, to get away from the damn white room, from her cage in Mr. Lemaitre's house.

Jason told her to ease back into her routine slowly, but she was bursting with pent-up energy, and besides that, the only way to stop thinking about Mr. Lemaitre...*Master*...was to throw herself full throttle into her act's development. She had other parts to learn too, narrative elements that would be woven throughout the production. Some were as simple as sweeping across the stage in a theatrical way. Others involved acting and choreography, and interaction with other performers playing their own roles.

None of this worried her. It was all easy, even exciting, and she'd accomplish it all long before *Cirque Élémental*'s premiere in the spring.

By then, she'd no longer be his slave.

This idea both exhilarated and depressed her. She was less than a week into her four-week servitude and she already felt like Mr. Lemaitre had scrambled her brain. Whenever she saw him, a needy, aching longing took over her whole body, and she wanted his attention more than she wanted life itself, but at the same time, he frightened her until she could barely breathe from it. Add this to the fact that he scorned her as much as he fucked her...

Her feelings didn't make any sense.

But work made sense and that was something she could do well. Work was something measurable, something useful that made all her other agitations go away.

Agitations? But you wanted this, Tina. You're living your "dream."

"Hey there. Valentina?" Jason's voice jolted her from her thoughts. She looked at the clock and was disappointed to realize that practice, contractually limited to two hours a day, was already over. While she'd been busy daydreaming about her Master, Andrew, Roman, and Danil had packed up and headed off. Adei lingered, giving her a strange look. She'd gotten that look a lot today. He and Jason exchanged glances and then he left too.

"I thought Mr. Lemaitre kept a lot of slaves," she said. "Why is everyone gawking at me?"

Jason pulled at his lip, then let out a soft breath that flared his nostrils. "Do you want to have lunch?"

Oh no. She'd come to recognize that tone all too well. "Actually, I was going to grab something quick and head over to the gym—" she began.

"I think we should have lunch."

Damn.

She followed him to the cafeteria, trying not to think too hard about the determined expression on his face. People stared as they walked down the corridors, and continued to stare as they filled their trays and sat down at a table.

Why all the looks? It wasn't inappropriate for them to have lunch together. Jason was in charge of her act. She turned her back to everyone and took apart her turkey sandwich, eating the tomato slices first. She wished she could put tomato on some of her art. The red was so vibrant. The texture of the shredded lettuce clinging to the turkey caught her attention next. She poked at it as she bit into the tomato.

"So," said Jason. "I've considered your request to add the series of flips to the finale."

"And?" She looked up from the lettuce and knew he was going to tell her no. "I can do it," she said. "I used to do flips on top of my three brothers in a stack. Boom, boom, boom." She used her hands to illustrate the concept. "They never dropped me. Never."

"Somehow I believe that."

"So why?" She shoveled the lettuce into her mouth, then reassembled her sandwich and took a bite. "I like the challenge," she said after she swallowed. "I want it to be hard every night."

"I know you like things to be *hard every night*," Jason said, with a bit less patience in his tone. "But you can't incorporate skills into the act that can't be replicated every show, day after day. Every skill in the act should have a one-hundred-percent likelihood of perfect execution."

"I could do it perfectly one hundred percent of the time."

"Valentina."

"I could! It's the speed. It's easier to balance moving fast than moving slow—"

"Valentina, enough." He brushed a crumb from the corner of his mouth. "Look, the answer is no. If I didn't tell you no now, then Genevieve would tell you no when she saw the flips. And if she didn't say no, then Lemaitre would."

Just hearing his name made Valentina go tense. She took another bite of her sandwich, her throat suddenly tight and itchy. "I'm just trying to be myself," she said. "I came to Cirque du Monde to be an artist, to express my—my—" She waved a hand. "Whatever it's called. My vision."

"Is that so?"

"Yes, it's so." She glanced up to find him staring at her with one eyebrow raised. "You know, when you look at me like that, I want to throw my plate at your face."

"I wouldn't do that. Your Master wouldn't be happy."

"He's not here right now."

"But you're his slave, aren't you? You're supposed to behave in ways he finds pleasing, whether or not he's here."

She looked around the cafeteria, like he might be watching from a corner somewhere. Yes, she'd been learning—via some very painful lectures and punishments—that her Master's will trumped everything where she was concerned. She pushed down uneasy feelings and forced a smile, giving Jason a flirtatious look. "You wouldn't tell on me, would you?"

"I would tell on you in a heartbeat, especially if you threw a plate at my face. Maybe I'll go tell on you right now for threatening me."

"No!" She reached out and grabbed his hand before she realized he was joking. Oh shit. Now he looked perturbed.

"What's he been doing to you?" Jason asked. "You're not yourself today. Honestly, you haven't been yourself in a while. Where's the Valentina that showed up here last fall ready to conquer the world?"

"You won't let me conquer the world. You won't even let me put fun stuff in the act, because it can't be *replicated*." She said the last word in a sing-song mocking tone.

"Let's forget about the fun stuff in your act because it's not happening, and that's not what I want to talk about." He leaned closer, lowering his voice. "What's going on with you and Lemaitre?"

"What do you mean?"

"I mean, why the fuck are you putting yourself through this? I told you, you aren't a good match. He's not Lugo in the showers, Valentina. He's not Adei. He's not even me. He can be a brutal, unfeeling Master and he's not one to fall in love with his slaves. If you think you'll be different, that you'll somehow get through to his heart, you're in for a disappointment."

She stared at the table. "I don't want to get through to his heart."

"Yes, you do. You've been in love with him since the first week." He took her hand hard, the way she'd taken his hand when she thought he was going to tell on her. "I love the way you fall in love with everyone and everything. I do. I love your recklessness and intensity. They're wonderful qualities."

"They're terrible qualities," she said, grabbing her hand away. "You complain about them all the time. Mr. Lemaitre is going to help me be a better person. More focused. More self-disciplined."

"He's going to help you be a better sex slave, okay? Period. That's it."

She shook her head. That wasn't true. Mr. Lemaitre had told her he would change her, that he would make her better and stronger. "You don't understand. You haven't been there for our conversations."

"Oh, I'm sure you're having lots of conversations," said Jason, rolling his eyes. "I know the kind of conversations Lemaitre likes to have with his slaves. They involve lots of lubricant."

Valentina put down her sandwich. "You don't understand anything. You think you know everything about me and Mr. Lemaitre, but you don't."

"I know enough. I warned you off him weeks ago, Valentina. I'm worried about the two of you together because I don't think your personalities mesh."

She took small sips of water, refusing to look at him.

"Hm, no comment," he said after a moment. "Listen, if the reality isn't what you thought it would be—"

She covered her ears. "Don't. Please don't."

"Valentina."

She shook her head. "Why are you doing this? I'm a grown woman. I can do as I like."

"Not for the next twenty-five days, you can't."

"I want this. I want to tough it out, okay? He won't hurt me."

"If I thought he would hurt you, really hurt you, we wouldn't be having this conversation." He sighed and ate the last of his sandwich. "I'm just telling you that if you ever want out, you can get out. He won't fire you. He won't send you away. There are ways to keep the two of you separate, if that's what you're worried about. In the end, it's a game. It's supposed to be fun. If it's not fun, if it becomes too much for you, tell him. If you can't tell him, tell me."

She knew he meant to help but he had no idea about her feelings. This wasn't a game to her, not in the slightest.

"I heard you were a hard Master too," she said, purposely keeping her voice low. "I see how you control Sara."

"There's a big difference. I love Sara."

Yes, and Mr. Lemaitre didn't love her. Could he emphasize it again? Ten, twenty more times before she escaped this lunch from hell?

"I need to go to the gym," she said. "I haven't worked out in three days."

"Go then. But don't forget what I said." He pointed a finger at her. "You're destined for great things, Valentina Sancia. I don't want to see any more ropes around your pretty little neck."

Chapter Eleven: Control

By the end of the first week, they'd settled into a daily routine—of her Master's making, of course. Day followed day, regimented and predictable. There were never any breaks.

Valentina awakened every morning to the sound of him unlocking her cage. Sometimes he'd get under the covers with her, and draw her face down to his cock. Other times he'd kneel over her and force himself down her throat, or order her out of bed and onto her knees to serve him. No matter what mood he arrived in, every morning was the same. A huge cock shoved between her lips.

It was easier to deal with once he stopped using condoms. She hated the taste of latex but she loved the taste of her Master, especially when she was sleepy and warm and just coming out of sexually charged dreams. When he came in her mouth she would swallow it, sinking into subspace as his container, his object. She felt utterly enslaved to his will.

After that he went to work and she had a small measure of freedom, since her practices didn't start until ten. She was allowed whatever she liked for breakfast, as long as she ate something healthy and as long as she ate it naked—her Master continued to forbid the use of clothing inside the house. Galvin cooked delicious breakfasts for her most days, omelets or waffles or crepes, not even seeming to notice her nudity. He was gay after all, in a relationship with a lover who called and texted during the day, and doubtless welcomed him home at night.

Galvin left right after he cleaned up the kitchen from dinner. Sometimes she'd watch him go with the wild idea of running after him, running to freedom, running to her private apartment where she could do whatever she liked whenever she wanted, without anyone holding her down or hurting her, or invading her body in one hole after the other. Mr. Lemaitre would look over at her and she'd know he knew what she was thinking, because he'd get that little smile that wasn't a smile.

You wanted this. You chose this, crazy girl.

After she ate breakfast every day, she showered and dressed in her practice clothes, and Galvin drove her to the huge headquarters building. By that time her Master was usually knee-deep in meetings or business, and she was forbidden to visit his office unless he summoned her. Which he often did. Sometimes an assistant came to get her and sometimes he'd show up himself, somber and formidable in his perfect suits and fancy Italian shoes.

He'd beckon her from across the gym or the practice facility, and she'd have to readjust herself from artist and performer to slave. And of course, everyone knew what he had come for. Everyone knew why he wanted her, and everyone would watch her cross to him and follow behind him to his office. Inside, she'd be shoved under his desk to perform a blow job, or thrown over the top, her legs pulled wide as he undid his fly and shoved inside her. If she wasn't wet, that was her problem.

But by the time she got to his office, she was always wet. There was something about being used...and used...and used merely for someone else's pleasure. When he craved her, he came and got her and fucked her. It was so simple, and so animalistically hot. Sometimes he'd start in her pussy and then decide halfway through that he wanted to fuck her ass. He used condoms for that. She didn't think he could get in otherwise, without the slippery smooth latex to ease the way. Even then, it took extra lubricant which he kept in his desk drawer.

Her nose had grown all too familiar with the polished surface of his desk. She knew the temperature of it, the scent of the furniture wax. Smooth wood surfaces had come to trigger an automatic response in her. Everything *clenched*. It still hurt to take him in the ass, even after a couple weeks of training with butt plugs. She thought it would always hurt a little, which was probably why he liked it so much. The worst part was the beginning when he first nudged the head in. After that, the ache became more bearable but it still felt scary and risky. He never injured her, but there was always that sense that he could if he were not so careful.

Valentina was such a pervert that all these thoughts about care and risk turned her on. *He could damage me—but he doesn't. But he could...* That was hot to her, especially paired with the dull, agonizing repetition of his thrusts. Sometimes, if he was in the mood for it, he would make her come, touching her in all the places that would make it happen: her pebbled nipples, her swollen clit. He'd slide his fingers between her pussy lips and find that exact spot and caress it in the same rhythm he banged her asshole, and she'd begin to quiver and shake, and in her climax, her pussy and ass would both contract and he'd feel even bigger and hurtier inside her, and oh... Sometimes she'd come again, just because the first orgasm felt so good.

But she'd always been that way. Very sensitive, very responsive. Her Master seemed to delight in it. *Are you coming again?* he'd ask, shaking his head. He only punished her for such excess when he was in a very, very bad mood. Most of the time he just punished her because he liked to hurt her. He was a sadist. That's how sadists were.

Valentina tried to enjoy the punishments as he did, but they were more difficult to adjust to than the anal. Once her back healed, he started taking her to his playroom, a dark, hot space carved out of the attic. Many evenings he scened with her there, fastening her to various pieces of equipment and breaking her down. There was a wooden chair with phalluses rising out of it, ones he could interchange depending on his mood. Sometimes he used a big dildo in her pussy, sometimes a big dildo in her ass. Sometimes two dildos, so she had to sit there feeling stuffed and restrained by her own orifices.

The chair had a wide leather lap belt so she could neither get up, nor work herself up and down on the dildos the way she wanted to. Once he had her impaled and secured, he'd torture her breasts with clamps, or a crop, or both. He'd make her keep her mouth wide open, whether or not he put his cock inside. The point, she supposed, was to make her feel she was nothing but a collection of holes to be filled at his pleasure. Sometimes she enjoyed her times in that chair, but other times she felt overwhelmed and scared. She could never walk correctly by the time he let her up.

There was another contraption he used a lot, a bench with a high back. He'd make her kneel on the seat facing the wall, so her breasts reached just to the top of the wooden back. Cruel, alligator-grip clamps were fixed to the wood with an adjustable lever, and these were attached to her nipples as she whimpered and cried. Cuffs topped the posts at either side of the bench, and once her wrists were buckled into them, she would be powerless to get away from anything he did to her. She couldn't move a centimeter without feeling excruciating pain.

Then, of course, he would pick up a strap or flogger or paddle or crop or any of the instruments that lined the walls, and beat her with it to the music of her screams. The pain of the beatings was bad enough, but the nipple-clamps-as-restraints added an entirely new level of hurt. Her hands would strain at the cuffs but he gave her no way to save herself. She was allowed to beg for mercy, but she couldn't beg him to stop. If she did, it earned her a rough assfucking against the contract wall, nose pressed to the line where she'd signed herself over to him. Three or four assfuckings later, she'd learned to bite her tongue.

There were other pieces of furniture up there too. A spanking bench with straps and restraints all over it, a St. Andrews cross that he hadn't used with her yet. She thought it would be easier to be tied to that than the high-backed bench with its horrid nipple pinchers, but knowing him, he'd find some way to make the St. Andrews cross horrible too.

The only good thing about his attic dungeon was that by the time he finished with her, he could do just about anything to her sexually and she didn't care. She took his cock in her ass, she took his semen down her throat, she jammed her tongue up his asshole, whatever he demanded, and she did it with pure relief because at least he wasn't beating on her. Well, except for the times he beat her and fucked her at the same time.

Sometimes she thought of Jason's words. *If you ever want out, you can get out.* Sometimes she really, really wanted out, but then her Master would gather her in his arms and carry her to the white room, and gaze at her in a way that made Valentina's heart tremble. He would shower with her and check her all over, talking to her about random things like her act, her practices, or a meeting he'd had that day. Sometimes before he locked her into her cage, he'd brush a hand over her hair so gently that her eyes glossed over with tears.

I love you, she would think. And after dreaming of him all night, she'd wake and pull out her sketch pad and try to capture all those brutal, affectionate qualities that comprised him, and again she'd fail. She'd close her pad and put it away and stare at the door in anticipation of his arrival, wondering if she was happy or miserable, or just very, very confused.

* * * * *

Michel stared down at the tickets in his hand, then over at the silent woman on his arm. They stood in a crush of patrons at the *Palais Garnier*, waiting to be seated for a *l'Orchestre de Paris* concert. Just last week, he'd learned in the course of their dinner conversation that Valentina had never been to see a live orchestra. The revelation had horrified him. He could barely conceive that someone as bright and creative as Valentina might have lived twenty-six years and not yet enjoyed the aural mindgasm of a live orchestra program. He'd immediately stood, abandoning their dinner plates, and dragged her to his home office. He'd purchased third-row tickets while she knelt at his feet.

And why not? He enjoyed spoiling his slaves now and again, taking them out for dinners or shows. In Valentina's case, he'd been so preoccupied with her luscious body that he'd done nothing but drill her holes for the past three weeks. Careless of him, to get so carried away.

He clasped her wrist tighter as an usher glanced at their tickets and gestured them toward the main floor. The congestion of people pushed them together. He smiled and steadied her when she stumbled against his front. She took a step back with a murmured apology and he slid a look down at her prim black-belted dress and mid-heeled pumps. Her hair flowed loose about her shoulders, a riot of color against her dark outfit. He studied that hair, thinking of her art back in her apartment, creative works so vivid and full of color. Why was he keeping her trapped in his bleak and colorless home?

Because she's sexy. Because she signed an agreement.

Because he led a bleak and colorless life, and he had wanted her to paint it rainbow-colored for a while.

She could get back to her artistic endeavors soon enough, and her other endeavors too, like sleeping with lots of men and throwing temper tantrums whenever life didn't suit her. They only had one week left, seven days for him to wallow in his mastery and control. Had he changed her at all? He didn't think so.

At last they made their way to their seats. More than a few heads turned. The Paris art community was large, but so was the Cirque, and people knew who he was. Their eyes passed from him to the pretty young thing beside him, and he knew their thoughts, not that he cared. Age was irrelevant when it came to attraction. He glanced over at Valentina, at her slim knees pressed together beneath the crepe skirt of her dress. Two hours ago he'd spread those knees and fucked her until he came, leaving her unsatisfied. He enjoyed, sometimes, making her smolder rather than bringing her to full flame. Without thought, he reached and slid a hand down between those knees. She let out a slow, small breath.

He could touch her wherever, whenever he wanted. He owned her, an intoxicating thought every time it presented itself. For now, he let her be; there were people all around them. When the lights went down, perhaps he'd caress her again, run a hand farther up her thigh, up to her hot, wet—

Orchestra, Michel. Not sex.

The musicians began to stream in from offstage, settling with their instruments into their carefully laid-out seats. They fussed with music binders and readjusted their stands, leaning to speak to one another in the casual, short check-ins of collaborative artists. Orchestra concerts weren't so different from Cirque shows. In both cases, everyone had to work together and do their part. Michel was slated to review a few of the acts from *Cirque Élémental* in the morning, including Valentina's revamped one. He believed he was perfectly capable of judging her without being influenced by their current relationship. He always put professionalism first...perhaps too much of the time.

Why did he feel like reaching over to hold her hand?

She leaned forward in her chair as the cacophony of tuning and warm-ups began. His spirits rose in anticipation, and she seemed affected too. *You're so similar to me*, he thought. *Too similar sometimes.* The lights dimmed and she sat back again, her lips slightly parted. From the first chords of Mozart's *Symphony No. 41 in C Major*, Valentina was gripped.

He had known she would be. Mozart's music wasn't only for the ears, but for the soul. As the music soared and complex melodies played against each other, Valentina's eyes grew wider and wider. Her hand gripped the armrest, then she looked over at him with an expression of wonder that made every frustration worthwhile. Forty-five minutes later, as the symphony concluded with booming brass and a sweeping crescendo of notes, she still stared in wonder.

The audience broke into applause and so did she, effusive, noisy clapping that was so very Valentina-like. He stifled a smile. "There's more, you know," he said when she finally piped down. "It's only intermission." He took her hand and propelled her out of her chair, and dragged her down the row, over knees and shoes, not caring.

"Where are we going?" she asked.

"Wherever I want, yes?" he said, turning back to her with a raised brow.

"Yes, Master," she whispered. Perhaps she worried he would make her leave. He could be ornery and cruel but he wasn't that cruel.

"Come this way," he said when they reached the lobby. He knew the Paris Opera House like he knew his own headquarters. He led her down a corridor and past an usher he silenced with a quelling stare. Another turn, and then he ducked with her into an unused dressing room. He took her over by the far wall. On the other side, one could hear the faint sounds of instrument tuning and casual chatting. She looked up at him, awed.

"It's them."

Them. The musicians she saw as amazing, superhuman, when she herself could do things none of them could ever hope to do. "You ought to have gone to a concert before now," he said, taking her face between his palms. "They have them everywhere."

"I don't know why—" she began, but he cut off her words when he pressed his lips to hers. He tasted her, shoving a hand into the mass of her hair, then curling his fingers into her nape. She wasn't the only one affected by fine music and talent. Her little gasps were new notes, her moans a lovely melody, if a simple one. She arched into him and her hands crept up his front, flattening against the lapels of his suit.

He wrapped an arm around her and pulled her closer, and kissed her harder because he couldn't fuck her, because he couldn't do all the things he wanted to do to her before the end of intermission. But later...

He thrust a rough hand between her legs, pushing aside her panties to stroke her pussy. She moaned louder, shuddering in his arms. On the other side of the wall, one of the musicians murmured something and another replied. From farther away, a shout of laughter, then the voice of the stage manager giving the five-minute warning.

"*Arrête*," he muttered, and he was talking to himself, because if anyone was out of control at the moment, it was him. He pulled her skirt back down and tore his lips from hers, and shoved his finger in her mouth instead. "You're all over me now, damn you. Lick it off."

She sucked his finger with abandon. *Dieu*, not helping. He pulled it away with an audible "pop" and took her by the elbow. "It's time to return to our seats. You want to see the rest of the concert, don't you?"

For a moment, she hesitated, her eyes hazy with lust. But then a long, sweet note sounded from the adjacent room and she remembered where she was.

"Yes, please, Master. I want to see the rest of the concert."

He could drag her home right now. He could use her to his heart's content. He was the Master, after all, and she was his slave, existing only to serve his needs. Instead he led her back out to the main floor and to their seats in the third row, feeling hot and confused, and inordinately proud of his self-control.

Chapter Twelve:
No

By the end of the concert, he had gone from feeling casually amorous to feeling crazed with desire. He steered her out to the pavement for the twenty minute stroll to his house. They walked along *Rue Cambon* and through the gardens of the *Champs-Élysées*, Valentina prattling the entire time about music and notes and how she was definitely going to learn the violin, or perhaps the drums, or perhaps the trumpet, or perhaps... She left off and leaned down to catch a stray leaf blowing by.

"No," he said.

She straightened, dropping it back again. It was a lovely scarlet red, so out of place in the winter landscape. He relented. One more week.

"Go on," he said. "You can use it on some self-portrait or other."

She picked it up with a sheepish expression that made him feel ashamed he'd stopped her in the first place. "Do you have a pocket?" he asked when she looked down, holding the thing between her fingertips.

"No, Master."

He held out a hand and she placed it in his palm. He slid it inside his coat pocket, then came up with something else...a makeup-smeared handkerchief. Sara's. He couldn't remember putting it in this coat but he supposed he had. He jammed it back down again, not before Valentina had seen it with her hyper-observant gaze.

"What's that?" she asked.

"Nothing that concerns you. A keepsake. Something I carry around to remind myself I'm human."

"I need one of those."

He looked over at her. "Do you?"

"Doesn't everyone? It's a good thing, to remember you're human."

She hadn't the slightest idea what he'd meant, and anyway, she already had a keepsake, a thousand of them probably, one of which rested in his pocket, red and crisp and criss-crossed with tiny veins.

They turned onto *Avenue Montaigne* and down the side street to his house. "What have you drawn in your sketchbook this week, *ma mignonne?*"

"Oh, nothing much," she said, looking uncomfortable.

"Are there many pages left?"

"Some."

He let the subject drop. It surprised him when she was reluctant to talk about something, since she tended to go on and on. He wanted her to talk about music again, about her vaunted hopes and dreams which might or might not amount to anything. The Cirque offered college programs. She could study music if she liked, for the future, when her body didn't allow her to walk on air anymore. She could study art if she wanted, and still work for Cirque in some design capacity long past the time her athletic skill gave way. He thought of her old and incapable, and shook it out of his mind. When she was old, he would be older, eighteen years older to be precise.

It suddenly seemed to him that time was his enemy. Every minute it took to get to his house, wasted. Seven days. That was all he had left. He fell on his slave just inside the door, ripping off her delicate dress, making quick work of her lacy bra and panties. She responded to him as if she'd expected this, taking his groping, grasping assault in stride. He unzipped and fisted his cock, then shoved it inside her pussy, shuddering at the tight hotness of her. Electric arousal swarmed his pelvis and his balls, and he thought he could never be deep enough inside her, no matter how much he hurt her or pleasured her.

Merci, she whispered, clutching at him, and he thought, *quoi? Merci?* Why was she thanking him? For ripping her dress? For taking her to the concert? For holding her leaf in the pocket of his coat, now discarded on the foyer floor?

She gazed at him, stroking his shoulders, running her fingers up into his hair. He captured her hands because he didn't want her affectionate caresses, but he couldn't take away the starry adulation in her gaze.

"Stop," he said, gripping her hands hard. "Control yourself."

"It's only...I hear music even now. I hear music in the way you make love to me."

He pulled away with superhuman effort, a chill chasing the heat of his passion. "*Making love?* Is that what we're doing?"

Her lip trembled. He would always remember it, that little tremble in her lower lip.

"You're my slave," he said. "Not my lover. I think you'd better remember that."

She stared up at him, the night's magic fading from her gold-hazel eyes. Michel watched it happen, feeling actual, physical pain that he'd caused it.

"I just want to fuck you," he said in a rough voice. "Just lie there and let me fuck you. And don't come. I don't want you to come tonight."

A beat, and then her soft, accented voice. "Yes, Master. I serve you."

She blinked and blinked, turning her face away from him. He let her, because to take her chin and force her to look at him...that would cause him more pain, and he didn't like feeling pain. He focused on the pleasure instead, the pleasure of holding her down and having his way. At least, he thought it was pleasure he felt. She messed him up so badly sometimes, he wasn't totally sure.

* * * * *

Valentina lay in bed later, in her cage, clutching her pillow to her face. She wasn't going to cry. She absolutely wasn't. She knew he could see her and she'd embarrassed herself enough for one night. It wasn't only the aching horniness that upset her...the fact that he'd left her purposely unsatisfied. It was his coldness and anger, his insistence on keeping her cut off from the mystery and wonder of his inner self, his emotions and feelings. There was a line around her Master's heart and she wasn't allowed to cross it.

Why? Why was he like that? And how could she love him so much when he held her at arms' length? Sometimes it seemed he had no interest in her beyond controlling her and fucking her, and while the controlling and fucking turned her on, some gaping hole was opening inside her soul that she wasn't sure would ever be healed.

His touch still excited her every bit as much as it had the first time he took her hand. She still got that butterfly feeling in her stomach when he talked to her, or looked at her, or even just sat beside her at their oddly formal dinners. But to reach out and touch him...to even suggest they made love...that infuriated him, when in her heart she knew they sometimes made love.

And the concert, what was up with that? He'd done it for her, and kissed her during the intermission like a lover, and then brought her home and fucked her like a whore, and sent her off to bed in her cold iron cage.

Ugh. Tears came against all her intentions. She turned away from the camera and pressed her palms against her eyes, and tried to think about something else. Her leaf. She had to remember to get it back from him at some point, or maybe she wouldn't, because it would remind her of this night when he'd both thrilled her and broken her heart. *But he does not define you, Valentina. When he lets you go, you'll still be you.*

Or would she? Tomorrow she had to perform for her Master, expose not just her body, but her very being as an artist for his critique. If his opinion was negative, it would kill her. She played one of the main characters in his show, so even after her time as his slave was up, she would still be part of his life. As long as she stayed with Cirque, she would be part of his life, and he part of hers. She screwed her eyes shut, wiping away tears. Maybe she should go through the steps of her act in her head. That would distract her.

She welcomed Adei, Andrew, Roman, and Danil into her thoughts, picturing their formations, the skills when they lifted her or tossed her in the air, the way they caught her, the moment when she did the arabesque on Adei's hand, where she would have done a few flips if Jason wasn't such a stick in the mud. She scrunched up her face, angry that the tears wouldn't stop. Even now, all she could think of was her Master watching from the sidelines, frowning. Scowling at her.

"Valentina."

She turned. He stood beside the bed, unlocking her cage. He still wore the clothes from the concert, his tailored shirt and suit pants. She swiped at her cheeks, embarrassed to be caught crying, but he snapped at her, "Leave them."

She obeyed, blinking out more tears as he took her hands and buckled cuffs around her wrists. He hooked the cuffs to bars on either side of the bed so she was trapped on her back. Only then did he sit beside her and brush fingers through her hair, and smooth his thumbs over the trails of tears on her cheeks. A tender gesture, but his eyes weren't tender. He stretched out on the mattress beside her and took an mp3 player and earbuds from his pocket. He put one of the earbuds in her ear, and the other in his, and laid his head next to hers.

"Listen to this," he said.

She was his slave. Her job at moments like these was to accept what he asked of her. The strains of a classical music concerto swelled in her ear, complex and beautiful, but she couldn't enjoy it, not when he was in one of these moods. Why was she restrained by the cuffs? Why was he lying beside her, fully clothed, so detached, not touching her? His gaze swept over her body, then he reached down and used one hand to shove her legs open.

Just like that, she was aching. Wet.

But he wasn't going to fuck her, not while he was fully dressed. Not this again. Not more arousal when he wasn't going to let her come. Or maybe he'd let her come. She stared into his eyes but there were no clues there, nothing but a slow blink and his glacial blue gaze. He squeezed both her thighs, then delved his fingers between her pussy lips, to the wetness there.

"Handel," he said with his French lilt. "The greatest composer of all time."

The music had turned mournful, or perhaps wistful. He stroked her clit, smoothing her pussy juices over the swollen, unsatisfied flesh. If she could have grabbed his hand and made him stop she would have. Instead, she started crying again, noisy, hot tears in time to the flutes and violins in her ear. She wanted to hate him but she still loved him. She wanted to be unaffected by his sensual caresses but her hips started to move. She drew her legs together, trying to force his fingers away.

"No." He pushed them apart again and slapped the inside of each thigh, once, twice, three times, the blows harsh and discordant compared to the pretty music in her ear. "Keep them open, damn you."

She whimpered, tears running down the sides of her face. The stinging heat of his slaps only increased her arousal. His lips were set in a grim line as he masturbated her for his own thrills. There was a point to this, and it had nothing to do with her.

She knew for sure he wasn't going to let her come.

She steeled herself not to play along this time. She tried to shut off her nerve centers where he teased her so mercilessly, light, stroking touches over her swollen button. Instead he moved to her nipples, her super-sensitive nipples that betrayed her every time. Each pinch, each tap of the taut buds created a deeper pulse in her pussy and clit. She squeezed on nothingness, her whole consciousness centered on her arousal and his deft, teasing touch. *Don't feel. Don't feel anything.* But that was impossible for her and he knew it. She met his gaze with her most pleading expression. "Please, please let me—"

"No."

Her eyes felt itchy and achy. She wished she could stop crying, or at least wipe the current tears away. She tossed her head from side to side, fighting in the only way she could. She wanted to come so badly. She was *so close.* If only he'd touch her a little harder, stroke her more steadily. If only he'd touch her nipples again. If he'd only...*ohhh*...

His hand left her just at the peak of her apex, before she could ease into climactic release. He took the earbud from his ear and sat up, and placed it in hers, so the music sounded twice as beautiful and twice as clear.

"I hate Handel," she cried over the scales in her ear. "I hate Handel and I hate you."

His hand went to his waist, to the buckle of his belt. "I hope so, *mignonne.* It's good for you to hate me sometimes."

She whimpered as he doubled over the belt and grabbed her legs. He wrenched them up into the air, holding them against his side. With his other hand he punished her, delivering sharp, brisk strokes to the backs of her thighs and the sensitive underside of her ass. It hurt too badly to scream. All she could do was make frantic, gasping cries until he stopped. It wasn't a long beating, only eight or nine licks. A long beating would have diffused all the needful pressure in her pussy and given her some respite. Instead, he left her with a raging horniness she couldn't control.

"You're going to leave me like this?" she yelled as he threaded his belt back through the loops.

"You're my slave, aren't you? Or have you forgotten again?"

Oh no. "No, Master. I haven't forgotten. I haven't!"

But it was too late. He undid his pants and went for the condom and lubricant. When he returned he yanked her legs up again and pushed them down against her stomach to get them out of his way. She was helpless to fight him with her wrists still cuffed to the bed. She felt his cock pressing against her ass, pushing its way past her tense ring. "Who do you serve?" he asked.

"I serve you," she said through gritted teeth. *And I can't wait for you to release me, because you make me crazy.*

She was crazy, pure and simple, because this violence turned her on. Her pussy was so wet she could feel her juices dripping down to mix with the lubricant he used on her asshole. The music flowed on in her ears, centuries-old melodies and harmonies while he fucked her as a punishment and reminder. She felt so full of him, not just her body but her mind and her *heart.* Finally, her Master came with an especially deep thrust, pumping hard and then going still. He stared down at her with that fierce, intent look she'd come to know so well, that look she'd always remember. That *possessive* look.

After a few moments he pulled away, releasing her limp, shaking legs. She stayed where she was, more frustrated and unsatisfied than ever. His shirt still hung loose and his hair looked as wild as his expression. He pushed her legs apart again.

"I want you to lie here like this, legs wide open, until the music's done. I'll be watching so don't try to close them. After that I'll let you up to clean off, but you're sleeping cuffed tonight."

In other words, no hope of a stolen orgasm even if she'd been brave enough to try. She wasn't brave enough, though. Her ass hurt, and her unsatisfied pussy hurt even worse. She relaxed into the explicit position he ordered and let the cool night air soothe her pitiful clit as Handel's sonatas went on and on, taunting her.

Crazy didn't even begin to describe the way she felt.

Chapter Thirteen:
Bobble

Michel sat at the tables flanking the headquarters stage, ready to critique the latest progress on *Cirque Élémental*. Jason sat to his left, marking out the order of performances. All his other directors were there, looking excited and nervous. Good, they ought to be. This was the point in the game where the acts needed to look polished, because they still had staging to complete. Set building, costumes, makeup to plan in its final form, not to mention programs and promotional campaigns.

Unfortunately, Michel wasn't in a very good mood. He hadn't slept well. He doubted Valentina had either, considering her beleaguered expression when he woke her, but routines had to be adhered to. He had knelt over her and buried himself in her throat while she remained restrained in the cuffs from the night before. "You wanted this," he'd reminded her as she struggled beneath him.

Six more days.

"Michel?"

He turned to Jason. "Yes?"

"Did you hear anything I just said?"

He didn't appreciate Jason's bemused expression. "Apparently not."

"We're going to do the acts in order, including the interval skits, so you can give feedback on those too. The ones that are done, anyway."

"Yes, fine." He flicked a hand. Interval skits were the last thing on his mind, but he was impressed that Genevieve already had such things in hand. Well, she was one of the best Mistresses the Citadel had ever known.

The Citadel. He hadn't been there in weeks. He assumed all was in order at the club or Jason and Sara would have told him. Strange though, that he hadn't even thought about the Citadel lately, or his private room there...

"Not in the most attentive mood today, are you?"

"What?" Michel snapped at Jason. "Why do you keep talking when I'm obviously not listening?"

"Because these are notes you need to know. Do you want to reschedule this for some other day?"

"No, of course not." Michel gave a big dramatic sigh, like it was everyone else's fault his mind was stuck on Handel concertos and tears. It was only one person's fault. Hers.

No, damn it. His.

He squared his shoulders and attended carefully to the rest of the questions and explanations from Genevieve, Jason, and his other directors. If he expected one hundred percent from others, he needed to give one hundred percent himself. At last the stage was set and the artists of *Élémental* began to show off their progress. Michel watched the acts with a critical eye. He expected technical excellence and precision at this point, but he also demanded something more, something best described as...heart.

Expressions, affectations, even the smallest hand gestures had to carry meaning in a Cirque act. He marked down which acts and skits had found this special "heart" and which hadn't, and noted improvements that might be made. Valentina played a part in one of the skits, gesturing and emoting to the non-existent back rows as only a fourth-generation Italian circus princess could. While he watched his slave, Genevieve described the costume she envisioned for Valentina.

Michel, meanwhile, envisioned Valentina completely nude.

Attention. Control. One hundred percent.

Michel refocused on Valentina as a performer, not a sex slave. More acts followed, including Sara's solo trapeze. Every time she took to the air, he thought she did it a little better. He could feel Jason shifting beside him; he leaned his way and whispered, "Your fiancée is something else."

"Your daughter's not bad either," he said with a smile.

A complicated trampoline act came next. It took some time to set up, time they would have to minimize in the final production. He added that to his notes, then looked up to see Valentina's hand-to-hand troupe taking the stage. In this case, anyway, there was no complex staging, no unwieldy equipment to move into place. There was only Valentina and four men who were strong enough to hold her over their heads and send her skyward, catching her every time.

He settled back as the act began. Showmanship certainly wasn't a problem. She had that "heart" he wanted in abundance, and her intensity seemed to fuel her partners. The four young men had been great athletes in other acts. Now, working with Valentina, they had grown into performers. They were a pleasure to watch, strong and sure in their movements as they created formations and tossed and caught Valentina, then rolled into another section of the act. Valentina's balance was a miracle, as was her confidence as she teetered on her partner's palms. He stared at her, remembering the night before, remembering her tears, but now...now...

When the bobble happened it shocked him, because she'd lulled him and everyone else into believing her movements were effortless, her balance a foregone thing. Worse, the bobble was followed by a shriek and a pitch toward the earth that Andrew tried to halt by grasping her ankle and holding tight. Valentina's head hit the stage so hard it bent sideways, almost to her shoulder. The dull sound of impact echoed in the mostly-empty theater. Someone screamed.

Jason vaulted over the table and ran to the stage, breaking through the concerned cluster of her partners. Michel stayed where he was, too petrified to draw breath. *No, no, no, no, no.*

It was his fault. He'd kept her up late. He'd bound her for hours. If she was paralyzed now because of his selfish, over-rigid mastery... But she was moving. Her toes were moving, her legs were moving. She pushed everyone back and stood up. Michel forced his muscles to fire again, made himself stand and walk over to join them.

"No, it was my fault," she said to Andrew. "It was my mistake."

When she noticed him, she shrank back a little. "Please, Mr. Lemaitre, let me do it again. I can do that skill so easily."

"You're not doing anything until you've been checked out at a hospital." His voice sounded a lot angrier than he meant it to be.

"But I can do it."

"Then why did you fall?" he said, cutting her off. "What caused it? A waver in balance? A lack of concentration?" *A cage-bed, and cuffs, and Handel?*

Jason held up a hand. "I think we should get her to a hospital before we start yelling about what she did wrong."

Yelling? He hadn't realized he was yelling. His heart pounded hard and fast and his shoulders ached with tension.

"I don't need a hospital," she said, moving her head from side to side. "As you can see, I'm perfectly fine."

"You could have a cracked vertebrae or a concussion." Jason stilled her head between his hands, then felt over her scalp for the knot where she'd bumped it. Michel felt jealous that Jason touched her so tenderly, so gently. He wanted to push him away. "I'll take her in," said Jason, turning to him. "You should stay here and finish the critiques. Everyone was really excited to perform for you."

Michel didn't want to leave Valentina's side. But Jason was right. There were performers who wouldn't be able to sleep tonight without some feedback from him.

"Call me," he said to Jason through gritted teeth. "Call me from the hospital." He turned to Valentina. She wouldn't meet his eyes.

* * * * *

Valentina endured a battery of tests at the hospital, scans and x-rays, and a lot of complicated questions that Jason translated into English for her. She felt tired, but not tired in a head-injury way. Just tired in an exhausted, frustrated way.

Stupid, *stupid*. Of all the stupid times to make a mistake.

If she wasn't so tired from the night before she wouldn't have fallen, not that she would ever tell her Master that. He had left her plenty of time to sleep...she just couldn't drift off with her legs spread and her hands cuffed to the sides of her bed, and her pussy aching for relief.

When they laid a hot blanket over her and told her to rest, she closed her eyes and fell into a dream-addled sleep. In her dreams, she visited a shop hoping to find a gift her Master would like. She ended up buying a baby giraffe but then it wiggled too much for her to hold it, and managed to get away. She chased it for a while, fretting over what would become of a baby giraffe in Paris, and then a bear had risen up and roared at her, *How about me?*

She realized the bear was offering itself as a gift and she led it down the road toward *Avenue Montaigne*, but then she noticed the bear was terribly angry. She realized there was no way she could control it and that it might hurt her Master. She decided to run away from the bear but in the course of doing so, she tripped over the baby giraffe. It had shrunk down to a toy size. When she picked it up, she felt annoyed that it was a toy and not a real giraffe at all—after all her worry. She stalked back to the shop where she'd bought it, intending to demand her money back, but then she heard her Master's voice.

"If she can't do the skill—"

"She can do the skill." That was Jason's voice. "She's never fallen before today. You made her nervous."

Valentina looked around the shop for her Master and Jason but the shop was fading along with her dream. She registered the warmth of the blanket and remembered that she was in the hospital. She peered through slitted eyes to find dusky, late afternoon sun filtering through the windows. Jason and her Master were there, conversing in low, sharp tones in the corner of the room.

"You're harming her." Jason's voice again, very angry. "I couldn't stand the way she cowered when you came over to talk to her. You're making her skittish and hesitant. Weak."

"I can do what I like to her. She's mine."

"For six more days."

"Keeping track, are we?"

"Damn right, I'm keeping track."

A soft, feminine voice interrupted their spat. "Daddy, Jason. You're waking her up."

Both the men glanced over at her, frowning. They started to argue again, this time in whispered French.

Valentina looked at the woman beside her bed. Sara, Mr. Lemaitre's daughter. She was only a few years younger than Valentina, and universally loved. She didn't look a lot like her father, being half-Asian, but she shared his piercing blue eyes.

"How are you feeling?" Sara asked. "Any headache?"

Valentina considered a moment and shook her head. "No. I only fell asleep because I was so tired. I had a...a long night."

Sara looked uncomfortable. Valentina flushed. She and Sara hadn't really hit it off, and being her dad's slave only made things worse. Valentina tried a friendly smile, then nodded over toward the two men. "Please, do you know what they're fighting about?"

"I don't speak French that well, but I'm sure they're fighting about you."

Valentina pressed her fingers against her eyes. "Mr. Lemaitre is so angry with me. I drive him crazy and now I've messed up my act."

Sara tilted her head, her guarded expression transforming to something a bit more sympathetic. "Everyone makes mistakes. He knows that. I'm sure he's not angry."

As if to dispute Sara's words, her Master's voice rose along with Jason's, in sharp, bit-off tones.

Sara looked back at her. "Okay, yes, he sounds pretty angry, but not about your act. He's angry because... Well. I think he's angry because he loves you and he's not quite sure what to do about it."

Valentina stared at her. "What? He doesn't love me."

"I know my father, okay? He's definitely falling in love with you, if he's not there already. Believe me, I find this as awkward as you, but I want him to be happy and I think you make him happy in some weird, torturous way."

Her Master turned away from Jason with a French expletive Valentina recognized. There wasn't the smallest hint of love or even affection as he stalked over to her bedside.

"I hate being in hospitals," he said, scowling down at her. "I hate looking at my performers in hospital beds."

Valentina pulled the blanket up a little and scowled back at him. "I'm fine. I said so at the theater but you made me come here anyway. The doctor said there was nothing wrong with me, not even a strained muscle."

"Yes, by some act of God. I've never seen such an ugly fall."

"If Andrew hadn't grabbed my ankle—"

"Andrew has been set straight on that account. As for you, I don't want you to do the act anymore."

All her breath left her. She turned toward Jason, taking in his irritated expression. Tears gathered in her eyes, tears of disbelief and pain. "Are you...are you serious?"

"I am completely serious. I don't want you to do the act anymore, but Mr. Beck has convinced me otherwise. Fortunately for you, he has more faith in you than I have."

"Michel." Jason's voice floated between them, a warning.

"When you sign on to do an act," her Master said, his face reddening, "you are signing on to do it perfectly every single time. When you create an act that's too difficult to perform—"

"I fell during an easy part," she interjected. "It was only an accident."

"There can be no more accidents. No one else has accidents."

"Well, sometimes they do," came Sara's quiet voice.

He lifted his eyes to hers. "Whose side are you on, *ma fille?*"

"Your side, daddy," she said with surprising steel in her voice.

The doctor came in and Valentina let out a sigh of relief that the uncomfortable conversation had been interrupted. The doctor checked Valentina one last time, gave her a clean bill of health, and handed over discharge papers. "Tonight, you rest," he said in English, pointing at her. "Absolutely no activity. Call if any headache or pain."

She looked sideways at her glowering Master. His frown deepened and he looked away.

* * * * *

Her Master left her alone for one night to recuperate. Valentina spent it locked in her cage, ignored and despondent over failing him. If she could take that bobble back, she would. Horrible, careless loss of concentration, and now both her Master and her boss were displeased. She tore pages out of her sketchbook and shredded them into little pieces just to have something to do. She had plenty of pages left, after all, and not much time before her indentured servitude ended.

She'd never realized how busy he kept her until he had to let her rest.

137

Fortunately, the next night they were right back at it, up in his dungeon attic. He strapped her down in the dreaded chair, with only one dildo this time, invading her ass. Then he tied her legs apart, one to each front leg of the chair. He never explained anything he did to her, only did it with a dreadfully intent look on his face. It scared her to death. Once she was tethered around the waist, legs spread, ass impaled, he brought out a little vibrating egg and slid it into her pussy. It created a tight, uncomfortable feeling, but it aroused her too, because it didn't only vibrate inside her. It also rubbed against the glass dildo in her ass, causing an answering vibration so her entire pelvis felt enervated.

He watched as she shivered in her bonds. Something in his regard, his haughty manner, ratcheted her horniness even higher. He was nude so she could see all of his hard, sexy body, down to the rising cock between his legs. She loved the way he flaunted his masculinity, the way he shoved it in her face, daring her to ignore it.

"Master," she asked after a few moments. "Am I allowed to come?"

"If you can," he replied.

Oh, she didn't like the sound of that. He crossed to his collection of painful implements and selected a thick rattan cane, and came to stand beside her. "Why don't you tell me when you're close to coming and we'll see how things go?"

Oh. Fuck.

Sometimes he let her come as much as she wanted. Sometimes he didn't let her come at all. And sometimes, like now, he let her come, but only while she was enduring some capricious and unavoidable form of pain. He'd explained it to her once...something about conditioning, and equating pain with pleasure. She wondered if she'd ever enjoy sex again without having evil things done to her.

The vibrating toy inside her did its job. Within a few minutes she was squirming on the dildo in her ass, aching to climax. She didn't have to tell him because he knew everything about her body and her sexuality by now. But of course he wanted her to tell him, because that was tantamount to asking him to hurt her.

She looked over at him. "Master..."

"You're almost there?"

"Yes, Master," she whimpered, bracing.

He brought the cane down across her spread thighs in a white hot streak. She gave an agonized cry, clenching her fists at her sides. The orgasm that had hovered so close fled in the panicked processing of the cane stroke. When she'd regained her composure she stared at him, tears in her eyes. The egg buzzed on. Her asshole clenched on the dildo holding her to the chair, so she couldn't even shimmy away when he hurt her.

Now the throbbing, pinkening cane track added to the mixture of discomfort and excitement she felt. Her nipples ached to be tormented. He'd conditioned her so well to pain that she craved it. She squirmed in the chair, not even trying to distract herself from another rising climax. Either way it was going to come as she suffered the scrutiny of his cool blue gaze. His cock grew so stiff she wondered if he pulsed like she did, if his blood beat in his veins just like hers.

"Master, I'm about to come again."

She screamed as he hit her thighs with the cane, then fell silent, sucking in breath through her teeth.

"Do you want to come, Valentina?"

His voice was so calm, so measured. She gazed up at him, fighting to be his slave, fighting to accept these things he did to her. "Yes, Master, I want to come very much."

"It comes at a price, doesn't it? Your pleasure? Who do you serve?"

"I serve you, Master."

"Do you enjoy it when I hurt you?"

"Yes, Master," she said, and she wasn't lying. Every time he dealt her pain, her body's reactions amped up. "Please let me come. Please." She stared at his cock. When he moved forward, offering it, she took it in her mouth. Oh God, now she was really going to come. She felt filled, air tight in every hole as he drove toward the back of her throat. Her ass clenched, her pussy buzzed, her mouth and nose were filled with the delicious scent of her Master. She moaned around his hardness a moment later. He knew exactly what she meant to say.

He pulled away and caned her on the thighs but it was too late...his encompassing possession had stolen her control. He drove back into her mouth, fucking her face as she shuddered through an orgasm of astounding power. She could barely breathe but she wasn't sure she cared. He withdrew from her mouth and left her slumped there as he returned the cane to the wall. She watched as he walked away, ogled his tight ass and all the masculine curves of his body.

He returned with a small tin of oval, potent breath mints, and popped one into her mouth. She understood by now this meant she was to rim her Master's asshole. He turned around and she parted his muscular cheeks in the manner he'd taught her, and went to work. Her Master had demonstrated this technique on her own asshole so she knew exactly what it felt like, the extra sensation created by the mint's spiciness. He'd shown her exactly what he desired, using her body as a model. Now she'd become skilled at manipulating the mint on her tongue to bring him maximum pleasure as she caressed his puckered hole.

She had never, ever rimmed a man before she met her Master, had never wanted to, but now she didn't mind doing it because his groans and growls affected her so powerfully. Her pussy was so wet she had to squeeze it to keep the buzzing egg inside. Even though she'd come just a few minutes ago, she wanted to come again. She started wiggling and humming against his asshole.

"No," he said. "Don't come."

At her moan of disappointment, he stepped away and went for the nipple clamps. She shook her head, like that might actually deter him. He only smiled and attached a painful clip to each nipple. These were the clover clamps, the ones that felt too horrible to turn her on. He gave the chain a little tug.

"Open your mouth."

When she did, he put in another breath mint. The first was almost gone. It took three mints all together before he gasped and reached a climax. He caught the semen in his hand and turned to rub it over her belly and chest. The resulting movement and pull of the clamps hurt enough to wash away any remaining pangs of arousal.

"Good girl," he said, his eyes sex-hazy and warm. She felt a thrill through all the pain, the same thrill she felt every time she assisted him to one of his shuddering orgasms. It gave her warring feelings of submission and power, to affect her Master that way. For a while he knelt, looking at her, massaging her chest, and then he seemed to snap from faraway reveries and return.

He went from lazily satisfied to businesslike, a transformation she dreaded. As he took off her clamps, took out the egg, untied her legs, lifted her from the chair, she stared into his face wishing for some spark of connection, some sign that he felt the same deep longing she felt.

But no. Nothing.

Three more nights after tonight. It wasn't long enough to make him fall in love with her. It wasn't long enough to make him see that they belonged together, damn it. She wished she could be his forever because his power soothed and comforted her, and made her crave him day and night.

No wonder he made her sleep in a cage. If not, she would never have left him alone. She would have followed him from room to room, a nuisance of a pet, touching him, begging for attention, curling at his feet wherever he sat. And at night, she would have cuddled in his arms and clung to him, drowning in the scent and feel of him. She wanted his warmth so badly. She wished she could sleep next to him just once.

Later, when he drew the bars of her cage closed and locked her in for the night, she took long slow breaths to calm herself.

Inside, though, she wanted to scream.

Chapter Fourteen:
That's It

Michel had dinner with his daughter every Saturday night. It didn't matter if he was busy, or she was busy, they made time for it. He'd been absent from her life for twenty-two years and this was one way he tried to make it up to her. Over dinner, he listened to all her week's news, mainly a thousand and one ideas about her upcoming wedding to Jason and a thousand and one requests for his opinions on the reception afterward.

Michel finally reached over and took her hand. "Don't ask what *I* want. The reception is for you and Jason. It should be everything *you* want. I'll go along with whatever you decide."

"But..." Her blue eyes clouded a little. "Don't you have an opinion? Don't you care?"

"Of course I care. How could you suggest I don't?" He squeezed her hand and let it go. "If you want to have a May wedding and a party afterward at my Marseille villa, let's do it. It's beautiful there. It might be chilly at night though. You could wait until summer to get married...or fall..."

"We don't want to wait until fall, daddy."

She wanted his opinion, but only so far as it supported what she'd already decided. Brides were delightful to deal with, especially when they were your only child and you couldn't really get flustered with them.

"If you wait until fall," he said, "the show will already be well into production and everything will be settled down."

"And I'll have to find someone to stand in for my act. No. It's better to do it before the premiere, don't you think?"

Michel sighed. She was so young to be getting married. When he was her age, he was still traveling the world, busking, learning about circus. At twenty-two, he'd accidentally knocked up Sara's mother, then left her like the heartless man he was. So many heartless people in the world. So many ways for a vulnerable young woman to be hurt. He wanted to plead with Sara to wait, wait another year, another five years.

But putting it off wasn't going to change anything. Sara adored Jason beyond any reasonable measure, and Michel knew Jason adored her just as much. Michel tried to be happy for them, but he held so much distrust of love and commitment. His mother had murdered his father, for God's sake. Love had driven them to violence so many times. If Jason ever hurt Sara...

"Daddy, what's the matter?"

He forced a smile and poured her some more wine. "Nothing. Absolutely nothing is the matter."

She drew in a breath and let it out in that impatient, endearing way she had. "Jason and I have been going over the guest list for the wedding. We're wondering if we should invite Valentina."

"That depends on whether you want someone seducing the male guests in a back room while you're making your toasts."

"Daddy, I'm serious."

"Okay, then. No. I wouldn't invite Valentina. We're only going to remain...involved...for a few more days."

Two days to be exact.

He felt angry at the thought. Some part of him was virulently angry about having to give her up. Not angry enough to ask her to continue as his slave, because that would cause all kinds of other uncomfortable feelings, like the feeling of not being able to let her go.

Sara studied him with far too much acuity. "I hope you weren't too hard on her about that fall. Bad days happen to everyone."

"I wasn't too hard on her." Well, tying her to the dildo chair for an hour while he edged her and caned her across the thighs wasn't really so bad, compared to some of the things he'd done. "I don't punish people for honest mistakes," he added. *I punish them for scaring me half out of my mind.*

"You were horrible to her at the hospital," Sara said.

"I wasn't."

"You were." She paused a moment, chewing. "You yelled at her and scowled and stomped around like a hornet."

"A hornet, Sara?"

"Yes, a hornet. Or whatever. Something angry and stinging. And I know why."

He reached for his wineglass, fortifying himself with a large swig. "It's difficult enough that we must arrange space for one another at the same fetish club. Please, can we not discuss my private life?"

"You and Valentina aren't private. Everyone at Cirque knows what's going on with the two of you. I know more than anyone, because I've been in her place."

He choked. "You certainly have not."

Her delicate skin deepened in a blush. "I mean that you loved me and you wouldn't admit it, and you hid your feelings from me. Now you're doing the same thing to Valentina and I think it's really sad. I mean, do you have any idea how painful that was for me, your rejection?"

"I have some idea." His chest ached a little, the way it always did when he remembered that time in their relationship. "I said I was sorry."

"And I forgave you. We're fine now. But what about Valentina?"

"What about her?" His voice sounded too defensive, even to his own ears. "Honestly, this is none of your affair."

"It *is* my affair. Families look after each other. Families want each other to be happy."

"Sara—"

"And here I am planning a wedding to celebrate love, and I see you with this girl who you obviously have feelings for, and I see how she's changing you. I see the way you look at her, like you've never looked at anyone else. You're smiling more, you're laughing more, you're frowning more. You're doing everything *more*. You're falling for her and I think that's a wonderful thing."

"Sara," he said more sharply, holding up a hand. "When you're in love, you tend to see love everywhere. But I assure you, Valentina and I are not in love. I'm not falling for her and we don't have a future together. I could explain it to you in greater detail, but I would find it terribly awkward and so would you."

"It's not awkward to love someone. It's wonderful. Magical."

You have no idea, he thought. *You haven't seen the faces of love that I've seen.* Whimsical, guileless Sara had made him into a father at this late stage in his life, and now she wanted him to fall in love too.

"Why are you fighting it?" she pressed.

"Why are you pushing it? Valentina would not make a suitable grandmother for your children."

"Oh God. First of all, who says Jason and I are going to have kids? And even if we were...if we're talking about suitable grandparents..." She arched a doubtful brow in his direction.

He put a hand to his heart. "You wound me."

"Well, it's true. Both of you are a little...different. But the pieces of you fit together just right."

"How would you know?" An impatient edge crept into his tone. "How do you know what's going on between us? It's not the loving scenario you envision. It was an ill-advised entanglement to begin with, one that will shortly be over. I assure you, we will both be relieved."

She started to say something else but he cut her off.

"While we're on the subject of grandparents, Sara, perhaps I should tell you why I've never talked much about your *grand-mere* and *grand-pere* Leveille. Perhaps I should explain where I'm coming from. There's enough bad blood in this family—"

His voice cut off as Sara visibly flinched.

"I didn't mean your blood," he said. "You're the only good thing...the only good thing in my life," he finished with some difficulty. He took a breath and ran a hand through his hair. "Can we not talk about this?"

"You brought it up." Of course, his daughter would know how to be brutal. "Tell me about my grandparents. Tell me about this bad blood. I'm curious."

He needed more wine. Where was the damn waiter? "Have you ever loved someone so much that you wanted to kill them?" He said it softly, because in some way he didn't want her to hear. "Do you know the feeling of being destroyed by love? Your grandmother—my mother— killed my father, but it could just as easily have gone the other way. That was how they loved each other. And me... Well." He forced a pained smile. "Thank God you're so much like your mother. I'm glad about that."

"No, I'm just as much like you. You don't have any bad blood, daddy, if that's what you're getting at. So my grandparents were fuck ups. You got away from them. You explored the world and you learned stuff and created a big circus that brightens millions of people's lives. You're one of the best men I've ever known."

A forced laugh joined his forced smile. "That's not true. Jason's a great man, but me..." He shook his head. "You're kind to humor your father."

"I'm not humoring you." Sara pushed away her plate and placed her napkin on the table. "I'm inviting Valentina to the wedding, okay? As for the rest of it, you need to figure it out."

"There's nothing to figure out."

She shook her finger at him. "There's plenty to figure out, but I have faith in you. You're really smart."

He bit his tongue. *I love my daughter. I do, even when she's pummeling me into a heap.*

"Oh, and Jason and I are flying to California in mid-March so I can meet his family. Unless you want to come with us, the Citadel is yours that entire time."

"I wish I could come with you, *ma chère*," he said, seizing on this new, less threatening turn in the conversation. "Jason's family is going to love you."

No bad blood there, he added silently to himself. He was sure of it, or he'd never let her go.

Michel took his daughter home shortly afterward. She hugged and kissed him at the door as always, but there was tension between them he didn't like. Well, brides-to-be were a ball of nerves, weren't they? And so was he.

He didn't want to think about why.

* * * *

One more day.

Mr. Lemaitre had warned her at the start that she would regret giving herself over to him. He seemed to believe that returning to her own life and her own control was something Valentina should be happy about. And she was happy, a little. There was some sense of relief that after tonight she wouldn't have to answer to his whims anymore. She wouldn't have to submit to his sadistic play times or his huge cock coming at her from every direction. She wouldn't have to report to his office during the day whenever he had a horny craving for her.

She also wouldn't be close to him anymore.

Not that he had ever let her close. He put her away in a cage every night, but still, she was in his life. She was at his house. She was a room or two away from him even if he never allowed her to cuddle in his arms. She'd been awakened by him every morning and done BDSM scenes with him every night, not just play scenes, but intense, heightened scenes she'd become addicted to.

Who else would be able to excite her that way? She ticked through the list of men she knew at the Cirque. There were plenty who were strong and attractive, but none of them were Michel Lemaitre. None of them came close.

Her mind got all caught up when she tried to figure out why he attracted her so much. There were no words to explain it. She had tried to draw pictures of those feelings, pictures of how she felt about him, but she hadn't had any success at that either. None of them were good enough. Maybe when she returned home she would work some more on her portrait of him, but now that she knew him better, she worried it would be all wrong.

She didn't even want to think about going home.

Her Master had given Galvin their last night off. She wasn't sure what that meant and she was afraid to ask. Was he going to finish their thirty days with such horrifying activities that he didn't want anyone else in the house?

She wasn't expecting any Valentine's Day romance, that was for sure. She looked down at her plate, at the meal Mr. Lemaitre had cooked himself. *Coq au vin*, and it was the best she'd ever tasted. What would she do without him? The idea was so depressing she could barely breathe.

"Eat," he said when she paused. "The vegetables too."

She shivered, feeling especially naked tonight, even though she'd been naked every night she'd been under his hand. When she was home, and free, would she eat dinner naked every night to recall these times with him? Maybe. Yes, she probably would.

"If you can cook like this," she said aloud, "why do you pay someone else to do it?"

"Time, *mignonne*," he replied with heaviness in his voice. "I have very little of it. But it's our last night together, and this is my favorite dish."

He'd cooked this for her, his favorite dish. She wanted to cry. *Tina, pull yourself together.* Across from her, her Master took a leisurely sip of wine and leaned back in his chair as if this night were like any of the others.

"What will you do with your time once it is your own again?" he asked. "Return to seducing every single heterosexual man at the training center?"

"I was never that bad."

"You were. You even broke up Silas and Peter's relationship, and they'd been together as long as I could remember."

"They were on their last legs. They would have broken up by the end of that month anyway," she protested. "And obviously, neither of them was one hundred percent gay."

"None of us are one hundred percent anything. Anyway, I'm only teasing you. You may do as you like. After tonight you'll be free, at least when it comes to service. I'll probably still have my fingers all over your career."

Oh, that imagery didn't help. "I hope you will, Master. I mean, Mr. Lemaitre."

"It can be Master for one more night."

"Master," she repeated quietly. "I'll miss calling you Master."

He stared at her a moment, then down at his plate. "We'll take everything into the kitchen and leave it for Galvin. I'm not in a dishwashing mood tonight."

Valentina couldn't frame a reply to that. No matter how hard she tried, she couldn't imagine her Master up to his elbows in soap suds, or loading the dishes into his gleaming oversized dishwasher. She didn't want to imagine him that way.

Once they carried their dishes into the kitchen, her Master led her to the white room. He was still dressed in his work pants and a white shirt, and she was still naked. *Please, please tell me to do something. Tell me to get on my knees. Tell me to suck your cock.*

Instead he took her sketchbook from the top of her packed belongings. Oh no. She didn't want him to look through it but if she tried to stop him, he'd punish her and look at it anyway.

He flipped through the pad, expressionless, studying page after page of half-drawn, scribbled, smeared, and scratched-out renderings of his face and body. She wanted to sink into the floor and disappear. "I didn't really... I wasn't really able to...draw anything."

"Except me. You tried, anyway." He turned one page to the side with a dubious expression.

"I couldn't get it right. I'm sorry."

"No." He shook his head. "No apologies. I know more than anyone that art is a matter of trial and error. Some works take years. A lifetime."

Valentina nodded, biting her lip, but she knew there'd be no "lifetime" with them. If she hadn't been able to draw him while living as his slave for thirty days, she wouldn't be able to draw him when they were merely boss and performer. She wanted to tell him *you're too much of a puzzle*, or *you're too complicated*, or *you're too great and beautiful*, or *you're too...* Whatever. She could never explain why she'd been unable to draw him, and they would all seem like excuses anyway. Better to let him believe what he probably thought right now—that she was talentless.

He tossed it on top of her neatly stacked suitcases and gestured to her. "Come here. Kneel in front of me."

Thank you, God. In this, at least, she wasn't talentless, especially after a month of his training. He reached down and wove fingers into her hair, brushing them against her nape, tugging until she felt some pain.

"Oh, Master," she sighed. He didn't permit her to go on and on when they were scening but all the words screamed in her brain. *That feels so good. I'm going to miss this. Please hurt me. Please force me to do whatever you wish.*

He let go of her hair and tipped up her chin, so she gazed at him from the floor.

"I wonder...how have you changed, *mignonne*? What have you learned?"

She thought hard because she knew she ought to say something wise and submissive at this moment. But all she could think was *I've learned that I love you. I want to be with you.* He wouldn't want to hear that. He'd been perfectly clear the entire time that this was temporary, that he'd wanted to play with her and control her, but only for a while.

"I've... I've learned to be more attentive to other people. To be less absorbed in myself," she finally said.

"I would agree with that."

His softly spoken words sounded like high praise, especially after all her struggles to please him.

"And I think I've learned to be less impulsive," she continued, feeling emboldened. "You've taught me to think before I speak and before I act. I'm so grateful for that."

His mouth turned down a bit. "Valentina without her impulsivity. I don't know... I'm happy to have curbed it a little, but I think it will always be part of who you are, just as controlling and subduing people will always be part of my nature. But yes, you've progressed. Become more balanced, perhaps." He studied her with an expression of gravity. "I haven't had to fuck you against the contract wall in some time, have I?"

"No, Master."

"But it would provide a certain delightful symmetry if I did it tonight. Don't you think so?"

She swallowed hard. "Yes, Master."

Were there to be no trips to the attic torture room this last night then? No beatings, no mindfucks? No restraints or tests of pain? Only this, the ultimate symbol of surrender? It was the way they'd begun, and he was right. It only made sense to end the same way.

He lifted her and led her to the wall and pressed her against it. "Stay."

She closed her eyes and leaned her forehead to the words as she waited. She heard him undressing, heard the scrape of the drawer and the lube's cap flicked open. She remembered how panicked she'd felt the first time, how certain she'd been that he wouldn't be able to force his way in there. He'd proven her wrong so many times since then. He was about to prove her wrong again. She felt his thickness sliding between her ass cheeks as he took his place behind her. He pressed his thighs to the backs of her thighs and trapped her against the wall, his willing, trembling victim.

There were no words, no commands, only his calm, steady breathing as he positioned his cock against her hole. He was slicked up. She wasn't. He'd stopped giving her extra lube about halfway through the training, when she'd learned to compensate by relaxing her tense muscles and letting him in. He squeezed her ass and she arched back, offering her tender orifice to be impaled.

He didn't wait. *Oww...* Oh, it still hurt, even when she relaxed and cooperated. Because of his size it would always hurt, at least at the start. She moaned and let the pain fill her, wash over her and make her into that most delicious of things, an obedient slave. With surrender came pride and pleasure and arousal. As the pain eased into a lesser discomfort he forged deeper, grasping her hips so there could be no escape.

Her hands balled into fists against the wall, then relaxed as he began to move. He slid in deep, so deep, then out again so she felt alarmingly empty. Then in again... It wasn't a drilling. When he was in her ass, there was no need for him to be rough or brutal. The fact he was there was brutal enough, and she felt a low-simmering anxiety the entire time. There was a kind of pleasure in that fear, and a pleasure too in being so filled and so controlled. She made a small sound, a little moan of contentedness that she couldn't contain.

And then it occurred to her: this was how she'd changed. The first day when he'd done this, all she could think about was herself, how scared she was and how much it hurt. She hadn't thought once about what he got out of it, or what she, as his slave, ought to have been getting out of it. She'd only thought, *I wish I could come, but I'll never come this way.* She'd shivered and shaken and wished for it to be over because it wasn't what *she* wanted.

Now, she wished it could on forever because it brought pleasure to her Master. She wished she could be his forever, to control and use, with his beautiful eyes and body, and his wild dark hair, and his stern, French-inflected voice. At her moan, he turned her head and lowered his mouth over hers. While he pinned her to the wall with his cock, he kissed her, deep and hard, his fingers curled around her chin. After a while he thrust his tongue in her mouth, and then he bit her. It wasn't a kiss after all. He was devouring her, and she answered back with her own desperate passion.

"You've changed me," she gasped when he pulled away. "I see now. You truly changed me."

"I know."

He kissed her again, stealing her breath. His lips were hard and commanding against hers, as rich and warm in flavor as a fine wine. His fingers trailed over her body and then down to her pussy lips. He parted them and found her clit, stroking it with proficient skill. Her moan tore wide and became a begging cry into his mouth. His stroking felt so good. Her hips bucked back against his cock, and then forward against the teasing joy of his fingers.

"Oh, please, Master. *Please.*" She pleaded for him to let her come because she wouldn't be able to come unless he helped her. Unless he let her. As good as it felt, she knew he might stop pleasuring her at any time, only to enjoy her sagging disappointment and distress. Or he might let her come. She didn't know. He stoked her clit in rhythm with his strokes, not too hard or fast, but lazily, as if he had all the time in the world to play with his toy.

Her hands spread against the wall, pressing against the words he'd written and her own name. Her nails scraped over the silly hearts. He still held her head and kissed her, occasionally letting his lips meander over her cheek and across her jaw. Her frantic panting mounted as her orgasm curled and built, aching to break wide. Her Master stopped kissing her and pressed his cheek to hers. Her pussy was so wet now she could feel his fingers gliding through the moisture. The warmth of his body engulfed her. A strangled sound rose in her throat and he groaned against her ear.

"Now, then. Do it. Come for your Master."

His rasping words took the rising winds of her climax and spun them into a cyclone. If he hadn't held her, she would have fallen to the floor. The orgasm took all the strength from her body, concentrating it in her mad, contracting core. Hot satisfaction drowned her. He drove his fingers into her pussy and she clenched around them as he drilled her asshole, fucking her fast and hard until he went rigid behind her. His heart beat against her back, and he shuddered with a restrained kind of resonance, so different from her crazed gasps and cries.

He remained motionless and she did too, except when her ass contracted randomly and involuntarily around his cock. She felt so close to him, so protected and nurtured. Then her eyes opened and she stared at the words in front of her. *I belong to Le Maître*, and today's date, February fourteenth.

She turned her head and saw him looking at the words too. He pulled out of her, leaving her bereft. He lifted her chin for one last, fleeting kiss.

"You've done it, *mignonne*. You survived." His lips turned up in a faint smile. "And I did too."

"What happens now?" Her voice sounded tight and a little sharp. She'd felt protected before, but now she felt scared.

"It's time for you to get ready to go," he said, stroking her shoulder. "It's time for you to fly away to freedom. Clean up and I'll take you home."

He walked away. She felt rage, panic, anxiety, all of them attacking her when she was least able to withstand the assault. "That's it?" she cried. "'*Clean up and I'll take you home*'?"

He turned back, his previous warmth and tenderness disappeared. "That's it. Your term of service is over. I hope it was everything you dreamed."

"Everything I dreamed?" She searched his eyes. There was nothing there now, only distance. Irritation.

"Why are you repeating everything I say? I am still your Master until I take you home. I've asked you to clean up and prepare to leave. Let's not end this on an unfortunate note."

She wanted to scream at him. *An unfortunate note, really?* But mimicking his cool words wasn't going to change anything. She took one last look at the words on the wall and then closed her eyes and turned away. She couldn't bear to see them anymore.

Chapter Fifteen:
Deal

Valentina was not the first slave who'd shed tears at their parting. Surely, she wouldn't be the last.

Michel tried not to be affected by her quiet sniffling and sobs as he drove her to the Cirque compound and her dormitory. Honestly, he'd feared worse, which is why he'd been so remote and cordial with her at the end.

He felt regrets, of course, but also a sense of relief. He'd survived a month with his tempestuous sex slave, and enjoyed it for the most part. He'd changed her. Perhaps. Whether he'd changed her for better or worse, he wasn't sure. He'd been a little depressed when he'd leafed through her sketchbook full of scribbled-out drawings. Apparently his control had stymied her creativity—the very creative spirit that made her who she was.

Not good.

So, it was out of the question to try to extend any connection between them. Part of being a good Master was knowing when to let go because your control was damaging rather than improving a slave in your care. That, too, had happened before, and would certainly happen again. Not that he hadn't selfishly held onto her until the end of her term. He was human, after all.

It was after eleven when they pulled up to the dormitory. He made her compose herself before they got out to unload her things. It wouldn't do for everyone to see him moving his sobbing, weeping slave back into her place. Or perhaps it would enhance his reputation as a hardass. In the end, he just wanted her to stop crying, so he ordered her to, and she did.

She opened the door to her apartment, calmer now, and he resigned himself to stay awhile, until he was sure she was okay. Ending a single scene could create a wretched case of sub-drop; ending an entire relationship could trigger a much worse one, even if the sub in question had known all along this would be the end. He helped her put away her things and monitored her outward emotions. She seemed sad but not depressed. Being among her art and personal possessions surely helped ease the sting a bit.

Then he remembered and shoved his hand in his pocket. "Here. This is yours."

It was the curled red leaf she'd picked up on the way home from the symphony. Valentina reached out and took it. "I had forgotten."

"It's just a leaf, I suppose. One can find them anywhere."

"That's not true. This one has memories." She went over to the jury-rigged easel that held her self-portrait and considered where to place it. He noticed the piece of red cellophane on the table from before. She slathered both of the items with glue and placed the cellophane in a spot near the middle. She added the red leaf just above the figure's shoulder. It looked perfect there.

"*C'est belle*," he said. "Is it finished?"

She shook her head. "They're never finished until someone takes them away."

"People take them away?" Unreasonably, he wanted to take all of them away and keep them for himself, not that he had a place for them in his monochrome house. Valentina's place vibrated with color. He felt trapped all of a sudden, and anxious to escape.

"Well," he said.

She gripped her hands in front of her. He could see her eyes go glossy with tears. "Please wait, Mr. Lemaitre. I have to...to go wash my hands."

She scurried to the kitchen to soak off the glue she'd slathered on her fingertips. Michel stared at her self-portrait. Candy. It had candy on it, round red bonbons that looked like frosted jewels.

"Will you still..." She called out to him over the patter of the water in the sink, then waited and shut it off. "Will you still see me? Ever?"

"I'll see you all the time," he answered as she shook off her fingers and dried them on a towel.

"I mean, will we ever play together again? Perhaps at the Citadel?"

The Citadel, he thought. He'd never even taken her to his back room. It seemed a terrible omission. "I don't think so. I don't go much anymore. My daughter goes with Jason now and...you know." But his daughter would be in California for a week. Perhaps then... *No.* "I don't think it's a good idea for us to play casually."

"Why not? We obviously do well together. I mean, in that way. We turn each other on."

He considered her, fighting questions in his own mind. He looked away and flicked at a piece of lint on his shirt. "You're more of a full time project. And I won't do full time with you again." As he said it, he understood why. Because he would lose himself, and worse, she would lose her creative spirit, her spark.

Her lips trembled. The gathering tears fell. "Didn't you like our time together?"

He gave a frustrated sigh. "You're right back to being that silly, dramatic girl. Why ask such a question? Did I enjoy our time together? What do you think?"

"I don't know! I don't know what to think. How can you so easily release me? How can you just walk away after all we shared?"

"I told you, thirty days. It's better for these things to have a finite life."

"These *things*? What is this *thing*? You mean all the fucking and service, and all the things I did for you because I lo—"

He grabbed her and put a hand over her mouth, muffling the word he didn't want to hear. "Stop. Don't," he growled. "This is not going to be. You don't love me and I don't love you. We are two very headstrong personalities who just spent a month in an emotionally heightened dance. Now the dance is over. You understand?"

Her hot tears wet his fingers, sliding between them. Her body shook, her fiery hair making a halo around her beautifully familiar features. "I am not for you, and you are not for me," he said in a softer voice. "This is something we've both known from the start."

"That's not true," she forced out past his fingers.

He let her go and turned away, and picked up her sketchbook from the table where she'd placed it. "Look," he said, leafing through the pages. "This is who you are with me." He gestured around at the explosion of art cluttering her apartment. "This is who you are without me."

"I don't care."

"You should care. I do."

She put her hand over her lips, right where his fingers had been, and sat on the edge of her couch. "Who will I be with now?"

"You don't have to be with anyone." His voice betrayed more jealous anger than he wished. "Why not be with yourself for a while? You don't have to sleep with every single man in the world—"

"I don't," she yelled at him. "That was always your take on things, but I'm selective."

He gave a bark of laughter. "I'm not certain you understand what the word 'selective' means."

She crossed her arms over her chest, visibly fuming. By some miracle of control, perhaps the control he'd taught her, she managed to keep any further retorts inside. He could leave now. She had clearly unattached herself from his mastery, if she'd screech at him like this. She was back to her old self, voluptuous in emotion. She would obviously be okay...but he hated to leave things in a spat.

He sat beside her and took her hand, and put his other arm around her, holding her close. "It will be okay, you'll see. You won't miss me."

"I will," she bawled, turning her head into his chest. "I miss you so much already. I'll never survive."

"You will."

"How? I'm falling apart and it's only been an hour since you let me go."

"The first hour is the hardest."

She sobbed harder. "This isn't funny. This isn't a joke."

"Of course it isn't. None of this has been a joke to me." He let go of her hand to wipe away her tears and brush her hair back off her face. "I'm so glad to see you this way, because it means I didn't do any lasting damage. You're the exact same Valentina you were thirty days ago."

"That's not a good thing." She shook her head, burying her face in her hands. "I don't like being this way."

"But the world needs you this way." He stood up and crossed to her portrait, with the candy and leaf-ribbon hair. "You see how beautiful you are." He touched some swirls and dots around the border. "I wish I could have this to remember you by."

They were fatal words. A fatal mistake, as much as he meant them. He did want her. He would not have her, but he wanted something of her.

In that moment, he wanted her portrait more than life itself.

"Can I have it?" he asked, turning back to her. "Then it can be finished, no? If I take it away?"

She stared at him and he thought, in that gold-hazel gaze, that she could see everything inside him. Everything that made him powerful and everything that made him weak. She was still angry with him, still in her mood. She lifted her chin and said, "You can have it, yes, but only if you sleep beside me all night. Not just sleep beside me. You have to hold me against you, in your arms, all night long."

He narrowed his eyes. The little bitch had gone right for the center of his terror, poking at the tender, roiling spot that frightened him the most. "I sleep in my own bed. Alone."

"Then you can't have it."

Now he was the one to cross his arms over his chest. "Why would you want that? It's uncomfortable to sleep beside someone."

"I want it. I want to know how it feels."

"You'll be asleep through most of it."

"No, I won't. I'll stay up all night so I don't miss a moment."

"And I suppose you'll talk at me all night, and keep me up, and expect all kinds of flirtation and affection and half-drowsy sex acts until we wake in the morning and find we've fallen in love?"

"No. I just want to sleep beside you for one night."

His jaw worked. Damn her. He could walk away now. He could leave her portrait behind. Hell, he'd stared at it long enough that he could recreate his own approximation. Grab some leaves and cellophane and candy and some brightly colored paints and throw them at a canvas until they took on Valentina's form.

"I snore," he said.

"It doesn't matter. I told you, I'm not going to sleep."

Damn her. "Okay. One night."

"In your arms."

"In my arms. How charming. But I can touch you wherever I like and fuck you if I feel like it."

She rolled her eyes. "Of course you can. Those rules will stand for as long as I live."

He'd barely gotten over the fact that she rolled her eyes at him when he realized the message in her words. She was still his. She intended to remain his forever, willing and available for his needs. This detachment wasn't working. Somewhere along the line, he'd lost control of her.

He'd lost control of himself.

"It's late," he said, hiding his misgivings in a gruff, impatient tone. "If you want to cuddle in bed, let's cuddle in bed."

He stalked into her bedroom and undressed. She undressed too, watching him like he might go back on their deal and leave. But no, he was staying. All she'd specified was that he had to hold her, so he could do it any way he wanted. Grudgingly, stiffly, with tension and detachment. "Which side do you want me on, Mistress?" he asked, taking in her narrow bed. He'd barely fit in it himself, much less with her beside him.

Indignation colored her cheeks. "Why 'Mistress'? Am I forcing you to do anything? You wanted the painting and this is my price. Artists deserve to be compensated. You of all people should know that."

He grabbed her and pulled her over his lap, and started walloping her bottom in an impromptu spanking she very much deserved.

"Wait— Hey!" She flailed, trying to escape him. "You can't do this. You're not my Master anymore."

"I'm giving you this spanking as an irritated friend. Be still."

She was not still. She kicked and complained that the spanking was unfair, but it seemed totally fair to him and so he spanked her ass cheeks until they were scarlet and until she drooped in capitulation across his thighs.

"There," he said with one final stinger. "I'll sleep much better now."

He let her up and she backed away, rubbing her bottom. "Why did you do that?"

"You said I could touch you wherever I liked. Get into bed."

He'd gone rock hard from spanking her, and now he wanted her. As soon as she crawled in next to him, he turned and spread her legs open with his knees, grasping her heated ass cheeks in his palms. Her sniffling complaints disappeared the moment he pressed inside her. Fucking her was like being stimulated from the inside. She was so tight, so electric. She reacted with her entire being, whether you were hurting her or trying to make her feel better than she'd ever felt in her life.

Ah, he would miss those reactions.

He held her tight and thrust into her, fucking her for his pleasure, knowing the more selfishly he acted, the more it would feed her submissive needs. She struggled beneath him, his inextinguishable flame. Within minutes, he could feel her climax unfolding.

He knew it not only from her cries and the rhythmic clenching of her pussy, but from the way she practically levitated from the bed. He'd done so many scenes with her, planned, careful, controlled scenes, but he'd rarely indulged in the simple pleasure of throwing her down and fucking her. He was glad he'd thought to do it now. Some elemental, Neanderthal exhilaration built in the base of his cock, setting off jolts of sharp pleasure in his balls and thighs. He pumped his orgasm into her with growling satisfaction.

After a few moments, she wrestled her way from under him. She said she had to go clean up but he knew she just wanted to go to the bathroom and look at her red, hand-printed ass in the mirror.

"*Viens*," he bellowed from the bed. "*Tu me rends fou.*"

She poked her head out the door. "What does that mean?"

"It means get your ass into bed right now. My spanking hand is twitching."

She hurried to the bed, mumbling something like *Does it ever stop?* She had better take care. He'd be only too happy to spank and fuck her in alternation all night long.

She slipped under the covers beside him, smelling sweet and feminine, and gave a sleepy sigh. "Mr. Lemaitre," she began.

"Shh."

"*Monsieur—*"

"No." He put a finger over her lips. "No talking. Lie in my arms and be still." He gathered her close, then closer, aligning her body to his. When had he last slept against another warm body? Never. Perhaps as a child, before he went into foster homes. From a very young age, he couldn't bear to have people near him when he slept.

There was something very cozy about it, certainly. She felt soft and warm curled against him, her cheek pressed to his chest. One of her hands crept up to his shoulder and rested there. It felt alien to him, like a bird perched there, a dove or pigeon. While he lay trying to figure out how he felt about all this, Valentina grew very still in his arms. He could feel her relax, slowly, incrementally. She was drifting to sleep.

Up all night, indeed.

He held himself completely still so he wouldn't wake her. When she'd fallen fully into slumber, her hand lost its grip on his shoulder and slid down little by little. It only stopped when it came to rest against the thumping beat of his heart.

* * * * *

Valentina awakened to the sun shining on her face. Who had opened the shades? She fluttered her lashes and blinked, and then she remembered. Mr. Lemaitre. He stood beside her window, gazing through it without expression.

"You said you would sleep with me all night," she said.

He turned toward her with a frown. "I did sleep with you all night. Now the night's gone. It's broad daylight."

"But...I thought..." She winced at the whining weakness in her voice. She'd wanted to wake up in his arms the same way she'd drifted to sleep in them. Maybe some morning sex? He'd already gotten dressed. He looked like he was ready to go to work.

She sat up in bed, holding the sheets against her chest. "Why are you up so early?"

"Why are you lying in bed so late?"

"You lied to me. You don't snore."

He gave a sharp laugh. "How would you know? You fell asleep in thirty seconds flat."

That annoyed her too, that after all her excitement to sleep beside him, she could remember precious few moments of it. "I tried to stay awake but you're very comfortable to sleep with."

"*Merci*," he said, looking back out the window.

She lay down, clinging to her scant memories of the night before. She remembered his chest rising and falling beneath her cheek, his strong thighs nestled against hers. And the smell of him—sandalwood and cologne and his own masculine scent. She didn't want to forget any of it.

"I suppose you're going to go now." Some part of her wanted him to go because he made her feel so agitated and needy. And rejected. Why couldn't he have just held her until she woke up? Why get up and stand across the room like some hovering specter?

"I was going to go into the office, yes," he said. "And you have a practice later." He came to the bed, reached down and ruffled her tangled hair. This was the time at his house when he used to unlock her cage and demand his morning blowjob.

He obviously had no intention of doing that today.

"I'm going to take the painting now," he said instead. "Thank you for giving it to me. Thank you for giving yourself to me for a month, Valentina. I know I didn't make things easy for you."

"I didn't want you to."

He gave a soft breath of a laugh. "Well, I enjoyed our time together." He leaned down and kissed her forehead. It lasted a mere second, not long enough. He let go of her and started for the bedroom door. "You needn't get up. I'll see you at work, *mignonne*."

Just like that, he was gone. She tilted her head back, blinking at the sun again, and then collapsed into her pillow. Somehow, she had to go on in life without him. It was a good thing she was so strong.

She peeled herself out of bed and brushed her teeth and showered, and puttered around her kitchen in her bathrobe, trying to find something to make for breakfast. The loaf of bread she'd bought weeks ago was disgusting and moldy. She threw it away, along with some other long-spoiled items. She would have coffee then, and boxed cereal with lots of sugar. Mr. Lemaitre hadn't allowed any sugary cereal at his house. See, there was a bright lining to everything. Now she could once again eat all the sugary cereal she liked. She filled her bowl almost to the top, and then stopped when she heard a sharp knock at the door.

She knew immediately who it was.

Maybe he'd forgotten the portrait. But no, it was gone. She opened the door and there he stood, distant and haughty and handsome as ever. She didn't say anything, only stared at him.

"May I come in?" he asked.

"You just left."

"I came back. May I come in?"

He asked the second time in bitten-off syllables, so she stood back and let him enter. He paced across her living room. She watched him, puzzled. "Is everything okay?"

"Yes. No." He turned back to her. "Would you be interested in...extending?"

"Extending?"

"Extending our association. Our power exchange." He shook his head as if to clear it. "Extending our Master/slave relationship."

"But just last night you said I was not for you, and you were not for me. You said our dance was over."

He looked up at her ceiling and let out a long, ragged breath. "Yes, I did. Yes, all of that is true. Forget what I just said."

"Forget what you said about our dance being over, or what you said about extending?"

"Just..." He swung an arm at her, heading for the door. "I'm going to be late." He reached for the knob, then turned back again. "One more month? We were making such progress."

Valentina's heart hammered in her chest. He wanted her back. More slavery. More pain. Part of her felt elated that he wanted her. Part of her felt flattered. Part of her felt scared.

Part of her felt really, really pissed off.

"You made me cry," she said. "You pushed me away and made me cry, and now you want me back?"

"I tend to be very capricious in my desires."

"That's not something to be proud of." She took a step back as he advanced.

"I know. That's why you should say no to me. '*No, I don't want to be your slave anymore.*' Say it."

She put her hands out to stop him. "You always want me to do what will please you. *You.* I always have to be what *you* want, when *you* want it. Lover, slave, pet, whatever you're in the mood for, but I only ever get what you give me. I never get to choose who you are, what you do."

"Yes, that is the lot of the submissive partner."

"It's not fair though, is it? It's not fair that I must always meet your needs and you never meet mine."

He took her in his arms, circling her waist in an unyielding grip. "Are you sure I don't meet your needs?"

Just like that, her anger and resistance fled. His touch alone had the power to melt her. Add in his artfully sensual lips and his piercing light blue gaze and she was burnt to a crisp.

"I want you, but you hurt me," she whispered.

"You like to be hurt," he whispered back. "You like to be excited and endangered. You like everything I do to you. Let's be clear about that."

She pushed against his chest, pulled at his arms until she extracted herself. Well, until he decided to let her go.

"One more month," he said, following as she tried to put distance between them. "It will be nearly time for the premiere then, a more natural stopping point. I can't explain why, but right now things feel unfinished. Do you know what I mean?"

She did know what he meant, but another month? Thirty more days to fall in love with him and then lose him? How could she protect herself?

"I can't," she said, suffering at the look he gave her. "I just can't."

"What if we negotiated?"

She regarded him suspiciously. "People warned me at the beginning that you were not the negotiating type."

He shrugged, his lips pursed in an impatient line. "Even when we don't negotiate, that is a negotiation." He reached for her again.

She skittered away, flustered. "No, I don't..." But she did know what he meant. Everything, always, was by choice. Even giving up choices.

"I can't give you as much as I gave you before," she said as his arms once again trapped her. "I can't give you all of me all the time."

"And I can't be manipulated with retreats and safewords every time you're not in the mood."

"Then how can things work? What is there to negotiate?"

Her frustrated outburst didn't seem to rattle him in the slightest. "I want two hours a night," he said. "Two hours of devoted service, and the rest of the time is your time." He thought a moment. "But you still have to sleep in the cage."

"If you only want two hours a night, why can't I sleep at home?"

"Because I want you in my cage. I like you there."

Him and his damn cage. "I want Sundays off." It was difficult but she held his gaze. "No service at all on Sunday, and I get to sleep that night in your bed."

"Valentina," he said, as if she were ridiculous. "Where would I sleep?"

"I get to sleep *beside you* on Sunday nights," she clarified, and then realized he teased her. She pouted and pushed away from him. "I like serving you but I need breaks. I need times to live my own life."

"I agree with that."

His quick capitulation caught her off guard. "You agree that I need breaks?"

"I agree that you need breaks, and I also agree with your conditions. Sundays off, and Sunday nights in my bed, if you must persist in this silly cuddling fetish."

"It's not silly." *No more silly than you asking for another month*, she thought, but she didn't dare say it aloud. Twelve hours a week he'd have control of her, and she didn't want to anger him unnecessarily.

"I have one more condition," she said. "I want a place to work in your house. A place for my art. Either that, or you let me come and go from my apartment when I wish."

"I've already told you that coming and going is out of the question. That's not slavery. It's hooking up." He thought for a moment. "I don't have any free rooms for you to use as a studio, and I don't want your scraps and paper and leaves and candy cluttering up my place."

"You don't have a corner somewhere in the sun, with a table, where I can set up two or three projects? I don't have to bring everything."

She waited, worrying, hoping. This negotiation stuff was hard. He might say no, and then she'd have to decide to go anyway, or somehow find the guts to say "No, thanks" to more time with him.

Which she could never do. Which he probably knew.

"Three projects," he finally said in exasperation. "That's the absolute limit. You can have the corner by the window in the living room. Only the corner."

He did it to be kind. He knew she would have come anyway, spent another month with only a sketchbook if that's what it took to be in his home, staring up at him from her knees. She threw her arms around his neck. "Okay, only the corner, I promise. Thank you."

Later that night, after he locked her in the cage, Mr. Lemaitre went to the contract wall with his big marker and scratched over the previous dates. He added *for two hours a night, not including Sundays*. No ending date. She stared at him from behind the bars, wondering if he really grinned before he left the room, or if it was only a trick of the light.

Chapter Sixteen:
Demands

It happened slowly, all the little encroachments.

First it was an extra, brightly colored coffee cup in the drainer beside his.

Then it was her art, spilling from her corner in his living room onto side tables and windows, and even his blank, neutral walls. He kept his home uncluttered because he liked his mind uncluttered. She couldn't seem to grasp this concept, not even after repeated lectures and punishments in the attic, pinned by her nipples to the spanking bench. One day he found paint drips on his carpet. He put her in the dildo chair for two hours and tormented her until she screamed that she would respect his personal space and his home's pristine decor. Then the very next day he found a silk plant shorn of leaves, sacrificed for collage parts.

He ought to have been glad. She was proving that she could be his slave and still remain her true self, an impulsive, creative bundle of trouble. But this didn't soothe him. It threatened him. If she could be his slave sometimes, his abject, unresisting slave, and still remain Valentina in all her uncontrolled beauty...

Damn her. She was stripping his peace of mind as efficiently as she'd stripped his designer silk plant.

Sara insisted he was in love with Valentina but it wasn't love Michel felt. It was lust mixed with irritation. Somehow Valentina managed to be two very different things: a slave whom he owned and controlled, and a mystical creature he could never own or control. If she was one or the other he could resist her, but when she was both, she defeated him. She was elusive, complex, infuriating, all the things that made it impossible for him to send her away, although he really wanted to.

Then, on Sunday nights, he was forced to fulfill her nightmarish cuddling requirement. She curled up beside him in his bed where no one ever, ever slept and stayed there all night pressed right against him, smelling of sex and life and flowers and warmth. The deliberately muted design of his large white bed, accented with calming steels, blacks, and grays, was shot to hell by the garish red-orange hues of her hair.

He had to allow it—he had promised—but he didn't have to enjoy it or become used to it. The first Sunday he lay awake all night, just as he had when he spent the night at her dormitory. The second Sunday he slept off and on, but still woke too early, tangled up in Valentina's tentacle-like arms and legs. The third Sunday he took out his frustration in endless fucking. He woke her up three or four times during the night, even assfucked her once, and still she curled up next to him and sighed like this cuddling was the greatest thing on earth.

As he dealt with these encroachments, Cirque du Monde entered the final production stages of *Élémental*. They closed *Tsilaosa* the second week of March, tore down that set and started building the new one with state-of-the-art upgrades that were equal parts headache and wonder. The directors made final decisions about the order of the acts and the skits in between, and Michel sat in on hours of meetings and consultations. He had to watch Valentina do her terrifying hand-to-hand act three, sometimes four times a week. She never made a mistake, not once, but afterward he would find himself with the beginnings of a migraine from all the tension in his shoulders and neck.

Jason would probably have noticed and mocked him if he wasn't so caught up with Sara in the planning of their May nuptials, to take place at Michel's Marseille villa. In her corner of Michel's living room, Valentina worked on a wedding gift for the couple. She'd adapted her portrait of

Jason into a portrait of both of them, embellished with all manner of shiny and colorful things. Jason's heart was still a key, and Sara's a tiny, gilded lock. Michel watched her work on the magnificent thing with injured pride. So far, she'd made no artistic renderings of him aside from the rough, scratched-out disasters in her sketchbook.

He realized it was petty and pompous to expect an *objet d'art* from his devoted little slave, but he did. What would he even do with it once he had it? He'd put Valentina's portrait in his closet, in an archival-quality box carefully sealed so the candy bits wouldn't attract pests. She never asked about it but he felt ashamed for not displaying it. The self-portrait had so much life, it felt like keeping Valentina herself in a box, suffocated beneath layers of acid-free tissue paper, but to display it would result in its eventual disintegration, and he couldn't bear that.

Sometimes after he locked Valentina away for the night in her cage, he stared at the portrait of Jason and Sara with its beautiful colors, and lock and key, and seethed with jealousy. *Do me next. Me, Valentina!* A painting of him wouldn't have colors and locks and keys... What would it have? How did he seem through her eyes?

He should have been glad she didn't make art about him. He worked hard to keep their relationship appropriately distant, to keep their power differential in place. Valentina seemed addicted to the act of falling in love. When he didn't keep her busy enough, she read romantic novels and watched classic movies about couples, sobbing and talking to the characters on the screen. She marveled about things like rainbows and glitter and the magical innocence of children. *You're a child yourself*, he wanted to snap at her. *You act like one.* He was careful not to give her the least reason to go swooning and falling in love with him.

And yet, despite all his efforts, she was taking over more and more of his life. Even his daughter! To his chagrin, Sara and Valentina had become something like friends. He saw them talking to each other at work with greater and greater frequency. They weren't comfortable friends, at least he didn't think so. Their body language didn't suggest girlish confidences and gossip or whatever it was women did. Still, they talked and knew each other, and it seemed like one more area of his life where Valentina had barged in and made herself at home. Valentina knew the time when Sara and Jason would leave for California, even though Michel hadn't told her.

She asked if they could go to the Citadel now that his daughter wouldn't be there for a few days.

Jesus, he supposed they should. Michel wanted to go—he missed the place—but he was conflicted about it. He still remembered Valentina hanging from that noose, and before that, he remembered her weeping outside the door to his back room, crying *Oh please! Why won't you do that to me?* He remembered other things too, so many nights spent in his back room doing vicious things to begging, groveling slaves for their pleasure, and his. Was he losing his nerve?

He would see other slaves at the Citadel, past partners he'd never cared much about, and he'd feel compelled to compare them to Valentina, about whom he had come to care an alarming amount.

Then again, maybe he needed to take her there and place her among his other slaves, in the gritty, dark, alternative side of his life. Maybe it would be good for them both.

* * * * *

Valentina suspected Mr. Lemaitre was coming to love her. She couldn't be one hundred percent sure, because he still acted the same way. Stern, demanding, distant.

But he allowed her to do things and see sides of himself he'd kept hidden before. He smiled at her sometimes now when he unlocked her cage in the morning, and sometimes he even stayed to have breakfast with her before he hurried off to work. Over dinner he talked to her about business decisions he had to make, or ideas he had, or even sometimes his hopes for the future. This was a great change from before, when he'd mainly just lectured her on etiquette and occasionally fucked her bent over the table. Maybe it was the whole difference of letting her wear clothes, since dinnertime didn't fall within her two slave-hours.

Mr. Lemaitre stuck to his word about only demanding two hours of service a night, and it was always after dinner, not during, or before. He paced their scenes so they ended on time, with just a little time at the end to give her aftercare. A hug, a few words, some questions to be sure she was okay. That was pretty much all she got but it was enough to reassure her that she meant something to him, that she was more to him than a willing body.

And oh, she was willing.

She'd been unsure if their new arrangement would soften things so much that their encounters would lose their thrill, but the opposite happened. When he was in charge of her all the time, his mastery became an ongoing, diluted thing. When he had only two hours, his mastery became sharp and cutting as a knife. For those two hours he would consume her, and then, just as quickly as he took over her and turned her inside out, he would set her free. It was a roller coaster ride of ups and downs, of danger and then sudden safety that left her reeling and hungry to do it all over again.

Now, tonight, he was taking her to his famous back room at the Citadel to play. He hadn't been to his back room in weeks and so no one else had been there either. At work, word had gotten around that he was returning to the Citadel since his daughter was away. People caught Valentina in the corridors or backstage at the theater and asked her, *Is it true? He's coming back again? Are you excited? Scared? Can I come?*

But she had no control over who could come or not come, or what might happen in her Master's back room. No one had control but Mr. Lemaitre. That was what was so exciting about the whole thing. That, and that she was going to be there as his primary slave.

Last time she'd been in his back room, she'd had to watch him with his other slaves, and she'd been so jealous. She'd marveled at their self-discipline and the way they suffered to please him. Now, she knew she could match them in self-discipline and sacrifice, and that made her proud.

As Valentina waited in her Master's cavernous bathroom, she ran a finger up and down one of the ribs of her black velvet corset. He'd given it to her at dinner, turned it over and shown her the copper-orange thread outlining the boning, thread chosen because it matched her hair. It was impossible to see the thread from the outside because the velvet was so plush, but Valentina loved the secret of it inside, right against her skin. He'd also had her name stitched along the side seam, not Valentina, but *La Vampa*, her circus persona. She'd almost cried when he showed her. She'd taken it and crushed it against her heart and told him she would keep his gift forever. The corset had hooks for wide black garters, six of them, and he'd given her black silk stockings to wear with seams up the back. He laced her so tight she felt squeezed and hugged by the garment, so tight that he had to do the garter hooks for her, kneeling at her feet.

I love you, she thought, looking down at his thick black wavy hair. *I love you. I love you.*

She wished she could say it out loud. Her Master had put on one of his favorite Handel concertos, turning up the volume on his fancy, whole-home audio system that made it sound like the orchestra was right there, whatever room you were in. In his granite-walled bathroom, the music echoed and seemed to dance in the air. Her Master hummed along at parts, tilting his head back as he shaved.

I love you. The phrase repeated in her head to the accompaniment of the music. His body was so strong and sexy. His hands, his brows, his lips, his ass, his cock flaccid and resting on a thatch of dark hair. Every single thing about her Master was fetish-worthy. She'd been with a lot of men— a *lot* of men—but none of them had ever affected her as he did. None of them had ever made her feel breathless and excited like this. Just being near him, being in the same bathroom with him as he dressed...

"*Une image dure plus longtemps,*" he said.

She blinked at him when he turned to her. She'd learned a lot of French, but found herself too distracted to translate at the moment.

"Take a picture, it lasts longer," he repeated in English. When she continued to gape at him, he smiled and said, "You're staring."

"I can't help it." Her insides felt as warm as her face. He picked up a white towel from the counter and wiped away the last traces of shaving cream, and applied the sandalwood-scented lotion that permeated her dreams. What was it about a man grooming? She watched his chest and arm muscles contract as he put away his razor and straightened his lotions and bottles. The music in the background swelled, notes chasing one another and then blending into a resonant harmony.

"This is so perfect," she blurted out.

He turned away from her to go into his dressing room. "What's perfect?"

"This," she called. "This moment. This music and my corset and stockings and...and you."

He came out wearing a pair of black leather pants that clung to him in all the most compelling places. "You're excited about *le Citadel?*"

She sucked in a breath, staring at his hard chest, his abs, the trail of dark hair disappearing down the front of his low-waisted pants. "It's not...no. That's not what I mean. I mean this moment feels perfect. So many times when I'm with you, everything feels perfect."

His eyes narrowed the slightest bit. "Sometimes when I'm with you, things feel perfect. Other times I want to strangle you. This is life, I suppose."

She didn't know what gave her the bravery to speak. Perhaps it was the intimacy of being invited into his bathroom to watch him shower and shave, or the intimacy of watching him dress, or those damn leather pants. "I wish we could stay like this forever," she cried in a rush. "I feel most perfect when I'm with you. I don't want to be your slave for a month, and then another month, as if it's the dates that matter. I want to be yours, all yours, forever and ever my whole life."

The more words she spilled out, the more her voice rose in intensity. By the end it was practically a shriek. Would he be angry at her outburst? Dismissive?

No, he laughed. Not a sweet, agreeable laugh, but a harsh mocking laugh that felt like a punch to her heart.

"Valentina, you're so outrageous. So ridiculous sometimes. The things you say."

He disappeared back into the dressing room, leaving her to clutch her chest in agony. Ridiculous. *Ridiculous?* She stood up from her perch on the edge of his bath tub and stormed after him into the dressing room.

"You hurt my feelings. You just stabbed my feelings to death."

"To death, eh?" he echoed, nonplussed. "I'm sure you'll have some new feelings in a second or two. You always do."

"You mock my feelings?"

"Yes, I mock your feelings." He turned to her as he pulled on a shirt. "When you fling them at me willy-nilly all hours of the day, it grows tiresome. And a little mock-worthy, if you must know."

Her mind swam with such hurt that she wasn't sure for a moment what to say. She'd bared her heart and all he did was laugh and belittle her. "You gave me a corset," she said. "A corset with my name embroidered inside. You have feelings too."

"I gave you a corset because it pleases me to see you wear it. It makes me horny." He paused to pinch her nipple beneath one of the molded cups. "And it has your name embroidered inside so you don't lose it when you leave it behind after one of the myriad sexual encounters you'll indulge in once I set you free."

Her hand shot out and cracked across his face. The slap echoed in the starkly organized dressing room, over the barreling notes of the concerto. Both of them froze. He stared at her like she'd grown a second head. Slowly, he rubbed a palm against his cheek, over the red imprints of her fingers.

"*Vesuvius*," he murmured. "You little bitch."

"I love you," she said. "*I love you.*"

Again, that horrible, mean laughter. This time, when her hand shot out to slap him, he caught it in midair. "Once is enough. Don't do this. You will lose everything you've gained." He held her hand there between them, his expression serious as death.

"What have I gained?" She tried to yank her hand back but he wouldn't let go. "What have I gained, Master? I love you and you won't love me back. I care for you, I adore you, and all you do is mock me and laugh at me."

"Oh, I do much more than that," he said, using her hand to yank her close. When they were nose to nose, he ran his fingers down to her bare ass and squeezed. "You, my dear, are having a meltdown. This is not the time or place for it." He squeezed harder, until she whimpered in pain. "There is never a time or place for it in my world. I don't know what brought on this *ridiculous* display"—he emphasized the word that hurt her so badly—"but it's over. And every time you begin again with your love and perfect-ness and feelings, you'll be mocked again."

"I love you," she said, pushing away from him. "I love you, I love you, I love you."

He stalked past her to his fourteen rows of shoes and hundreds of belts. He chose a black belt from the middle and turned to her, doubling it over between his fingers. "Go ahead. Say it again."

"I love you." She didn't even hesitate. She screamed it. He could beat her for a million hours and she'd still scream it because she loved him and it was killing her trying to keep her feelings inside. He stalked toward her and pinned her facing the wall, and striped her ass with a volley of strokes. Instead of screaming in pain she just kept screaming, *I love you, I love you,* and sometimes *te amo*, and sometimes *je t'aime.*

"Enough," he barked over her babbling. He pulled her up and shook her. "You want love like a child wants candy. You're a junkie for it."

"It's better to be like you? A hard, emotionless man?" She struggled away from him, or perhaps he let her go. He flung the belt aside and threw wide his arms.

"You and your love, Valentina. You're so deluded. You think love is delicious and sweet. You want to hoard it and gorge on it until your stomach aches and your teeth rot out of your pretty head. But you can't demand love of someone," he said, his voice rising in fury and sharpness. "It's one of those things, like slavery, that requires consent."

Her ears rang from the volume of his outburst. She stayed very still, her throat gone dry, her ass throbbing from the belt strokes. He'd never, ever used a voice like that with her. It occurred to her that for the first time ever in their relationship, he had lost control. The music flowed on in the background, the pleasant, harmonious notes too light for this fearsome moment. She put her hands over her ears. "I'm sorry." She began to say it in the same hysterical way she'd professed her love, and in the same way, she couldn't stop repeating it over and over. "I'm sorry, I'm sorry, *I'm sorry.*"

She jerked when she felt his hands on her, but there was no more violence, no more of that hoarse, furious voice. He took her in his arms and cradled her head against his rapidly beating heart. "Okay," he said. "It's okay." And then, a few moments later, "I'm sorry too."

She took long shuddering breaths against the soapy-fresh scent of his skin, against his sandalwood-lotioned neck. "I'm sorry, I'm so sorry." It was only a whisper now, which he silenced with one of his fingers pressed over her lips. When she finally calmed enough to breathe normally, he drew back and leaned down to look in her eyes.

"Let's forget this ever happened. It wasn't a good conversation. It was a conversation we shouldn't have had." He pushed her hair back from her face and used the pad of his thumb to brush away her tears. "You see now why it's better to do things my way?"

It took a long time for Valentina to produce the words of agreement he wanted to hear, because she didn't believe them. But she eventually managed to force them past her lips. "Yes, Master. It's better your way."

He studied her another moment, then nodded. "Hang up my belt then, and meet me downstairs."

Chapter Seventeen:
Back Room

Michel felt empty, as if someone had reached inside him, scooped out everything, and left a vast, echoing shell.

Damn her for her ridiculous emotional outbursts, and damn him for entertaining them long enough for the episode to blow up into a disaster. He should have cut her off at the start, told her to be quiet and wait for him in the car. Now he was stuck with the memory of beating a woman while she screamed hysterically that she loved him. He'd have nightmares about it forever. It was precisely the kind of thing he set up his life to avoid. He had the same feeling now that he had after his mother and father screamed and fought each other, the same shell-shocked paralysis that had dogged him through much of his early life.

He glanced in the rearview mirror. He'd put Valentina in the back seat, needing distance and peace. He'd offered her the choice of wearing a gag or committing to absolute silence. She chose absolute silence and understood it would last all night. He wouldn't mind the noise of the Citadel. In fact, he looked forward to it, because it would drown out the other noises in his head. Her screaming and whimpering, her crying, her manic *I'm sorry*'s.

No one on the planet was more fucking sorry than him. He was sorry he'd indulged himself, sorry he'd wallowed so long in Valentina's tempting charms. He'd become lazy, stupid, and slow over her, so slow that he hadn't seen this breakdown coming. A screaming match in his dressing room?

No.

After tonight, he'd start working again on releasing her. He thought perhaps he could offer her money to rent space in an art studio. Paris was full of them, and it would occupy her time when she wasn't performing. It would keep her out of his hair. Maybe he could hire her a gigolo to stay at her dormitory and keep her busy. Maybe he'd buy her a house so she could spend hours and hours painting the walls and making it into as much of a mess as her corner in his living room. Maybe he could visit her on occasion and see what she'd done to the place...

No, he couldn't visit her. He had to let her go, completely and finally. How had he gotten himself into this situation, after so many years of caution and restraint?

A restless anger seethed in him. It wasn't anger at her, it was anger at himself, but when they arrived at the Citadel he helped her out of the car with a bit more force than was necessary. There was a fine line between a Master and a bully and he was teetering on the edge of it. As for Valentina, she looked beautiful in her black velvet and stockings, and her shock of red hair. Her eyes were still a bit red from crying. How telling, that even though both of them felt miserable, they'd both been eager as ever to come here and play.

Should he play with her? Misgivings dipped and danced in between the anger, creating a mess of disquiet in his brain. Once inside the club, he walked around and invited upwards of fifty people into the back with them. He invited women he thought were pretty, men he thought were handsome, and every heavy hitter and mind fucker who'd ever gained his respect. He invited old friends and people he barely knew but was curious about. It was probably too many people but it created the noise and distraction he needed.

Thirty minutes later, his private dungeon writhed in an orgiastic party of epic proportions. Bare, supple bodies paraded around the room. Cocks grew hard, pussies shone between spread thighs. Music thumped below the screams and sighs of the players. Michel sat on his great leather chair with Valentina at his feet, observing the proceedings with a sense of pride. There was no shame here. Women were openly lustful and men flaunted their erections. These cocks were fondled, worshipped, or tortured, depending on who they belonged to. They were forced into pussies, mouths, and assholes, both male and female.

Meanwhile, Valentina lavished attention on his cock. She caressed and licked it in slow concentration. He'd taught her well, and she was always so beautifully eager to please.

"Don't make me come yet," he warned. "Amuse me, but don't make me come."

She stared up at him, her nose buried between his balls. She was the only clothed woman in the room because he wanted her trapped in her corset, just as he enjoyed trapping her in his home, in his cage.

No. No more trapping. You have to let her go.

He wouldn't think about that now. Not tonight. He reached down and tugged on her hair, then thrust so deep in her throat that she choked and pulled away. The only answer to that, of course, was to repeat the action until she submitted. It only took a couple more ball-tightening thrusts before she stared up at him in capitulation, gagging, tears brimming in her eyes.

These were the tears he lived for. The face-fucking tears, the sexy-hurt tears that were part of a BDSM scene. He didn't like the other tears, the ones in the dressing room from true emotional pain. He felt a tenderness for her, remembering how he'd hurt her. He pulled out of her mouth to let her breathe.

"You're okay?" he asked over the low thrum of the music.

She nodded, sworn to silence. Was she really okay, or was she only nodding because she loved him, as she had professed so dramatically? He looked away, pursing his lips. If he leaned forward he could see the angry stripes he'd left on her ass with his belt, ten or more of them, clear as day. He'd intended to put her on the rack here and play with her, perhaps even let others play with her, but they were bad bruises and he didn't want to risk further damage.

Bad bruises...because he'd lost control.

He bellowed a string of curses in English and French. A few people playing nearby stopped and looked at him. Valentina sucked his cock faster, harder. He stopped her, taking her face in his hands. "I don't want to come yet. Toy with me, slave. Make it good for me," he said, infusing his words with an edgy sensuality.

His job here wasn't to hash over his personal issues or his complicated relationship with the slave at his feet. His job here was to be a good host and to give his fellow perverts a night to remember. Unfortunately, for some reason, he'd invited in more men than women, and now many of the men stood around the room pumping their dicks, inactive. The solution to this seemed all too obvious.

He looked down at Valentina, pushing her head back with a firm grip in her hair.

"I wonder, do you still have a taste for every cock that comes your way?"

She stared back as if she didn't understand his words. What was there to understand? There was a need in the room and his slave could fill it. She loved cock, didn't she?

"Go lie in the middle of the floor," he said, loudly enough for at least half the room to hear, the half of the room that wasn't busy fucking each other. "Lie down on your back and spread your legs."

People moved out of the way to make a space, because he was the Master here, Le Maître, and he wanted a show. He was the Master and people did as he asked. Even Valentina, who stood and backed away from him, didn't dare deny his orders. She walked to the area he indicated and lay down in the middle of a circle of observers.

"Good girl." It was almost silent now. "Spread your legs as I told you. Don't make me get the whip."

It didn't occur to him until much later that she might have preferred the whip to what he was about to do. He pointed to a man named Girard, who looked particularly frustrated jacking his own cock. Girard was a bottom, so he didn't mind taking orders. "Put on a condom and fuck my slave," said Michel. If he was in a really cruel mood he might have said something disparaging about Girard's size, since he possessed probably half Michel's girth, but he wasn't feeling that cruel or petty, and Girard probably would have gotten off on the insult.

No, he wasn't feeling that cruel, only very relaxed and sure he was doing the right thing. Valentina liked cock and she'd had quite enough of his over the past few weeks; she was probably dying for some variety. And there were perfectly hard men standing around with nothing to do, men who would probably never in their lives have a chance to fuck a pussy as delectable as Valentina's.

"Put your hands over your head and spread your legs wider," he ordered. "Show us how much you like it." There was total silence as Valentina complied. Such a good slave. Not one word or motion of protest, only complete submission. He stared a moment at her glistening pussy, watched her arch her back and sigh as Girard moved into her. Too soon, his pumping ass blocked out Michel's view.

Ah, well. He could spend the time deciding who went next. He lined up three more guys, some of them dominant types who liked submissive pussy, some of them, like Girard, subs who were eager to be forced to perform. He made sure they were all wearing condoms. When the fourth guy had trouble mounting Valentina, Michel provided lube. Through all of this, Valentina kept her hands over her head as he'd ordered her. He watched her carefully for signs of dismay or protest but she was beautifully surrendered, a slave for the ages. If she was dry, well, that was bound to happen after four guys had fucked her.

He tagged a pair of men next, and told one to use her mouth and one to use her pussy. By now guys were lined up ten deep, taking places without even asking his permission, and Michel started to have the first inkling that what he was doing might be a bit beyond back room fun. In between this group and the next, Valentina looked over at him with a gutted, bewildered look.

She didn't have a safeword. She'd never had a safeword. Slow, he was so slow. And so cruel.

One of the dominants he knew, one he respected, walked by his chair on the way to the door. "While you're at it, why don't you put a noose around her neck, you fucking asshole?"

Michel pretended not to hear him. He decided that guy wouldn't be invited into his back room ever again. But after one more pair of men fucked Valentina, Michel decided that particular scene had gone on long enough, and yelled at everyone to get out.

* * * * *

Valentina lay very still on the floor. Her pussy hurt. Her mouth tasted like latex and a little bit of vomit, because the last guy had thrust in her *too hard. My Master is going to come save me now*, she thought. *That's what this whole scene was about, right? He's going to make me endure this and then he's going to come and gather me up and soothe me...*

But he only sat staring at her from his chair. He looked unhappy. Angry. After all she'd gone through, the scene, the gangbang, he didn't even look turned on. This upset her so much that she started to cry. Or maybe she was crying because a dozen cocks that weren't her Master's had just pressed into her one after the other, without respite.

I didn't like that, she wanted to scream. *I hated that. I hate you.*

He finally got up from his chair and approached her, standing over her. "*Calme-toi, petite.* Don't cry. It was just a scene."

That made her cry harder. With a grim noise of frustration, he went toward the wall. She braced for some kind of punishment, but he brought back a blanket and wrapped it around her. "Let's take you home and get you cleaned up."

Yes, she wanted to get cleaned up. She wanted to clean this entire night off her memory forever, from the moment he'd given her the velvet corset until now, when he hauled her up without the least bit of tenderness and bundled her out to his car.

"I want to go home," she said, shivering in the back seat.

"We're going home."

"I want you to take me to my home."

His piercing eyes flicked at the rearview. "No," he said in a hard voice. "You're going back to my place and you're going to spend the night there."

"I don't want you to touch me."

He looked away again. "Our two hours are over. So if you don't want me to touch you, I won't."

Our two hours?

I hate you, I hate you, I hate you.

As much as she had loved him earlier this evening, she hated him now. She hated him for refusing to care for her and love her. She hated him for giving her to other men so carelessly and coldly. It hadn't even turned him on. So why?

"Why did you do that?" she asked. She meant to sound angry, but the words came out as a thin whine. "Why did you let all those men fuck me and breathe on me and sweat on me...?" She fell silent, unable to say more.

"I did it because I felt like it." She could see his frown in profile, his immovable expression. "I did it because you're my slave and I thought you needed some cock."

She wanted to rip his cock off and shove it up his ass. "I hated it. I hated every second of it."

"I'm sure you did. But you went through it anyway at my direction, which is the very definition of slavery. Good girl."

She shot him a scathing look, even though he couldn't see it through the back of his head. "I don't think it's the definition of slavery. I don't think I'm that good of a girl, because I hate you right now."

He gave a bitten-off laugh. "From love to hate in one night. Of course."

"I want to go home."

"You're not going home. You can leave in the morning if you wish."

"If you try to touch me—"

"I'm not going to touch you," he said, cutting her off. "You and I have come to the natural end of things, don't you think? It's time for me to find a new slave, one who's a bit less mercurial. All this loving and hating is making my head spin."

She squeezed her hands in her lap and didn't respond. It had been a very long night and she was far beyond fighting, far beyond anything but surviving. At his house, he made her shower while he stood outside the glass with his arms crossed over his chest. She stayed in the steaming enclosure for thirty minutes, maybe forty, just wanting him to leave, until finally he reached in and turned off the water and ordered her out.

They had another standoff outside the cage. He insisted on locking her in. She insisted on being unlocked. He finally left in disgust, telling her she could do whatever the hell she wanted.

She sat on the edge of her cage bed, leaning against the slack, unlocked panel of bars for a long, long time. Hours, it seemed. She was like a captive bird so befuddled by freedom that she didn't fly through the door when it was opened. But she had to find the courage to fly. She knew that.

If she could only understand why he acted the way he did. She knew she wouldn't be attracted to him if he was an evil, soulless man. She might be an emotional basket case, but she was an intuitive emotional basket case. Mr. Lemaitre was missing some part of his soul that allowed him to feel love properly. Perhaps that was why, no matter how hard she tried, she couldn't finish a sketch or painting of him.

She got to her feet and set off quietly through his echoing, empty house. If he was watching on his cameras he would know, but she didn't care anymore. She went into his kitchen and opened the drawer where he kept things like scissors and screwdrivers and duct tape. She pulled out his thick black marker and returned to the white room. She stood just beneath the camera in the corner, and uncapped the marker and put it to the wall. She let her passion guide her, let loose the roiling emotions that wouldn't be still. Her intuition, her feelings, she let it all guide the sweeping movements of her hand.

She drew in reckless strokes that left great black swaths on the wall. She drew the Mr. Lemaitre she knew, who was stern, cruel, conflicted, complex, and not completely finished. She made his eyes pierce, she made his lips frown. She made his hair a great tornado of blackness on his head, the way it looked when he ran his fingers through it and set it on end. She made the Master she knew and the Master who was unknowable, and when she finished the spare likeness, it looked so bleak she started to weep.

She pressed her hand over her mouth. She didn't want him to hear her. He might not be watching but he could hear when she made sounds. She went to the closet where Mr. Lemaitre kept her clothes and threw on a black top and pants. She packed a couple bags of things and left the rest. She left the painting of Sara and Jason for Mr. Lemaitre to gift or destroy as he wished. She didn't care about anything anymore except getting away from the picture she'd drawn on the wall. Part of her wanted to scribble it away, but he would still be there beneath the obfuscation, glaring out from the wall.

Instead she took the pen over to the contract wall where it said *I belong to Le Maître* and crossed out *belong to*. She replaced the words with *hate* in big block letters. She stood back and looked at it through tears.

I hate Le Maître.

But that was a lie. She might hate the things he'd done to her. She might hate the picture of him on the wall. She certainly hated that he was not a complete person, but she couldn't hate him. He was her perfect other half and always would be, no matter how much that hurt.

So she crossed out the word *hate* and wrote *love.*

I love Le Maître.

Something about seeing it there after everything they'd been through... It seemed like something worth repeating, so she wrote it again, and again, and again, bigger and bigger until the words took up whole walls. Until the words overpowered the sad drawing of him. She was going to leave him alone the way he wanted, but she'd still love him forever and she wanted him to know.

Then she took her couple of bags and left through the back door, disarming the security system the way she'd seen him do a hundred times. If he was watching her, he didn't try to stop her. She was pretty sure, by this point, that he wasn't watching, or he just didn't care. Either way it didn't matter. It was past time for her to go.

Chapter Eighteen:
Sad

Michel hadn't used drugs or alcohol to inebriation for many years, but he fell into bed like a man passing out, and woke up with something very much like a hangover hurting his brain.

But not clouding his memory, no. He wasn't that fortunate. The events of the previous evening unwound in his head with perfect clarity before he was awake enough to block them out. Yelling, fighting, hurting, killing. Not actual murder, but the killing of a relationship with such complete violence that it couldn't be revived. He had done all those things the night before, subconsciously perhaps, but he'd done it. It was, after all, the way he'd been raised.

But it was for the best. It was time to return to safety and sanity. He would have to issue apologies and retreat from the Citadel for a while, and apologize to Valentina. He would send her a note and some flowers, not to excuse what he'd done, but to reassure her none of it was her fault.

As for him, he had finally gotten a work of art based on him. In the style of Valentina, it was direct, true, and illuminating. No buttons, candy, leaves, hardware, or cellophane, no. She had used harsh, monotone lines on his harsh, monotone wall, and captured every ounce of harsh, monotone pain in his soul.

But she hadn't stopped there. Over all four walls, she had written, over and over, *I love you*, because she knew exactly how to hurt him as much as he hurt her. She hurt him by being Valentina, who coated the world in love and emotion, not even caring who it stuck to. He couldn't even go in the room to repaint it, and he couldn't bear to let anyone else see it. So her graffiti remained, a nightmare he saw every time he closed his eyes. The energy of her words, the walls themselves, seemed to throb through every night. It kept him awake in his harsh, monotone bedroom where he slept alone.

Still, he went to work. He continued to live. He watched Valentina when she didn't know it, to be sure she was okay. She was Valentina, so of course she was okay. She was still fire, *La Vampa,* all-powerful. She continued to smile and laugh and embrace the world around her, and did beautiful work with her hand-to-hand act. He had all her things delivered back to her apartment, except the painting of Jason and Sara, which he planned to present to them at the time of their wedding.

Safety and sanity. He longed for it, and in her absence from his life, he found some part of it. Then Jason returned to town.

"Is it true?" he asked, storming into his office. He was red-faced, livid. "Is it true you ran a train on Valentina in your fucking back room last week?"

Michel didn't look up from his laptop. "Do you have an appointment?"

"I'm going to make an appointment on your fucking face in a couple of seconds. Answer my question, motherfucker. Did you let twenty guys gangbang Valentina last weekend?"

He couldn't help arching a brow. "Twenty? Is that the rumor? There weren't more than fourteen. And I've warned you several times not to call me a motherfucker."

"You are such a motherfucking asshole. You are such an unbelievable asshole to her."

Michel shut his computer with a sigh. "If you're not going to leave—"

"I'm not going to leave until you explain how this is appropriate courtship behavior. Are you taking relationship advice from the Marquis de Sade? Have you started smoking crack? Should I be concerned about your mental health? Has she broken your motherfucking brain?"

He gritted his teeth. "Valentina and I are no longer together."

Jason clutched his chest in feigned shock. "Oh no. You're kidding? You let fourteen other guys fuck her like a piece of meat in your back room, and she broke up with you?"

His theatrics weren't doing anything for the headache punishing Michel's temples. If he could get just one night of decent sleep... "She didn't break up with me," he said. "I broke up with her. I mean, I released her. We weren't dating, as you know. She was only my slave."

"Only your slave. Oh, okay, I see."

"It amused me to watch other men fuck her. There's no more to it than that."

"Except that you're in love with her."

Michel opened his laptop again. "I'm busy."

"Everyone knows you're in love with her, Michel, everyone but you. How can someone so intelligent be so clueless?" Jason made the universal sign for his head exploding, along with the requisite sound effects.

Michel rolled his eyes. "Are you finished?"

"No, I'm not finished." Jason planted himself in the seat across from Michel's desk. "I want to tell you something else. There were almost a hundred people in your back room that night—"

"There weren't more than fifty."

"A hundred fucking people disagree with you, and a hundred fucking people are out there gossiping about this to anyone who will listen. You know how gossip is in the circus. They're talking about it in Vegas, in Toronto, in Sydney, in Buenos Aires, fucking everywhere about how you've freaking lost your brain over a woman and what you did to her that night. And a lot of the people hearing this—they work for you. They respect you. You're their boss and they're scared that you're not really worthy of that respect anymore." He crossed his arms over his chest, a muscle ticking in his jaw. "And I'm kind of scared too. If you don't love her, what's going on? What's making you act this way? Is it the wedding? Is it letting go of Sara?"

Michel waved a hand. He didn't want Sara in this conversation. "This has nothing to do with my daughter, nothing to do with anything but me and Valentina being a really bad match. I messed up." He gave Jason a rueful look. "You told me. You warned me at the beginning that I was making a huge mistake and I didn't listen. I regret that. You have no idea how much."

"I have some idea how much, seeing as how I came into practice today and heard that you had fourteen guys shove their dicks into the woman you love."

"Enough with the love," Michel snapped. "You and Sara are about to drive me mad with all this love nonsense. You're as bad as Valentina. Love, love, love, rainbows and unicorns and hearts made of glitter. None of it is real, you realize."

"I'm about to marry your daughter. I think you'd better take those words back."

Michel studied the younger man, rubbing a finger over his lower lip. Valentina's artwork came into his brain, Jason's key and Sara's lock. "Maybe love works for some people," he admitted. "But not for me."

Jason blew out his breath and pushed Michel's laptop shut before he could return to his task. "Jesus Christ, I can't believe it. It's your thing with Sara all over again. '*I don't know how to love. I don't have feelings. Wah wah wah, I'm a big forty-five year old uber-Master who can't process basic human emotions like caring and affection.*'"

His mocking, sing-song voice had Michel's headache throbbing into a migraine. "Enough," he roared.

"No, it's not enough," Jason said, talking over him. "I stood by and watched you rip your daughter's heart out. That's on me, letting that go on as long as it did. I won't let you do it to Valentina. And to yourself, you fucking lunatic. You love her."

"I think I get to decide who I love. That is, if I wanted to love anyone romantically, which I don't. Do we have anything else to discuss?" Michel was sure his strident tones could be heard throughout the entire floor. At this point, he didn't care. "Do you have anything else to say to me before you fucking get out of my office, you fucking prick?"

Jason stood, scowling at him with an expression that would have lesser men ducking back. "I do have one last thing to say to you. Someday you're going to be sorry you sat by and watched fourteen guys gangbang the woman you love. You're gonna really fucking hate yourself for it, and you're going to deserve every fucking iota of angst you feel." He went to the door, then turned back, poking a finger into the air. "You won't ever forget these things you're doing to her, Michel. And you know what? Neither will she."

* * * * *

The evenings were the hardest time for Valentina. Even with the noise and bustle of the dormitories all around her, she felt lonely. She read books, she worked on her art, and practiced French a little bit, not because Mr. Lemaitre spoke it, but because she lived in France now and it would be a good language to know. She had lots of friends to help her practice the language, people who had been so nice to her ever since...

Well, she didn't want to think about that, but with all the gossip, it was hard to get away from it. People looked at her differently. Nicely, but differently. They were sorry for her. It sucked.

She ate ice cream when she felt really sad. She watched movies late into the night curled under a blanket on her couch, and sometimes she slept there because she felt too lazy—or lonely—to sleep in her bed.

She was having just such an evening when someone knocked at her door. She pulled the blanket up a little. She was already in her fuzzy pajamas, settled in for the night.

"Valentina?"

Another knock, sharper. Jason Beck. She considered not answering but he could probably hear the television and he'd just keep knocking. She switched the maudlin movie to a cartoon channel, then shuffled over in her slippers and opened her door. She kept it locked now that Mr. Lemaitre had had the deadbolt replaced, and her key.

"Were you sleeping?" he asked.

"No. Not yet." She stood back to let him in.

He looked around at the mess that comprised her life, the mess that had only grown in scope during the past few days as she tried to forget about her broken heart.

"Wow," he said quietly. The last time he'd been here, she'd had everything packed up so she could run away from the circus. So many things had happened since then. He walked over to her bird made of matchsticks and lightly touched one of the wings. He turned around and bumped into a bust made of plaster and colored tiles. He grabbed for it, barely rescuing it from a crash to the floor.

189

"I'm sorry." He placed it back on its wobbly pedestal, a laptop table Valentina had scavenged from someone's trash heap. "I hope I didn't mess it up."

She shrugged. "If you did, I'll fix it. There's more room over on the couch."

Jason moved across her living room and sat, still looking wide-eyed around her apartment. Why did her life and her work always elicit that reaction in people? *Because you're a freak. Obviously.*

She tried to think what normal people did when guests came over. "Can I get you something?" she asked, heading for the kitchen. "Some coffee? A glass of water?"

"Will you come sit with me? I want to talk to you about something."

She stopped en route and turned back around. "I know what you want to talk about, and I don't really want to talk about it."

"I do. Come and sit down."

Jason wasn't her Master. He didn't have the right to issue her orders, but he was her development director and she usually listened when he used that tone of voice. She came back to the couch and collapsed beside him with a sigh. She didn't want to look at him, so she looked at the TV where a cartoon cat and mouse were embroiled in an endless chase. In her peripheral vision, she could see Jason's hands tighten on his knees.

"So, I guess the first thing I want to know is, are you okay?"

"Of course I'm okay. I've been working, haven't I?"

His gaze swept her apartment again, all the scraps and odds and ends, and stuff hanging from the ceiling. She was glad she'd left her painting of Jason and Sara at Mr. Lemaitre's house. There was nowhere to hide it here and it would have ruined the surprise.

"You can work and still not be okay," he persisted. "I heard about the Citadel incident second hand, but what I heard was enough to worry me."

Valentina forced a brittle smile. "Now I've been involved in two Citadel incidents. I think it's best if I stay away from that place."

"What he did to you was wrong."

The certainty in his voice ruffled her a little. "Who are you to judge our kink, Jason? How do you know I didn't enjoy it?"

He gazed back at her, saying nothing. She felt angry, confused. Defensive. She didn't like being depicted as a victim. She didn't like that she probably was the victim in Friday night's scenario.

"I liked it at first," she said, lifting her chin. "I like when he makes me do vile, perverted stuff. I like being humiliated by him, and feeling used by him. That is my kink and I don't want to be judged for it."

Still, nothing from Jason, just that steady gaze. She looked down at her hands, then started tracing the panda faces on her pants. The rest of the words spilled out like a dirty confession.

"I did it because he asked me to, and with the first couple of guys, I enjoyed it. I'm not ashamed." The fact that she was saying she wasn't ashamed kind of gave away the fact that she was struggling with shame, but her coach didn't call her out on it. "It turned me on, him watching me while other guys fucked me. The fact that he could make me do anything—even that. That he had that much control over me. It felt kind of hot."

"I can see that side of it," Jason said.

"But then...then it started to feel bad and I didn't know how to stop it." This was where the shame really ate at her. She had reached a point in the scene where she didn't know what to do, where it had progressed past eroticism to something ugly, and she had felt powerless to make it beautiful again. "Everyone was watching and really...I didn't...I didn't want to mess up the scene. I didn't want to challenge him in front of everyone. I wanted it to be exciting for everyone, and hot and sexy." Her voice trailed off as Jason leaned forward, burying his face in his hands.

He looked up at her a moment later. "I want to fucking kill someone right now."

"It was just...just a scene that went bad. It's not this big disaster everyone is making it out to be. I could have stopped it, but I didn't because..."

"Because you're such a good slave," he said in a derisive tone.

"No. Because I thought he'd be able to save the scene. Up until the end, I thought he'd figure out some way to make it better, and hotter, because he's Le Maître and he's really good at this stuff."

"He usually is," said Jason grudgingly. "But in this case he fucked up."

Valentina hugged herself, feeling the same unsettled angst she felt every time she hashed over the events of that night. "Up until the end, I thought he'd do some magic to make it all mean something, to bring us closer together. To make it about some connection between us. But afterward, I realized there was no connection between us, that I'd been making it up in my head because that's what I wanted. And that's when I really felt devastated. That's when I really felt embarrassed and ashamed."

"A relationship with Michel Lemaitre is not for the faint of heart." Jason reached over and stroked the back of her hand. She wondered if he could feel it trembling. "I told you once, at the very start of all this, that it was a game. That it was supposed to be fun. Do you remember?"

She nodded. She remembered most of that conversation, all his warnings and truths. She should have listened. It was too late now.

"So, I was wrong," he said, drawing his hand back. "I don't think it was ever a game. Not for you, not for him. I think he's in love with you. I think he has been from the start."

Valentina stood, knocking the remote to the floor. The channel changed to a late night soap opera. "Why does everyone say that? Have his actions ever been the actions of someone in love?"

Jason stood too, switching off the TV. "We're talking about Michel Lemaitre. He's not normal. Neither are you. I'm trying to figure this out but it's not very easy, seeing as how both of you are half-insane."

His words hurt her. She didn't know why, since she'd long ago understood she wasn't a typical person. "I'm trying to be myself," she yelled back. "I don't know how else to be. I am very frustrated and very sad, and if he loves me, it doesn't help me because he's sent me away."

"Don't you get it? He sent you away *because* he loves you. That's the reason for everything he's done to you. He has this belief that love is a bad thing, which is, yes, very frustrating and sad."

"Well, what do I do?"

Jason shook his head. "I don't know. I wish you could fix him, but if that means you keep getting hurt... I don't know if it's worth sacrificing the small amount of sanity you possess."

It was a joke, a small glimmer of humor in the midst of this heavy exchange. Did Mr. Lemaitre love her? If he didn't love her proudly and openly, giving her everything in his heart, then it wasn't a love she wanted. She didn't want love that diminished her.

And she couldn't bear any more hurt.

"Has he said anything to you since last Friday?" Jason asked. "Anything at all?"

Valentina moved to a table near the window, to a pile of dried, denuded rose stems. She picked up a note card beside them. "He sent me flowers, and this."

Jason tilted the card to the light and read the note. "*Forgive me for any pain I've caused. M.L.*" He looked up at her. "Really? Seriously? And this didn't send you into a murderous rage?"

"I ripped up the flowers but it didn't make me feel better, and afterward I wished I hadn't. It wasn't the flowers' fault."

Jason tapped the note card twice on the table and put it down. Valentina stared at the words scrawled on the card, at the sentence she'd read so many times, and at the bare stems that looked as dried up as her heart. "I thought we were meant to be together. From the moment I looked in his eyes I felt a connection to him. I thought finally, *finally*, I had met my soul mate. Now I'm just trying to move on in life. Bad things happen and good things happen. The important thing is to keep going."

Jason let out a sigh. "Can I give you a hug? Friend to friend?"

Valentina moved into his arms. Jason was a great hugger, always warm and supportive. She let herself sag against him for a moment, and remember that she had at least one friend who'd be there for her no matter what.

"You're so badass, you know that?" he said against her ear. "Nothing defeats you. Maybe you are meant to be his soul mate, because you survived him without losing yourself, or changing. But Valentina..." He pulled back from her with a frown. "To be with him would mean so much sacrifice. Perhaps too much."

"Don't all people make sacrifices for love? Husbands and wives, and parents for their children? The love is more important than the things you lose." She shrugged. "But in this case, it doesn't matter because he doesn't want me to love him, and he refuses to love me." She lined the stems up side by side, then swept them up and moved with them to the trash can. "As Mr. Lemaitre says, love is one of those things, like slavery, that requires consent."

Chapter Nineteen:
I Do

May arrived before Michel was prepared for it. He had far too much to keep him busy, but nothing to fill the nagging emptiness in his soul.

Now he stood at the town hall in Marseille watching his daughter and Jason get married in a half-French, half-American ceremony. Sara floated in a gauzy, sparkling white gown, her black hair sleek beneath her veil. Whenever Jason looked at her, her eyes shone with happiness. Michel tried to feel happy too, for her and for Jason, but he was losing his daughter to another man less than a year after finding her, and it felt...deserved.

Life had a way of giving people exactly what they deserved. He was truly coming to believe that. Jason and Sara, for instance, deserved each other, because they were two of the most well-adjusted, kind, and caring people he knew. Theo and Kelsey, their best friends and witnesses, deserved each other. He had watched Theo and Kelsey's relationship go through terrible ups and downs a few years ago, culminating in a strong marriage. Looking around at the gathering of friends who'd come to support Sara and Jason, he saw other couples he knew to be in satisfying, enduring relationships.

He also saw people he knew to be single, and happy. Some of them chose to be single, some of them were between relationships. Some of them were in poly relationships, complex trios or even quads that they made work. Some of the people he saw were single and unhappy. They were selfish, or assholes like him. People got out of life what they put into it.

Like Valentina. She was here.

Her red hair distracted him so he could barely focus on his child's wedding. But of course they would have invited her. Sara and Valentina had grown progressively closer, even after he cut all ties with his ex-slave. He'd expected Valentina to be invited, but he'd hoped she would be too cowardly to come.

And then he remembered that Valentina was never cowardly.

He'd hated having her in his bed, and now he couldn't sleep without her. He'd become infuriated at her paint drips on his carpet and now he searched ten times a day for the faint stain left behind. He missed her excited voice and her brightly colored coffee cups. He couldn't bear to open the storage box in the closet with her portrait any more than he could bear to see her here among the wedding guests.

Valentina stood just a few feet behind him and to the side, so close and yet entirely lost to him. He'd hurt her so badly that he still felt the wound in his own heart. Perhaps he always would—fitting punishment for his treatment of her. As Sara and Jason recited their personal, handwritten vows, the words seemed to become his own vows to a life's love he had carelessly thrown away.

My heart is bound to yours, and yours to mine.

You are the magic of my days.

You are my breath, my endless heartbeat.

Why did it seem his heart had stopped beating the moment he excised her from his life?

"Do you take this woman to be your wife?" the officiant asked Jason in accented English, and Jason took Sara's hand and said with great conviction, "I do."

I do. I do, Michel thought. *Je le veux.*

I do want her.

Then why had he acted as he had? He had damaged their relationship beyond repair. Even now, weeks after, she still avoided his gaze. She turned her head when he looked in her direction, like some skittish, abused pet.

With this ring I promise to you perfect, abiding love.

Jason and Sara repeated the words to each other as they exchanged bands of gold. *Perfect*, Michel thought in grief. *How can the two of you expect love to be perfect, or even abiding? How can you vow such an impossible thing?*

Tears welled in his eyes at the hopelessness of it all, and at Jason and Sara's bravado, their stubborn insistence on pledging perfect, abiding love when it was such a risk. The happy couple kissed, but Michel didn't look at that. Instead he watched Jason's fingers curl around her waist to pull her close. So protective, that touch. So gentle.

Jason adored Sara. He loved her. Perfect, abiding love. Why couldn't Michel aspire to that? A cheer went up as the newly-married couple turned to their friends with brilliant smiles. Michel didn't know if it was the sun from the open windows blurring his vision, or the breeze blowing into the flower-decorated room.

* * * * *

Valentina wasn't hiding away. Not precisely. It was only that there was so much drunkenness and frivolity at the reception inside, and she wasn't in a frivolous mood.

She had seen something so beautiful today, the loving commitment of two people. After the ceremony, there had been dancing and toasts, and a delicious, extravagant meal inside Mr. Lemaitre's palatial Marseille residence. Jason and Sara had caught her into a hug and thanked her for their wedding portrait, which Mr. Lemaitre had given to them back in Paris. Sara had even cried. Valentina had pushed back Sara's veil and kissed her on her flushed cheeks, and caught a little taste of her happy tears.

Maybe those happy tears would act as a potion for Valentina. Perhaps in time she would find new excitement and new interests. There would be a new show for certain—the premiere was just a few weeks away. She had worn a bright red dress to the wedding for luck and good fortune. Perhaps the new show's premiere would bring a new love, if only she could move past old loves...

She blinked back tears of her own, but they were sad tears.

The party inside grew louder, and more revelers drifted out onto the terraces. A waiter offered her a drink but she declined. She never did well with alcohol, and now wasn't the time to have a drunken breakdown, not on Sara and Jason's special day.

She pushed away from the balustrade and walked toward the beach, away from the noisy reception hall. Nightfall brought cooler weather, and some guests had lit a bonfire down on the private beach, the flames licking up into the night sky. Valentina hid in the darkness just outside the fire's illumination until she was sure Mr. Lemaitre wasn't part of the surrounding group, then moved closer. The bonfire pulsed out heat but she still felt cold. She wrapped her arms around herself, her gaze fixed on the hypnotic dance of the flames. The distraction didn't work.

Nothing worked.

Again her thoughts returned to how handsome Mr. Lemaitre had looked standing beside Sara during the ceremony. There had been such gravity in his expression as he placed her hand in Jason's. For someone only recently come to fatherhood, he performed his duties with a natural, warm affection that made her want him even more. Horrible, that she still wanted him so badly. *I miss you. Why can't you love me as Jason loves Sara? Why did this have to happen to us?*

The sea breeze drew sparks upward into the darkness. She craned her head back and watched them rise, then closed her eyes with a sigh. When she opened them, her senses sharpened, noting a shadow in her periphery. Without looking, she knew it was him. She recognized the stance, the stillness.

She moved to slip into the shadows on the other side of the fire, but as she crossed the sand, the wind changed direction and smoke enveloped her. She tried not to breathe, but heat and the ashen taste of soot filled her nose and throat. She let out a hacking sputter that turned into a coughing fit. Her eyes watered and burned.

"Here." A deep, familiar voice accompanied firm hands on her shoulders. Mr. Lemaitre turned her to shield her from the smoke. "Walk this way."

She coughed and tried to swallow as they moved several yards down the beach. He handed her a glass of water that was perhaps his own glass of water. She didn't care. She swallowed a big gulp, letting the cold liquid soothe her stinging throat. "Take slow breaths," he said. He smoothed a hand over her back, up and down, until her eyes stopped burning and her lungs filled with friendlier air.

"I'm sorry," she croaked. "Did I cough on you?"

"A little. It's okay."

She blinked through lingering tears at his concerned features, and felt a pang of longing for the days she'd spent under his control. *Damn. I need that drink now.* She gripped the tumbler of ice water in her hands. Should she give it back to him? They'd moved some distance from the fire but the air seemed smothering as ever.

"Are you all right?" he asked. "Can I get you something?"

"I'm perfectly okay."

"Some tea or honey for your throat?"

"No, I don't need anything."

"Drink some more of the water."

"No, I..." At the look on his face, she bit her lip and took another drink, then handed the glass back. "I'm really fine, Mr. Lemaitre. Thank you."

He tilted his head with a ghost of a smile. "You might call me Michel by now, don't you think?"

She stared at him. Call the great *Le Maître* by his first name? "I'm not sure I can do that."

He shrugged and turned toward the sea. "Call me Mr. Lemaitre if you like. You've earned the right to choose."

"I'll call you Michel if you really want me to," she said, plucking at the folds of her dress.

"It's your choice," he replied tightly.

"Well, okay then. Michel." It felt horrible to call him that, like they were friends now. Chums. She wanted to wash out her mouth. She wanted to scream and throw things. She turned away, setting her teeth. "You don't have to stand here with me. I've tried my best to stay out of your way."

"Stay out of my way? Why?"

Because you hurt me.

Because I'm still in love with you and I shouldn't be.

"Because you're busy. It's your daughter's wedding," she said instead. "It's been a lovely day."

"I'm glad you're enjoying the festivities. Is this your first time in Marseille?"

"Yes, it's...yes. My first time." Making small talk with him was almost as painful as watching him from afar. "You have a very nice vacation home," she added in a fake, modulated voice that sounded nothing like her own.

"Thank you."

"How often do you come here?"

"A few times a year, when I'm not so busy. It's been hectic this spring, mounting a new show."

And dealing with you. He didn't say that part of it, but she heard it. He turned again to look out at the water. He'd taken off his suit jacket at some point, and loosened his collar like most of the guests. He still looked sharp and dangerous. Diamond hard, but then, she knew how hard he could be. She stood silent beside him, hot, cold, confused, ashamed, terrified he'd continue to make empty conversation with her, and just as terrified he'd walk away. The fresh, rich sea air couldn't cover the intoxicating memory of his scent.

"What did you think of the ceremony?" he asked when the silence strung out.

"It was beautiful." On this point, at least, she wasn't conflicted. "You must be so proud of your daughter. She and Jason love each other so much. It makes me feel..." She clutched at her stomach, not sure how to express the mixture of awe and joy she felt. "I don't know. Love is such a magnificent thing."

"Yes," he said, in a way that didn't sound like a yes. He blinked, looking down at the sand, and jiggled the ice in his glass. Then he said, so softly she almost might not have heard, "*Dieu*, I miss you."

She felt the four quiet words like a kick to the gut. She'd missed him too, so much that Jason and Sara's beautiful wedding had been a nightmarish agony. She missed him so that his nearness hurt like smoke searing her lungs. Anger washed over her, an eruption of temper spewing up from the empty spaces he'd left inside.

"It's your fault if you miss me, don't you think?" Her voice cracked on the last word. "You said we'd come to the 'natural end of things,' remember? You told me you wanted to get a new slave."

His lips pursed at the challenge in her tone. "I didn't get a new slave. I don't even go to the club anymore."

"But it's your club."

"Perhaps I'll go back someday. Perhaps Sara and I will work out a schedule so we won't run into one another. Perhaps I'm tired of the noise and drama and I don't want to return. Perhaps I don't want to return without...without you."

"Oh, of course." A harsh laugh tore from her throat. "Because the last time we went together, we had so much fun."

"Don't." His gaze faltered, revealing hidden pain. "Never laugh like that again, in that brittle way. I can't bear it."

She couldn't bear it either, the hurt in his voice, the tragic tone. How dare he act like the injured one? It was his choice to move her out of his life and keep her at a distance. "I don't think you have the right to tell me what to do anymore," she said, tipping up her chin.

"Even so."

Him and his *even so*'s. This conversation wasn't headed anywhere pleasant and she didn't want to cause a scene at her friends' wedding. "I think I'm going to head back to the house."

He followed. "Be careful of the fire."

"I'll be fine." She shied away when he took her arm and tried to guide her. She heard the clink of his glass as he shoved it into someone's hands.

"Wait. Please." He reached for her again, keeping pace. "Valentina, don't run away from me. Not today."

She didn't stop. If anything, she walked faster. They were on the other side of the fire now, on the sheltered side of the beach. "*Not today?*" she echoed. "What day would please you better, Master? What do I owe you?" She turned on him, her temper flaring hot as the fire. "What gives you the right to ask anything at all?"

"Nothing. I have no right," he said quickly. He held up his hands. "*Ma mignonne—*"

"No. I am not your little darling. I never was."

"Valentina, then. *Ma vampa.* Please let me...let me talk to you. There are things I need to say."

"There were things I needed to say too, and you wouldn't let me say them, remember? You beat me for saying them. You made me cry."

He halted with a stricken expression, his hands braced on his hips. The bonfire rose behind him in the distance, outlining his tall stature, his wild black hair.

"I loved you," she said, glaring at the man she *still loved*. "I gave you everything, every fiber of my devotion, every breath, every secret, every emotion for days and days on end. I did that for you, because I adored you. I gave everything to be your slave."

"I didn't want you to give everything." His voice rose along with hers. "You gave me too much, or perhaps I took too much. Either way, I told you from the start we weren't suitable for each other. If you had only listened—"

"Suitable? *Suitable?*" she cried. "What a stupid, horrid word. What a pathetic lie, to say we weren't suitable for each other."

"Valentina—"

"If you want to tell lies I suppose you may do as you please, but I'm not going to listen to you and agree, because I don't agree. I felt so much love for you. I still feel it"—she curled her hands into fists on her chest—"right here, living inside me. But that love should go to someone who wants it, someone who appreciates it."

"Valentina," he said in a sharper voice.

"My love should go to someone who returns it, and that someone obviously isn't you."

"Why did you never make a painting for me?" he interrupted, advancing on her again. As if to underline the angst in his question, an oversized wave crashed with a boom against the shore.

"I did make a painting for you," she said, walking backwards. "I made a sketch on your wall. You remember the *wall*, don't you?"

He made a dismissive gesture. "That wasn't a painting. That was a tantrum. Why didn't you make a painting of me while we were together?"

"I tried. You looked right at it in my apartment, but you didn't recognize yourself. That's how I knew it was bad work. I couldn't... I could never finish it. I suppose because there is some part of you I can't see." She stopped, planted her feet and stared at him, this man she'd never been able to finish. "There's something missing in you, some part of you I can't find. You won't let me see it."

"It's not that I don't want to!" He stretched his arms out in a wild gesture, and his voice seemed to strain against his will. "I think... *Dieu*. I don't know, Valentina. I don't know how to explain it. There's some part of me that's missing, yes. I know how. I know why. But I don't know what to do about it."

Back by the fire, some happy wedding guest whooped and whistled. Groups of people laughed on the terrace and muted music drifted from the reception room, but Valentina's world shrank down to the misery crumbling her Master's features.

"You're not missing anything," she amended. "I'm sorry. I only said that because—"

"Because it's true."

"It's not. Please, don't be upset, not today at Sara's wedding. Everything's okay."

He shook his head. "It's not okay. I did so many things to hurt you. I said so many things to you that weren't true." His voice roughened, turning hoarse. "I'm so bad for you. You're smart to...to stay out of my way. You've always been a smart girl."

"I'm not smart. I'm rash and emotional."

"You're awe-inspiring, Valentina. You're perfect and complete and I'm not. You can love and I...I can't." His voice broke on the last words. Valentina stared, paralyzed by his spilling emotions, then stumbled toward him and hugged him, pressing her cheek against the galloping beat of his heart.

"Nonsense, *monsieur*. How can you believe this? Everyone can love. You can love, I'm certain." She stroked his cheek, a calming touch. "Your heart's just locked up. I don't know why."

He clutched her. "Because I'm afraid."

"Then let me help you. Where is your key?" she asked, referencing Jason and Sara's painting. She placed her hand over his chest and gazed up at him. "Trust me, we can fix you. Just tell me where to find your key."

"Valentina..." He shuddered and curled his fingers over hers, squeezing them in a tight grip. "Valentina, don't you see? You are my key."

* * * * *

Michel led her farther down the beach, away from the fire. He needed cover and privacy. He could barely catch his breath for hoping. The way was there for him, if he was only brave enough to take it. *Help me love you. I need to love you or I'll die.*

He drew her into an alcove near a natural cluster of rocks. He sat atop one stone and she sat on another, her almond-shaped eyes reflecting the firelight from down the beach, her features framed by the red-gold magnificence of her hair. *You are the magic of my days*, Jason and Sara had said to each other. If it was Michel making vows, he would have said to Valentina, *You are the fire of my days*.

He started to talk over the pounding rhythm of the waves, to confess, self-consciously at first, then more easily. He explained to Valentina about his childhood, his parents, his days of wandering the world trying to find some peace. He talked about control and fear, and then he reached to draw her closer because what he really needed to talk about was the harm he'd done to her.

"I'm sorry," he said, burying his face against the softness of her hair. "I'm sorry for all the things I did to hurt you." He held her tight. He'd longed to embrace her for so long that now he couldn't loosen his grip. "I feel so much fear when I think about loving you. I'm so afraid of what I'll do to you. I'm afraid of hurting you, of destroying you. I'm afraid of suffocating you and taking away who you are."

She turned her face up to look at him. "You hurt me most when you were trying not to love me. Maybe... Maybe that means that if you allowed yourself to love me, all this hurting would stop. We've never dealt in locks and keys, you know. I gave you every part of me from the start."

"I know, and all I did was push you away. You should hate me."

"I did hate you, some of the time. But I never stopped loving you, even when I hated you."

His lips quirked into a half smile. "You left something to that effect all over my walls."

She laughed and buried her face against his neck. He twined his fingers in her hair, tracing the shape of her delicate scalp. "It's still there, you know. To remind me."

"Remind you of what? How awful I can be?"

"It's there to remind me that I love you. You're my key, Valentina. You're the fire of my days." He breathed in her scent, massaging her nape and then down the curve of her spine. "And you weren't awful. You were never awful. A Master has a responsibility to improve, to protect, to fulfill his slave's needs. I never should have rejected your love. I shouldn't have denied it existed. That was a callous, heartless thing to do."

"But you were afraid. Are you still afraid?"

"Yes." He touched her cheek, brushing away a bit of sand. "But as I watched Jason and Sara get married, all I could think about was you. That I felt all those vows and wishes for you. That means something, doesn't it?"

She turned her head a little. "It means love, Mr. Lemaitre."

"Michel."

"Michel." She rubbed her eyes. "Okay, I'll try to call you that. Michel...is it possible for you to love me and still be my Master?"

He gave a choking kind of laugh. "Of course it's possible. I've done it all this time, haven't I? Because I loved you from the start, as much as I tried not to." He nuzzled against her cheek. "You still want a Master, do you?"

"I need one," she nodded. "I need you."

He went rock hard as soon as she said the words. "Yes, you do need me, don't you?" He rearranged her legs and dress so she straddled him. His hands wandered down to squeeze her ass as he pressed his cock against her front. "Sometimes you're a very bad girl."

"Sometimes I'm awful," she said, "no matter your words to the contrary. I would like a Master to help me be better, and a lover to help me be happy. And a friend..." She lifted her face to look at him. "I'd like a friend who understands me."

A Master. A lover. A friend. He could be all those things if he worked at it hard enough, just as he was business owner, creative director, father, boss.

"Valentina, I want to be everything you need. You've brought me so much happiness and I'd like to do the same for you. With that said, I won't be perfect all the time."

"I'm the farthest thing from perfect, as you know."

He laughed, pressing his forehead against hers. It was a laugh of relief, a laugh exhaling weeks of stress and pain. "I like that you're imperfect. It brings variety to my days."

"And love is never perfect," she pointed out. "Sometimes it hurts. But for you, I'll put up with it."

There was a flash and a boom. Valentina's eyes widened as she clutched his shoulders. "Someone's shooting at us."

"No one's shooting," he said. "Look." High above them, a hundred sparking lights dispersed, fireworks he'd engaged for the wedding. She flinched as another rocket boomed. He squeezed her shoulders and turned her so they could look up at the sky together.

"Where are they coming from?" she asked.

"They're shooting them off the top of my house. Don't worry. Just enjoy them."

Behind them, on the beach and on the terrace, Michel could hear the drunken, happy wedding guests cheering with every boom and explosion of color. The air was just the right temperature, and the sky dark and clear. He realized Sara and Jason had been right, that May was a great time to be married. One of the thumping booms erupted into a great red heart in the sky, then turned orange and magenta as it fell away.

He looked over at Valentina, at the glittering sparks reflected in her eyes. "*Je t'aime, ma chère.*" The booms were steady now, building on one another to a climax. *Bang bang bang bang*, and then a hiss of lightning painting the sky in myriad, changeable hues. She turned and threw her arms around his neck. The racket of the fireworks seemed to shake the ground, their bodies, even their lips as they met in a passionate kiss.

Her lips were warm and responsive. Delicious. She tasted of wedding cake, sweet like sugar. Like candy. They reconnected there on the sand to the symphony of fireworks and the pounding of waves hitting the shore. He touched her everywhere, remembering. She still sighed the same way at this, or moaned at that. They hadn't been apart so long that he'd forgotten any of it, and he hadn't been with anyone else.

"I love you," he said every so often against her lips, and she'd echo him in her sweet, happy voice. At last the volley of fireworks died down and ended. Michel tore his hands from Valentina's curves and looked back toward the fire. He had no idea how long they'd been gone from the party. Even drunk, everyone would wonder where he'd wandered off to.

"I have to go back soon," he said. "It's Sara's wedding."

She nodded. "I understand."

He helped her up and they brushed sand off one another's clothes, then headed back toward his villa hand in hand. She had never stopped loving him. He could hardly imagine it. He felt humbled and incredibly fortunate. He'd been given a second chance—and this time he'd be much more careful.

"Where are you staying?" he asked when they were almost back.

"At the hotel with the others."

"Will you stay with me tonight instead?" He left no question what he asked for. He used his Master voice, deep and resonant with demand.

Her fingers squeezed around his. "That depends. Do you have a cage to keep me in?"

I do, he thought. *It's called my heart.* "I can't imagine spending the night with you and not having a cage nearby," he said aloud.

She laughed, her bright, easy laugh, but he sobered. He let go of her hands to trace her cheek. "Valentina, you forgive so easily. You frighten me."

"Because I forgive? Forgiveness is an act of love, and I love you." She reached to cover his hand with hers. "Anyway, you gave me time to learn, to adjust and change when I was confused in my life. When I was acting crazy, remember? How could I not do the same for you?"

His lips twitched. He didn't know whether to scowl at her or smile. "Was I acting crazy, Valentina? Really?"

She blinked up at him. "Will you be angry if I answer honestly?"

He burst into laughter, wrapping her in his arms. He'd been crazy, yes, but he was finally feeling sane again.

"Daddy?"

They broke apart as Sara ran across the beach toward them, followed by Jason's tall form silhouetted by the fire. "Daddy," she called. "Where were you? Did you see the fireworks?"

He greeted his daughter and kissed her cheek. "They were difficult to miss. Yes, we watched them together." He reached back to take Valentina's hand, their fingers easily twining together. Sara stared, then whooped and did an ecstatic dance, her full, white skirts shimmying in the breeze.

"I'm so relieved you two worked things out. It's the best wedding gift you could have given us, to see you smiling again." She waved back toward the house. "Jason and I have been busy socializing. And drinking." She laughed, stumbling sideways into her new husband. "We came to find you because we're probably going to leave soon. We wanted to...to thank you for everything."

"You are very much welcome for everything." He tried not to lose his composure at the catch in her voice, the sheen of tears in her eyes. He let go of Valentina to take his daughter in his arms. "I hope this day was everything you'd dreamed."

Sara clung to his neck, enveloping him in a hug. "It was more than we ever could have dreamed. Thank you for everything. *Everything*," she repeated with feeling.

Michel held onto her, his beautiful strong daughter who was now Jason's beautiful, strong wife. "I'm so proud of you. I love you so much."

She drew away, giving him a small, secret smile. "I'm proud of you too." She slid a look at Valentina, who was off to the side, exchanging quiet words with Jason. "I told you, daddy. I knew she was the one for you all along. Some things are meant to be."

Jason turned from Valentina and held out a hand to Michel. He pushed it away and hugged Jason too. What the hell. Jason was officially his son-in-law now, irritating, controlling bastard that he was. "If you ever hurt my daughter, I'll cut off your balls," he murmured in French.

"I know. I'll do the same if you hurt Valentina." Jason smirked at him as he pulled away. "Just saying."

Valentina watched both of them, and Michel had the distinct impression she'd understood every word of their conversation. "Have you been studying French?" he asked, one eyebrow raised.

"A little. We both have," she said, sharing a smile with Sara. "Let's hope both of you get to keep your balls for a very long while."

Chapter Twenty:
Mine

Even after midnight had come and gone, and Sara and Jason retired for the night, the party continued. Fortunately, her Master didn't seem inclined to watch the sun come up with the other revelers. After a few words with the party staff, he took Valentina's hand and led her toward the stairs.

She loved the way he gripped her hand, demanding her attendance. It reminded her of that first time at Cirque du Monde headquarters, when he'd taken her hand and led her through the corridors to his office. He'd been the lofty Mr. Lemaitre to her then. Now he was Michel, and he loved her.

He stopped at the top of the stairs and faced her. He placed his palms on either side of her head, gazing down at her with a thoughtful, almost worried expression.

"Oh," she said. "Please don't change your mind again."

"No, it's not that. It's just that I want to do everything right this time. I want to think before I act. I want to do violently debased things to you but I want to be tender too. I'll have to do both things to live with myself, and you'll have to put up with it."

Valentina desperately wanted both things. When he leaned in to kiss her, his fingers twisted in her hair so she felt the soft teasing of his lips as well as the sharp ache of his painful tugs. "Please, Master. Do whatever you want to me. I'm yours."

He got that look at her words, that feral intensity in his eyes. Wild laughter carried up from the main room downstairs as guests stumbled in from the terraces. "Come on, then. Come to my room."

He led her to a bedroom similar to the one in Paris, muted and cavernous, and mostly white and gray. He put the lights on low. There was a balcony to one side with glass doors that opened to the night sky. On the other side stood a monstrosity of a cage. It took up an entire corner, and unlike the sliding-panel bed-cages in Paris, this one was made with solid, immovable bars.

"For when you're awful," he said as she gawked at it. "Or when it amuses me to cage you. I don't want you in there tonight, although you're welcome to try it out. See if the view suits you."

Valentina couldn't resist. She crossed the tile floor and slipped inside the spacious cell. When she looked up, she saw the bars rose nearly to the ceiling. The floor felt hard and unforgiving beneath her feet. "This is scary," she said. "It's not so much a cage as a jail."

He pushed the door shut with a resonating clank and leaned against it, gazing in at her. "Admit it. You love it. You're wet as an ocean surrounded by these bars."

"It's not the bars making me wet, Master. It's that you're on the other side."

He reached forward and pulled her close, so she was pressed against the iron between them, and kissed her until she was dazed. When he released her, she stared into his eyes. She never, ever wanted to forget this moment trapped in his cage. Not just trapped in his cage but trapped in his heart where she'd always hoped to be. She looked away when the emotion got too much, and took in the soaring, gleaming bare white walls of his kingdom.

He made a soft, amused sound. "You can draw on these walls all you like, scrawl all the words you wish. Sometimes they'll be love words, and sometimes not, I suppose. No matter how much we love one another, we'll have those times when you wish to kill me, and when I wish to put you in a cage and throw away the key."

She smiled at his resigned tone. "I won't ever wish to kill you, and I won't draw all over your walls. Well, I don't think so. I'll try not to aggravate you too much. I know you prefer things to be calm and peaceful."

"I did, yes. I'm afraid those days are over for me, but that's okay. I needed a change in my life. I needed a spark to get my heart beating again." His hands caught her elbows through the bars, his fingers tightening on her skin. "You aggravate me every day, but you inspire me too. Do you know what it means to inspire a man like me, Valentina?"

Months ago, in his office, she'd fallen to her knees at that question. She did the same now, sinking slowly to the floor.

"Yes, that," he said, sucking in a breath as her fingers worked at his fly. "It means that, of course." She released his virile length, drawing it through the space between the bars. It was already rigidly, impressively hard. She began to lick and suck it, and worship it with passionate craving. He moaned as she opened wider, took him deeper. His fingers trembled against her scalp. "It also means I'm in love with you, *tesoro mio*, and I'm never letting you go." His words broke off in a groan.

She caressed him, luxuriating in his size and his scent. The skirt of her dress pooled around her knees, red for love, red for passion. He began to work at her buttons through the bars, then stopped her so he could open the door of the cage and come inside. There was plenty of room for two. It was big enough for ten, which made her wonder what kind of parties they might have in their future, but for now, he alone seemed enough to fill the large space.

He shrugged out of his clothes, tossing them aside, and then ripped off her red silk dress with a couple of powerful tugs. She didn't mind. This was Le Maître after all, the demanding Master in the cage with her, and she melted into white-hot desire. Her pussy went from wanting and aching to positively hurting. He grabbed her face in one large hand and kissed her so powerfully that her jaw ached. *Take me, take me, please...* His other hand squeezed her breast, then pinched her nipple in a punishing pressure. He backed her toward the bars, his cock prodding against her front. When she couldn't back up any further, he hoisted her so her legs were draped over his arms, and then he drove into her, balls deep, with one hard thrust.

Valentina remembered this pleasure, and yet the power of it struck her anew. The heat and girth of him spread her open, a conquering sensation that made her legs jerk and tense. His heat contrasted with the coolness of the bars at her back, making her feel trapped in the most vulnerable and exciting way. *Violently debased things.* Was that what he'd said? This was debasement and yet so much more. He moved into her with barely leashed force, lifting her with each thrust. She clung to him as he kissed her and fucked her, had his way with her like an animal devouring its prey. Just as she was rising to a blinding climax, he pulled from her as abruptly as he'd begun. He turned her around and pressed her hands to the bars.

"Stay. Don't move."

She obeyed, opening and closing her fingers against the metal. She knew what was coming next. She'd been put in this position enough times. She heard the lubricant's cap click open, heard the slippery sound of him applying it to his cock. Her arousal wasn't dissipating, only growing sharper and stronger. When he came back and delivered a glancing blow to her ass cheeks, she almost went off right there.

"Master, please," she cried.

"Hush." He took her hips in his hands. "Who do you serve, *ma mignonne?*"

"You, Master. I serve you."

"Show me." His words were both harsh and soft as silk, soft as the dress he'd torn and left in a heap on the floor. "Show me how you serve me."

She clutched the bars as he pressed his huge, lubed cock inside her asshole. It hurt, oh, it really hurt because it had been so long since he took her there, but it also felt like the most exciting terror on earth. As he drove deeper, he splayed his hand over her pussy, squeezing it in a possessive grasp.

"You're mine, aren't you?"

"Yes, Master. I'm yours." And where she used to think, *I wish you loved me,* instead she thought, *I know you love me.* She could feel it in his breath and movements, in his trembling restraint. Submission had made this act bearable, now love gave it a richness and closeness like nothing else. She belonged to him and he belonged to her, and it was always meant to be that way.

His fingers found her clit and teased it until she bucked back against him. She closed her eyes and words danced in her imagination, black words on a white wall. *I belong to Le Maître.* No dates, no starting and ending. Just...forever.

He put his hand around her neck and found her racing pulse, then tilted her head back against his chest. "Forever," he said. Was he picturing the words on the wall too? He would have stared at them also as he fucked her, as he pressed her nose against the letters. "Come for me," he said as she hovered on the edge.

They orgasmed together in a shaking, bar-clattering climax, his lips pressed against her cheek. Any words on a wall were forgotten. There was only his power and his warmth, and his hands curved over top of hers on the bars.

* * * * *

For weeks, Michel had fought himself, trying to resist her. Now he had her and he never intended to let her go. He took her to his bed and wrapped her in his arms, not because she preferred it, but because he did. He, this new Michel Lemaitre who had risen from the ashes of Valentina's flames.

Now he was the *ouroboros* twisted into a circle. Like the *ouroboros*, he must regenerate and reinvent himself. For so long, he'd been alone. He'd studied others from a self-erected pedestal and taken from those who enticed him—with their agreement of course. Otherwise, he'd kept to himself. But he could not, would not stay away from Valentina any longer. He was powerless to change the fact that she was his mate, his soul pairing. His legacy, perhaps. Eventually, certainly, his wife.

She shifted back against him and smiled in sleep, her hand flexing in his. He gazed down at her blazing red hair and thought that she even slept with energy. God help him, she was a wild thing. He didn't want to crush that wildness, but if they were to survive together, she would have to be somewhat tamed. In some things, he would let her be wild, and in others, he would require her submission. He envisioned a benevolent dictatorship, his orders balanced out by his hopeless fascination with her creativity and moods. Perhaps she believed she loved him more than he loved her. She was mistaken.

He stretched in his bed, pulling her closer. He wanted to wake her up and take her again but there was tomorrow still, and the next day. They had all the time in the world now. He had time to stretch out beside her and sleep, then wake to tumble and play with her. They could have breakfast together. Lunch, dinner. They could do that tomorrow, next week, next month. Forever. He would move her things into his Paris home, *all* her things, no matter how much mess they made, and they would be together as they were meant to be. He would give her spaces to live in all his houses. They would become *their* houses, his and hers, with cages and playrooms for the times they couldn't go to the Citadel, and well-lit studios for her art. Then, at night, she would sleep in his bed where she belonged.

All of this was clear as day in his head. Even the challenges were clear to him. Controlling her would be like bottling lightning. In reality, his life with her would sometimes be miserable. There would be fights and misunderstandings. But misunderstandings could be straightened out, and fights...fights could be arousing too. He opened his hand against the curve of her hip, slid his palm forward and down to rest on the heat of her mons. Even in sleep she responded to him, arching against his fingers. Mere seconds of touching and holding her, and he was painfully hard. A small shift, a readjustment, and he slid inside her pussy.

She opened her legs wider, drowsy and pliable. Her wet, hot sheath embraced him and pleasure mixed with an encompassing feeling of connection. He had felt love for her from the very beginning, had only hurt her and denied her because of his history, and his cowardice. Her stubborn bravery had saved them, fire and flame made real.

He opened his mouth against her ear, nibbled at her lobe as her hair tickled him. So soft, all of her so soft and bendy. She was waking up now, moving her hips to meet him thrust for thrust. She still held his hand. Without guile, she brought it to her lips and mouthed his fingers, closing her teeth on one fingertip. He was bitten, literally and figuratively. His cock surged, his balls teeming at the caress. He wondered what kind of caresses he might train her to do over a lifetime of mastery. So many pleasures to discover. He made her come, once, then again, fucking and playing with her until his own orgasm emptied him out. Replete, warm inside her, he fell into a slumber something like death.

He remembered nothing after that, until he came awake to the feel of her fingers brushing back his hair and tracing across his brow. She lay within his arms, her eyes sleep-tinged and puffy. She was as beautiful drowsy as she was awake.

"Michel," she said softly, her Italian lilt infusing his name with such novel tones. "Michel, I can still feel you inside me."

"Get used to it." He gave her a rough grope as she wiggled against him. When he pulled her closer she closed her eyes, drifting, humming a little. What on earth was she humming? And why?

He studied the woman in his arms and had the unsettling thought that he would never really know her, this *La Vampa*. If he was to represent her artistically, he would produce his own heart and set it on fire, followed by his brain and then his cock, in that order. Complete destruction.

And that was okay with him, really. Mystery and love, and fire. If this was to be his entire life, he couldn't be happier about it. He put his face beside hers and let her contented little hum resonate deep inside him, just like her laughter, and her wild, endearing love.

Epilogue:
One Year Later

Michel stared at the painting propped against the easel. It looked different than it had looked last week, or last month, or even last year when she'd shown it to him for the first time. Different...and still unfinished.

"It's not done yet? Really?"

He wasn't angry, but he pinched her ass through her white silk dress and pretended to be. "You said I could have it as a wedding gift."

Valentina managed to look both indignant and apologetic. "The rule is that you have a year to give a wedding gift."

"I thought it was a year to write thank-you cards. Whatever the rule, what are we to do about this?" He pointed to her self-portrait on their bedroom wall, and the empty space beside it. "Our decor is out of balance. Until you finish my portrait and put it there, your portrait appears disproportional."

She bit her lip. "I'm sorry, Master. I know you hate when things are out of whack."

"I'm going to whack you, little slave girl, if you don't finish this in the next week or so."

She skittered away as he followed his pinch with a good-natured smack on her ass. He knew from his groping investigations that she had nothing on under the wispy wedding dress she wore. She turned back to him when she'd put some space between them.

"The thing is, I want it to be perfect. It has to be perfect."

"But I'm not perfect." He shouldn't nag at her; it was spectacular so far. She'd recently added a bit more texture to his shirt, including a row of mismatched buttons and a feather blue eyelash he'd acquired from his daughter. Strangely, it was nowhere near his eyes.

But that epitomized Valentina's genius. Even the brushstrokes felt alive. He knew she changed the colors and shapes of them until they communicated exactly what she thought they should. "Look at your poor lonely painting," he said, indicating the bare spot on the wall.

"It doesn't look that lonely. It looks happy." She sidled back to slip her arms around his waist. "Maybe because the bugs haven't come for the candy."

"Yet." He tugged her chin up to give her a kiss. "I suppose I must be extra patient with you now that you're my wife. Perhaps I'll lock you in the cage and not let you out until it's finished." He'd erected one in their Paris bedroom that was exactly like the Marseille cage, and put it to regular use.

"That doesn't sound very patient," she said forlornly.

"For me, it is."

"What about our honeymoon?"

"Oh, I'd find it a lovely honeymoon. You. Me. The cage."

She shivered, melting into him. He cupped her face, rubbing behind her ears.

"Do you feel like something's still missing in me, *mon coeur*?" he asked softly. "Is that why you haven't finished?"

She pulled back, shaking her head. "No, oh no, it's not that. I feel like I have all of you now, every part of you. I love you so much." She went up on her tiptoes to kiss him, then turned and tilted her head to look at his artistic likeness. "It's only that, just when I think I'm done, I learn something new about you and I have to make changes. Even when it's done, I feel like it won't really be done. There is a lot still to happen between us. Anyway, it's only part of your wedding present." Her wide, earnest gaze returned to his.

"What's the other part?"

"Me, *monsieur.*"

She gave him one of her impish smiles, the type that never failed to make his cock stand on end. He swept her into his arms and carried her to their bed, and laid her back, pushing up the skirt of her dress as he came over her. He should probably take more care. The dress cost a lot, but ripping it off his bride—his *bride*, for God's sake—was worth all the fortune in the world.

"I never wanted to get married," he murmured in her ear. "This is all your fault. All this upheaval in my life."

"Yes, Master," she said as he stripped off the last of the gauzy material. "I should be punished. Severely punished."

He chuckled and shoved open her thighs. "I think fucking is a more traditional wedding night activity. We'll save the arduous, prolonged punishments for the honeymoon."

Valentina made a sound between a groan and a sigh as he shoved his fingers inside her. The honeymoon...oh, he had plans for the honeymoon, and plenty of time to put them into action. One of her younger sisters had come to Paris a few months ago to learn Valentina's part in *Élémental*, at least the nearest approximation of it she could manage. With Lucia to fill in, Michel could steal his bride away for two whole weeks to a remote castle in the Italian countryside. It had a real, honest-to-goodness dungeon, one of the main reasons he'd rented it.

Another reason–Michel needed the break, since there had been two of the Sancia sisters in his hair. He had nicknamed them Vesuvius One and Vesuvius Two. When they returned from Italy, Michel knew he would have to find Lucia an act in one of Cirque's other productions. Such talent shouldn't go to waste. In fact, he was in talks to bring all the family under Cirque du Monde's wing, the entire collection of sisters, brothers, cousins, father and mother, aunts and uncles. There were a good number of them, all talented and lacking inhibition or fear.

Earlier tonight, six of the young women from her family, including Valentina, had done a seductive, sensual dance at the wedding reception. It was a family tradition, apparently, of Iberian-Andalusian origins. The flame-haired women had shaken their hips and twirled and writhed with age-old moves of invitation until every attendee was on their feet, stomping along with catcalls and applause. By the end of it, he wanted to tackle Valentina right in the middle of the dance floor and fuck her into oblivion. He did not, however. Nor did he dream of taking all six of them to his bed as some of the other men undoubtedly did. One Vesuvius in his life was enough. More than enough. One volcanic, fiery lover, with talents yet to be explored.

"Do the dance for me again," he said, rolling away from her. "The one you did with your sisters and cousins."

"But I'm naked. I have no skirts to swish about."

"Improvise," he ordered. "I want sexy dancing. Now."

She scooped her slightly damaged wedding dress from the floor and draped it over one shoulder and down across her waist. She began a seductive hum, rolling her hips and then snapping them on the downbeats, using the dress to flutter about now and again. They had had chamber music at the wedding, and full symphonies at the reception, but somehow it wasn't as lovely as this improvised melody. So beautiful, her shape and femininity, and the power she held even when submitting to his commands. Without that power, she wouldn't fascinate him. She wouldn't challenge him so that his every day became about owning her and improving her, and loving her, and making her smile.

His cock bucked as she raised her arms in the air, their sinuous movements ending in prettily posed hands. She turned in a circle, then looked back at him over her shoulder. Their gazes caught and locked. *Come hither*, her eyes said.

I'm going to fuck you to pieces is what he thought. He reached out and grabbed the dress and yanked it toward him. She followed, falling onto the bed, right into his clutches.

"Fucking and dancing and making art," he said, pushing her beneath him. "That's pretty much all you're good for."

"I perform too," she reminded him.

"*Oui*, you somehow manage to do that without breaking your neck."

"Because I'm talented," she said, sighing as he caressed her.

"I know all about your *talents*." He felt drunk on love and lust for her. He felt happy. Ecstatic. Reborn. "You drive me crazy. Why on earth did I make you my wife? Am I crazy too?"

"I think you must be a little," she said with a grin.

His lips covered hers as he entered her. The dress slipped between them, cool silk against warm, fragrant skin. Valentina, *La Vampa*, Vesuvius, whatever her name, he loved her. He adored her elementally, like air and earth, and water and spirit.

Like fire.

THE END

A Final Note

I hope you enjoyed Michel and Valentina's fiery love story, the conclusion (at least for now) of my Cirque Masters series. I've had a lot of fun bringing the world of Cirque and the world of kink together in one yummy package for all of you to perv.

If you missed the first two stories in the Cirque Masters series, I hope you'll go back and check them out. The first book is *Cirque de Minuit*, Theo and Kelsey's dramatic love story about overcoming mistakes and healing the ones we love. The second book is *Bound in Blue*, featuring a cross-continental romance between Sara and Jason, as Michel tries to come to terms with being a father. (Spoiler: it's not easy for him.)

Many thanks to Linzy Antoinette, Candace Blevins, Tasha L. Harrison, J. Luna Scuro, and dear Doris for reading *Master's Flame* and sharing your thoughts, and thanks to my editors Lina Sacher and Audrey for helping me polish Michel and Valentina's story to a glowing shine.

If you liked this book, I hope you'll be kind enough to leave a review at your favorite online site, mention the title on Facebook or Twitter, or perhaps recommend it to a friend. Without your support I couldn't do this, so THANK YOU from the bottom of my heart for reading and encouraging me. To my Club Annabel peeps, to all my faithful readers: You are the magic—and fire—of my days.

Sign up for Annabel's Naughty Newsletter at annabeljoseph.com to learn more about upcoming releases and promotions. For more frequent updates, you can follow Annabel on Twitter (@annabeljoseph) or Facebook (facebook.com/annabeljosephnovels)

About the Author

Annabel Joseph is a multi-published BDSM romance author. She writes mainly contemporary romance, although she has been known to dabble in the medieval and Regency eras. She is known for writing emotionally intense BDSM storylines, and strives to create characters that seem real—even flawed—so readers are better able to relate to them. Annabel also writes vanilla (non-BDSM) erotic romance under the pen name Molly Joseph.

Annabel loves to hear from her readers at
annabeljosephnovels@gmail.com.